NUTWHISTLE FARM

A Novel

GEOFFREY EYRE

Mardle Publications

Also written by Geoffrey Eyre

A Plain Village
ISBN 978-0-9554608-1-4

The Poaching Gang
ISBN 978-0-9554608-3-8

The Case for Edward de Vere as Shakespeare
ISBN 978-0-9554608-4-5

Curlywigs
ISBN 978-0-9554608-5-2

Nutwhistle Farm

Published by Mardle Publications

www.mardlepublications.com

mardlebooks@gmail.com

© 2015 Geoffrey Eyre

Typeset by John Owen Smith, Headley Down

ISBN 978-0-9554608-2-1

Printed by CreateSpace

NUTWHISTLE FARM

1

Seven members of the Knight family lived at Nutwhistle Farm. The farm had been in their family a long time and the seven Knights who lived there did so in perfect harmony. They got on well together and overlooked one another's funny little ways. Birthdays and Christmas were observed with presents and special meals. Cross words were seldom spoken and even if the pace of life was somewhat slow it would have been hard to find a more compatible family than the seven Knights who lived contentedly year after year at Nutwhistle Farm.

A situation soon to change, although not for the better.

Joe Knight, seventy years old, owned Nutwhistle farm. His son Steve did all the hard work looking after their livestock and this left Joe free to make an independent living from his farm shop. This was set up in a hay barn and consisted of little more than a trestle table, a set of ancient brass-weight scales and piles of old cardboard cartons and recycled supermarket bags for his customers to bear away their purchases. There was a blackboard outside the farm gate on which was chalked the items for sale that day, together with their price. Seasonal produce such as bedding plants, cut flowers and vegetables were Joe's main sale items but at various times of the year his regular customers could also expect to buy jars of home made chutney, jam and honey, bundles of bean sticks cut to length, sacks of potatoes, bags of manure and topsoil, or duck and goose eggs laid out in a basket of straw. Anything and every-thing around the farm that could be exchanged for cash.

Joe sat on a chair behind the table waiting for his morning customers to arrive. Behind him, in cobwebbed dark corners of the hay barn, broken and obsolete machinery rusted away in the forlorn hope of finding a buyer in search of agricultural memorabilia. They never did.

'Who's this coming in, Zoe?' he asked his granddaughter. She was his assistant and sat on a second chair beside him. She was sixteen years old.

It took her a few seconds to identify the customer parking his car. 'I think it's the new bloke from the house opposite the pub. Wonder what he wants.'

'We shall soon find out. Any idea what he does for a living?'

'Not one of my favourite people, Gramps. He's a dentist.'

'Oh, plenty of money then,' he said, brightening quickly. 'What can we sell him, Zoe?'

'New people moving in usually want something for their gardens. Try him with some of those wallflower plants. I've taken off most of the yellow leaves.'

The dentist was a young man with a diffident manner. As this was his first visit to Nutwhistle Farm he took his time in crossing from the car parking area to the table set up in the old hay barn, looking around him as he went. It did not take him many seconds to realise that he had come to the wrong place. One look at the muddy farmyard puddles and tumbledown outbuildings changed his mind. He backed off in the hope of returning unobtrusively to his car and making a quick escape. He was not able to do so because Joe Knight saw him hesitating and captured him with a cheery greeting.

'Over here, sir. Good morning to you.'

Nervously the young man approached the table. 'Are you Mr Knight? I was told to ask for Mr Knight.'

'That's me, sir. Always pleased to meet a new neighbour. How can we help?'

'My wife wanted a kitten for our two little girls. Someone in the village suggested this was the place to ask.'

'They were right. And you're in luck, sir.'

'I am?'

'Our cat has just had some really pretty kittens.' Joe turned to his granddaughter. 'How many have we got left, Zoe?'

'I'm not sure. Three, I think. There were four when I

looked yesterday but the fox has had the biggest one.'

'Going to nip up and take a look for the gentleman then?'

'They're right at the top now. She's hidden them in a new place again.'

'Up you go then. I'll get a box ready.'

It was a tall barn and the bales of hay and straw were precariously stacked to the height of the medieval wooden tie-beams. Obediently Zoe squashed out the cigarette she was smoking and climbed up in search of cat and kittens. Tall and slim, her athletic progress upwards did not go unnoticed. Down below she had a small but attentive audience. A second customer had arrived, an elderly man this time, a bronchitic gardener who came regularly for sacks of farmyard manure. He may have been wheezy and white-haired but stood side by side with the dentist watching in silence as Zoe mountain-eered her way to the top.

She was wearing a denim miniskirt with bare legs, so it was quite a view. Joe had seen the same performance many times before and grinned to see the two men following every movement while pretending indifference. He was well aware of the pulling power of his granddaughter's long shapely legs and paid her just enough to put in a regular appearance when she was not at school, which was most of the time.

Having located the skinny black cat in her nest she called down to her grandfather. 'What sort do you want, Gramps?'

'What you got, Zoe?'

'I'll soon tell you.' She picked the kittens up one by one and examined them upside down from the rear. 'There's a black one and a ginger one both toms, and a tabby she-cat.'

'Did you hear that?' Joe asked his customer. 'Fancy a ginger tom? Make a lovely pet for your two little daughters that will.' Without waiting for a reply he found a small cardboard box, lined it with some soft hay and called back, 'Bring it down, Zoe.'

The young dentist would have preferred the female tabby but Joe was not giving him a choice. 'He's the nicest of the three,' Zoe offered as her contribution, placing the kitten in the box and handing it over. She had been well trained by her grandfather and knew that the appealing face of the bewildered kitten peering over the edge of the box would be irresistible.

'Only a tenner,' Joe whispered. 'You'll be a popular Dad when you get home. They'll remember this day, your nippers will. All you've got to do now is choose a name for the little fellow. Good day, sir.'

As soon as he had driven away the elderly gardener opened the boot of his car and Zoe obliged by carrying over a sack of rotted farmyard manure and depositing it inside. 'What a strong girl you are!' he said admiringly, trying hard not to stare from behind as she leaned over to position the sack.

'Make anything grow, that will,' she said confidently as he handed her the money. 'Lovely stuff that is. Just right for your winter pansies.'

'Thank you so much for your help,' he said as he left. He was wearing a tweed hat decorated with a fishing fly and raised it courteously as he eased himself carefully behind the wheel.

'Mind how you go,' Zoe said, giving the roof of his car a couple of parting swipes before returning to her seat behind the table. She knew well enough what went on in the minds of men, even men old enough to know better, and that included her grandfather. Joe held out his hand for the fertiliser money but passed over his tin of tobacco by way of fair exchange. Zoe rolled two cigarettes in her fingers, put them both in her mouth and lit them with the same match, passing one to her grandfather and smoking the other herself. After which they settled down again to await the next customer.

Nutwhistle Farm had once been situated in open country but building development in the surrounding villages had brought them many new neighbours. It was also close to a medium-sized market town which had been expanding steadily in their direction. The new houses came nearer every year. This encroachment created difficulties in the form of juvenile nuisance, criminal damage, marauding dogs and theft. Implements once left in the fields until needed again had to be brought in overnight and locked up. Gates and water troughs had to be secured in place, fences repaired and broken bottles removed from the fields before animals could be turned out to graze.

Joe Knight had long overlooked these minor irritations of modern country life. Far from being opposed to the incomers he had welcomed every new house that was built, viewing them as potential customers for his farm shop. He had a loyal following, mostly people from the town who liked to feel that they were buying rural charm along with their cheap fruit and veg. Joe was part of the attraction for the new urban town dwellers. He was rugged and whiskery, a big and slightly clumsy man dressed in a dark suit with a waistcoat, always with a grubby white shirt buttoned to the neck without a tie. In his fruit orchard he had two hives of bees and all the year round he wore his beekeeper's straw hat. Needing to make a success of his back door trade he had hammed up the part of the gruff old countryman, with just enough twinkly charm to discourage any complaints about the quality of the produce on sale. When he held out a large and none-too-clean hand for the money few of his customers had the nerve to tell him that their last sack of potatoes had contained an unusually large proportion of earth and stones, or that the cooking apples were bruised all over.

'Still no reply?' he asked sympathetically. Zoe had spent the morning thumbing away at her phone, sending one text message after another to her absentee boyfriend, whose name was Emerson.

Zoe admitted as much, sighing despondently. 'He's not answering.'

'I can see that he isn't.' Her grandfather pondered the matter and drew the obvious conclusion. 'You know what I think, Zoe? I think your young man may have gone for good this time.'

'Don't say things like that, Gramps. I love Emerson, you know I do.'

'We haven't seen him since that Sunday when he came to dinner with us back in the summer.'

'He said his mother was ill. Or was it his father? He had to go home and help look after them, whichever one it was.'

'That sounds suspiciously like an excuse to me, Zoe.'

'It will break my heart if Emerson doesn't come back.'

'A clever young man. Polite, too. He'll go far in life with good manners like that.'

'That's not much consolation to me, is it?'

Not liking to see his granddaughter so dejected Joe tried to cheer her up by sounding more hopeful. 'He came back once before. I'm sure he'll come back again. It's just a case of being patient.'

'I miss him all the time, Gramps.'

'Like I said, you've got to be patient. Emerson likes doing deals, he travels about a lot and one day he'll travel back in our direction. We shall all be pleased to see him, of course we will. Everyone likes Emerson.'

'That's what I'm afraid of. I don't want other people to like him. I want him all to myself.'

'You're a pretty girl, Zoe. He'll turn up again, when you least expect him like as not. Meanwhile we've got some more customers heading in our direction. Let's try and shift some of those apples. We've hardly started on the fallers, there's hundreds of them still on the ground in the orchard.'

Not surprisingly there were no takers for the fallen cooking apples. It was early in October, flower beds and vegetable plots everywhere were being dug over so sacks of farmyard manure were in big demand. Zoe had them all neatly stacked up awaiting a buyer and obligingly carried them out to the cars as required, while Joe trousered the cash.

Change had already come to Nutwhistle Farm. Joe Knight's faithful customers had noticed it even if Zoe hadn't, being preoccupied with her love life, or more accurately with her lack of a love life. The large blackboard by the farm gate had shown progressively fewer items for sale as the year moved through the seasons. Joe just shook his head when asked why there had been no field mushrooms on his trestle table this autumn. He made the same response when asked why there had been no marrows or knobbly but flavoursome cucumbers, both traditionally grown in hot, richly manured beds. Why had there been no intensely scented bunches of lavender for making lavender bags? No aromatic apple tree logs for winter hearths? Who else would supply their dark green sprigs of holly complete with berries for Christmas decorations? Their mistletoe? Their discreet brace of pheasants with no questions asked? They had good reason to be worried.

Once again Joe offered his tobacco tin and once again Zoe obliged by rolling two more cigarettes in her fingers, putting them both in her mouth and lighting them with a single match, keeping one herself and passing the other to her grandfather. She was a noisy cigarette smoker, sucking it in with big gulps of breath then blowing it out with tremendous energy. The gusts of smoke continued for a few minutes and then suddenly stopped.

'What is it, Zoe?' Joe asked her.

She drew her grandfather's attention to the farmhouse, about fifty yards from where they were sitting. 'Take a look,' she replied. 'Gran and Dad have been watching us from the kitchen window.'

Nutwhistle Farmhouse was old and looked it, with many extensions added in all directions over the years, mainly to provide enough bedrooms for the large families of the past. The kitchen was situated at the end nearest the barn and when Joe turned his head to look he saw that Zoe was right. His wife Martha and their son Steve, Zoe's father, were standing one behind the other with the curtain raised, staring in their direction.

The moment Joe turned his head to look the net curtain was dropped and the watchers moved away from the window. No one likes to think that they have been kept under surveillance and he reacted with equal amounts of indignation and curiosity. 'What do you reckon all that was about?' he asked his granddaughter.

'My ears aren't burning. That means they must have been talking about you, Gramps.'

'Very likely so,' he agreed. 'Very likely so.'

'Have you been up to something, then? Want to tell me about it?'

'No.'

'You can tell me. Go on.'

He squinted at her sourly. 'You've been expelled from school again. Perhaps that's what they were talking about.'

'I don't think so. Anyway I've finished with school now.'

'You mean they've finished with you.'

'What's the difference? I've decided not to go any more.'

'You never went very often in the first place.'

'Did you like school?'

'No. Can't say as I did.'

'Well then.'

He finished the conversation by handing her an empty plastic sack. 'Get yourself down to the orchard and rake up a few more apples. Make yourself useful. Sitting here arguing won't make either of us rich.'

2

Steve Knight was Joe's son and he did most of the outside work on the farm, helped by his wife Carol. They were both thirty-eight years of age, and Zoe was their only child.

Steve had been put to work by his father as soon as he was old enough to carry a bucket, shortly after his second birthday. Nutwhistle Farm was two hundred acres in size, and it was a mixed livestock farm, so the daily routine of feeding animals and clearing up behind them was hotwired into his brain as securely and permanently as a galley slave is chained to an oar. He knew nothing else.

Although Steve worked hard all day every day he was set to inherit the farm when his father died, and therefore did not see it as paid labour. He and his wife Carol loved the outdoor life, and looking after their many animals, and they also loved one another and got on well, at work and in the home. They were much too busy for it ever to cross their minds to wonder whether they were happy or not. They enjoyed family life and were on affectionate terms with the other five Knights who shared the farmhouse with them.

When it was time for his mid-morning snack Steve entered through the back door, kicking off his wellies in the scullery passage. So far the day had gone well, he was in a good mood and hummed a little tune as he padded into the farm kitchen on stockinged feet. He was surprised to find his mother at the far end of the kitchen, staring through a window with the curtain pulled aside for a better view. His mother was Martha Knight and she was aged sixty, ten years younger than her husband Joe.

'What are you looking at, Ma?' he asked, coming to stand behind her.

She replied, 'I'm looking at your Dad.'

Steve peered over her shoulder but was not aware of anything unusual going on at the farm shop. He could see his daughter Zoe smoking a cigarette while chatting to his father. They were sitting side by side in the hay barn and appeared to be relaxed and companionable as they waited for the next customer. It was a familiar sight, and he said so. 'I don't see anything wrong. What's up? Is there something going on I need to know about?'

It was at this moment that Zoe drew her grandfather's attention to the watchers at the window. For a brief moment all four stared at one another before Martha let the curtain drop. She returned to the stove and hefted the big brown family teapot to the table to pour Steve his mid-morning mug of tea.

As soon as he had removed his cap and drawn up a chair to the long kitchen table she cut him a thick slice of cherry slab cake, the family favourite. Only then did she reply to his question. 'Yes,' she said. 'There's something's going on.'

Martha suffered from painful arthritis in her legs and looked older than her sixty years. She seldom left the kitchen where she had her own easy chair near the stove. After providing her son's elevenses she returned to the chair, easing herself down slowly then flopping back with a grunt of relief.

'Well?' Steve prompted her, pausing in mid bite. 'What's on your mind? Nothing serious, I hope.'

There was no easy way to say what she wanted to say so she came straight to the point. 'It's your Dad. He's gone funny in the head.'

'In what way, Ma?'

'He told me he was going to die.'

This made Steve blink. 'Has he got something wrong with him then? Something he isn't telling us about?'

'He didn't say. That's not the worst of it though. Want to hear the rest?'

Steve looked worried, and stopped eating his piece of cake. 'There's more?'

'Last week he bought himself a suitcase. He tried to sneak

it up to the bedroom without telling me but I saw it and made him tell me what he wanted it for.'

'You don't mean he's planning on taking a trip some-where, do you? Not at his age.'

'No, he's cashing in all his accounts and filling the suitcase with banknotes. That's what he's doing.'

Steve choked on his mug of tea. 'Bloody hell, Ma. What's the old fool playing at? This is serious.'

Martha Knight was pleased at provoking a reaction from her son. 'I haven't told the others yet. I thought you should be the first to know.'

Steve worried his thinning hair with his hands, something he only did when he was agitated. 'But why? Why is he drawing money out of the bank? There has to be a reason.'

'Because he says he's going to die and wants to sort out the family finances while he's still alive. He doesn't trust the solicitor to execute his will properly and wants to do it himself.'

'You're right then. He has gone funny in the head.'

'He's bought some big brown envelopes, one for each of us. He told me he was going to write our names on them so that when he died we could open up the suitcase and our share of the money would be waiting for us.'

Steve's mind was soon ranging over the likely con-sequences, thinking of all the things that could go wrong and probably would. In a voice that trembled slightly he said, 'What about his will? Does that still stand? Do I still get the farm?'

'You'll have to ask him.'

'This is terrible. It gets worse the longer I think about it.'

'I tried to reason with him, you'll have to do the same. He thinks he's doing the right thing for us, and that we ought to be grateful.'

'This goes from bad to worse. Where is he keeping the suitcase?'

'Under our bed, the silly sod. The first place a burglar would look.'

'He must be crazy. Anything could happen to that money. He could lose it, he could spend it on something stupid. Or more likely it could get stolen. The wrong people soon get to hear about money under the mattress.'

'Last night he brought a loaded shotgun upstairs with him. It's underneath the bed with the suitcase right now.'

'Don't like the sound of that, Ma.'

'He locks our bedroom door during the day and keeps the key in his pocket. I couldn't get in even if I wanted to.'

'What makes him so sure he's going to die?'

'He hasn't been well since that bad turn he had just after Christmas. Do you remember?'

'Of course. He had the flu and took to his bed. Not like him to be poorly.'

'But could I get him to go and see the doctor? No, I couldn't, even though he was laid up for a fortnight. Obstinate isn't the word.'

'Dad never has had a good word for doctors.'

'If I was a bit more mobile I might have done something about it. I've had plenty of time to think it over since and I've come to the conclusion that it wasn't the flu. I think what he had was a stroke.'

'Strokes are serious. Hospital jobs.'

'Not if it was only a mild stroke. You must have seen the difference in him lately. He used to shave every Sunday morning when he put on his clean shirt for the week. Took a pride in looking smart for the Sunday dinner. He hasn't shaved for so long that he's almost grown a beard.'

'I still don't think it was a stroke, Ma. People who have a stroke are in a bad way afterwards. Can't speak, can't walk. Dad's not like that.'

'You start with a mild stroke and work up to a big one. He talks to himself in bed now, and says some very strange things. Having a stroke damages the brain. I can't get him to take a bath and his feet smell terrible. He's stopped looking after himself and can't remember things from one day to the next.'

Steve realised the truth of what his mother had been telling him and lowered his head to the table as a sign of dejection. 'I should have seen it for myself. There's been hardly anything chalked on his blackboard for weeks. He doesn't even bother picking the good apples off the trees, just asks Zoe to rake up the fallers.'

Martha used her apron to dab at her eyes. 'He used to pass the time making bird tables and rabbit hutches, and sold them as fast as he made them. He was always busy. If he had a spare moment he would cut a bundle of pea sticks, or bag up some topsoil. This time of year he would start carving faces out of pumpkins ready for Halloween. Now he just sits there selling apples. You couldn't give them away. It's a sad way to end up.'

'Do the others know about the money?'

'No. I told you first.'

'They'll have to be told.'

'It's up to you, Steve. You'll have to do something about it, and soon.'

'If he's cashed in everything then we're talking about a big sum of money. The money from selling the two cottages plus the money from selling the cows and the milk quota.'

'I know.'

'Dad promised to look after it for us. Invest it carefully so there would be more to share out between us when he died.'

'Does that seem likely to you now?'

Steve was really sweating by this time. 'The farm comes to me. That's what we all agreed, wasn't it? A farm this size is too small to split up but it won't survive without the capital to run it. We can only just make a living now.'

His mother put a consoling hand on his shoulder as she struggled up from her chair and hobbled to the stove to begin preparing the midday meal. 'I'll do everything I can to see that you get what is rightfully yours. You know I will.'

'Carol and me have never had a holiday or any luxuries. We don't want to be diddled out of the farm now.'

'You won't be. Not if I can help it.'

At the door Steve hesitated. 'We had better make certain of what he's doing before we tackle him about it. Dad won't like any interference. He doesn't believe in discussing farm business with anyone, not even me.'

'I think you should tell Carol straight away. She's your wife. She's got a right to know what's happening.'

'She's gone to the town to get some disinfectant for the sheep. I'll tell her as soon she gets back.' Once more he hesitated, troubled to see his mother still dabbing at her eyes. 'What is it, Ma? Is there something else upsetting you?'

She nodded, her head drooping. 'We've always been such a happy family.'

Steve went over and put a comforting arm round her shoulders. 'We still are a happy family. This won't change anything.'

'Oh yes it will. People always quarrel over money and I can see it happening here, and very soon. Remember what I told you. Things will never be the same again after this. Our days of being a happy family are over. Well and truly over.'

3

Most of Nutwhistle Farm was wet heavy ground unsuitable for growing cereal crops. Beef cattle fed on grass and maize silage provided them with their most reliable source of income. Pigs were the least reliable, being labour intensive and with the narrowest of profit margins. Steve and his wife Carol survived through unremitting toil and expert knowledge. They seldom needed to send for the vet, being able to treat most conditions themselves, as well as mending broken machinery and carrying out essential building maintenance.

Fathers and sons never see eye to eye about how to run a farm so Joe Knight did the sensible thing by going into semi-retirement when Steve finished at agricultural college. Steve married Carol the same year and they took over the day-to-day work on the farm. This left Joe free to make a living with his back door trade. It provided him with a tax-free cash income, enough to pay the running costs on his battered Land Rover and a few luxury items such as his weekly bottle of brandy and a few ounces of hand-rolling tobacco.

Carol also came from a farming family so she knew what to expect as a farmer's wife. When they started their married life as twenty-year olds she and Steve were full of enthusiasm and eager to succeed. Eighteen years later and they both looked older than their age, ground down with continual work, most of it outdoors in all weathers. There are no days off on a livestock farm since every day of the year is the same as another to a sheep, a pig, a chicken, or an ever-hungry half-ton curly-coated white-faced prime-beef Hereford.

Once young and pretty Carol was now prematurely aged and weather-beaten, her youth and femininity used up in eighteen years of gumboots, overalls and soiled hands. She and Steve were not big people but looked even smaller because neither carried an ounce of spare flesh. The other members of the family were much bigger, and less worn down with constant toil, even their teenage daughter Zoe was a head taller than they were. As the two smallest people on the farm they never seemed to mind or even notice that they did all the work. No one could remember seeing them dressed in anything other than their working clothes.

It should not be deduced from this that they were unhappy. On the contrary they loved their animals and the farm and being able to organise their own work. They toiled, but they toiled cheerfully, because always at the back of their minds was the prospect of one day being the owners of Nutwhistle Farm. A future now at risk.

After hearing the bad news from his mother Steve had to wait until Carol returned from the town before he could share it with her. Although they lived in the farmhouse, together with the other members of the family, they had a few rooms of their own in a kind of granny annexe so that they could have some privacy as a married couple. They kicked off their gumboots at the door and were soon sitting down for their customary lunchtime snack. This was two mugs of tomato soup heated in the microwave accompanied by digestive biscuits and triangles of processed cheese.

As soon as they began eating Carol said, 'What's the matter, Steve? You seem a bit agitated. Has something upset you?'

'It's Dad. Ma thinks he's gone funny in the head.'

His wife received this information calmly. 'He is seventy, Steve. I know it's a shame when these things happen but a lot of people get Alzheimers earlier than that.'

'Not Alzheimers. Ma reckons he had a stroke.'

'Wouldn't we have known about it if he'd had a stroke? I don't remembering him going to the doctor, or the doctor coming to see him.'

'She says it started when he had the flu just after Christmas. She says he still hasn't got over it properly. She says he hasn't been the same since. She says he's getting worse.'

'It's called old age, love. Comes to us all in the end.'

'Yesterday he told her was going to die.'

Carol was still unmoved. 'He doesn't look any different to me. What makes him think he's going to die?'

'Ma asked him the same question. Want to hear the bad news?'

'I thought that was the bad news.'

'It wasn't. Ma says he's started drawing all the money out of the bank. And everywhere else that he's got money squirreled away. He's stuffing banknotes into a suitcase and hiding it under their bed.'

'He's doing what!' Carol's reaction was more violent than he had expected. She swore viciously and jumped up from the table, spilling soup from her mug. 'This sounds like a disaster waiting to happen. The silly old bugger could lose the lot.'

'Steady on, Carol. It hasn't happened yet.'

'So you hope.'

'Dad isn't senile. Ma says it's to do with his will.'

'And that's supposed to make me feel better?'

'He wants to divvy up the money himself so that we can be paid out in cash when he dies. Which he seems to think will be quite soon.'

'I'm not believing this. Even your Dad couldn't be that stupid.'

'Ma says he's putting the money in big brown envelopes with our names on.'

'You've got to do something, Steve. This could go horribly wrong. He needs to be stopped.'

He said miserably. 'I know. I know.'

'We've talked about this before. About the money. About you having some control over the business side of the farm.'

'I know. Don't keep on at me.'

'That's what you always say. Well, now you've got to do something. You can't shirk it this time.'

This touched a nerve because in the last few months Carol had become increasingly uneasy at the way his father continued to exclude Steve from the financial control of the farm. This had seemed natural when they were first married and from time to time Joe made vague promises that he would gradually hand over the finances to Steve. Now that they were approaching forty years of age Carol thought the time had come and urged Steve to tackle his father on the subject. Steve was uncomfortable at the idea and took the easy way out by allowing things to go on as before.

For a family that never quarrelled the first cross words were soon spoken. Carol said bitterly, 'Your father still treats us as if we were children.'

'It isn't quite like that. He lets us run the farm.'

'He lets us do the work.'

'We've got along very nicely until now.'

'Yes, until it's too late, if what your mother tells you is true. I don't like unpleasantness any more than you do but we need to know how much money there is in that suitcase. And more importantly how much is still left in the bank. If any.'

Steve folded his arms and stared miserably at the table, his cheese and biscuits uneaten. 'I hear what you're saying, Carol. This time I'll do something. I promise.'

'If he isn't competent to handle the money any more we've got to stop him doing it. He likes to bet on the horse racing, even though he's never won anything to my knowledge. If one of his cronies in *The Shorn Lamb* gave him a hot tip he's just as likely to put the lot on a horse and lose everything we've worked for.'

Steve wiped sweat from his face with his sleeve. 'It's a family matter. I think we should all tackle him about it. We need to have a meeting, the sooner the better.'

'No, Steve. No, no, no. You can't sort these things out with a meeting. You've got to face up to him yourself.'

Still he wriggled. 'I'll have a word with Alice when she gets home tonight.'

Carol was exasperated and angry. 'That's what you've always done, Steve, hidden behind your sister. She can't stand up to your Dad either, even if she isn't so afraid of him as you are.'

'I'm not afraid of him.'

'All right then, speak to Alice. And if neither of you are brave enough to ask him what the hell he's playing at, then I will!'

4

Alice Knight worked at a large supermarket where she had a supervisory role as a shift leader. It was a full-time job with wages high enough to provide her with clothes and cosmetics, and to keep two old cars on the road, one for her and the other for her son Ronnie. Alice was a single mother and had kept the family name, both for herself and her son. They were the sixth and seventh members of the Knight family at Nutwhistle Farm.

Alice was two years older than Steve and had maintained this advantage in size and seniority ever since, the big confident elder sister helping to bring up her smaller, younger and timid brother. Alice closely resembled her father in appearance and at age forty was a large-framed heavy woman with a formidable presence. At the supermarket no one argued with her. If called to settle a dispute at a checkout till she stood no nonsense from stroppy customers. Few had the courage to complain when she was around.

Steve was anxious to tell her about the suitcase as soon as possible. 'I've got some bad news, Sis,' he said when they were able to talk on their own later that evening. 'Ma told me about it this morning.'

'How bad? Is someone ill?'

'Sort of. Dad has lost his marbles.'

'He lost those a long time ago. What's he been up to now?'

Steve was aware that he had not succeeded in winning his sister's full attention. She was reaching for the TV programmes but he put a hand on her arm. 'This is serious. It's about the money. The money he promised to invest for us.'

'The money from selling the cottages, do you mean?'

'That is exactly what I mean. Dad has been cashing in all his investments and drawing money out of the bank and building societies.'

'Since when?'

'A few days ago, according to Ma.'

'Is she sure?'

'She said Dad has bought himself a suitcase. She couldn't think what he wanted it for and then she discovered he was filling it with bundles of banknotes and hiding it under their bed. He keeps the bedroom door locked, which is some comfort, I suppose.'

Alice threw the magazine aside. 'What is the old fool playing at? Have you said anything to him about it?'

'He told Mum he was going to die. She says he's converting everything to cash so that he can allocate the money himself. He doesn't trust the solicitor to execute his will properly.'

'What makes Dad think he's going to die?'

'All connected with his state of mind, I suppose. Reckon we've got a crisis on our hands, Sis.'

Alice began to look worried as the news sank in. First she swore, which made her feel better but did not help to solve the problem. Then she shrugged, knowing a hopeless situation when she met one. 'I'm as much to blame as you are, Stevie. I should have tackled him years ago about how he was investing the money. I took the easy way out, the same as you did. Just left him alone to get on with it.'

'Dad has always had a good head for business, Alice.'

'He might have had once.'

'Christ, you don't think he could have lost some of the money already, do you?'

'It's a possibility. Not deliberately. Just muddled it away.' She rummaged in her handbag for a packet of cigarettes and lit one with a hand that trembled slightly. 'Have you told Carol?'

'Yes. She wasn't pleased.'

'I bet she wasn't. I shall have to tell Ronnie. Can't keep quiet about it at his age.'

'Ronnie's got a right to know. He was due to have some

money left to him. And Zoe. She gets a share too. That's what Dad promised us.'

'Where is Dad now? Can we do it tonight? Have it out with him, I mean?'

'No. He went off in his Land Rover just before you came home.'

Alice frowned. 'He hardly ever goes out in the evenings. Where do you suppose he's going? Or who he is going to see?' When Steve made no reply she stared at him until the significance of his silence sank in. 'Oh God,' she wailed. 'You don't mean he's been seeing Betty Hounsome again, do you?'

'Afraid so, Sis.'

'This goes from bad to worse. How long?'

'Since her last husband died. Not long. Three months at the most.'

'Long enough. If there's money to be had from a man you can be sure that Betty is soon on the trail.'

'Her husband was a bookmaker and left her everything. She wouldn't be short of money.'

'Stevie, I went to school with Betty Hounsome. I knew her first husband and I knew her second husband, and I can tell you that she came out of the divorces a lot richer than they did. Sex and money, that's what motivates Betty and if she finds out that Dad has gone soft in the head and keeps his money in a suitcase under the bed she won't rest until she's charmed every last penny out of the silly old sod.'

Steve swallowed hard a few times but then came down on his father's side. 'You know how tight-fisted Dad is. He won't be easily separated from his money. Not even by Betty Hounsome'

Alice was still angry with herself. 'I've often had it in mind to ask him about the money and how he was investing it. Never seemed to find the right time, always too busy. You know how it is.'

'I do. Yes. I have the same problem. Always too busy.'

'I'm not sure he would have disclosed anything even if we

had asked him. Probably told us to mind our own business. He never likes being questioned about anything.'

'I'm not a great one for confrontation myself.'

'Exactly. We've all kept our heads down for the sake of a quiet life.'

'Ma thinks he had a stroke. Just after Christmas when he took to his bed for a few days. Is it likely?'

'I don't know enough to say. He's been gradually going downhill for a good few months now. Could be just old age.'

'As soon as possible then? To tackle him about the money.'

'I'm not off until Sunday, it will have to wait until then.' Alice squashed out her cigarette and folded her arms, trying to calm down and think more clearly. 'Dad would have needed to give several weeks notice to draw out some of the money. For a really big account it could have been months. How did we miss all this, Stevie? There must have been correspondence from the building societies, financial statements, share certificates, a lot going on. Didn't you have any idea? Surely you must have had some suspicions?

'Dad meets the postman every day and takes the mail back to his office to sort out. The answer is no, I never suspected anything. Not like this anyway.'

'He's outwitted us in other words. Crafty old sod.'

Steve felt more relaxed now that he had alerted his sister to the situation. Because she had reacted so strongly he believed she would do something about it, and that the damage could be limited. He said, 'We've got Mum to thank. She told me the moment she found out. I hope it's not too late.'

Having given the matter some thought Alice was less hopeful. She lit another cigarette and looked even more worried. 'I've got a bad feeling about this money, Stevie. I don't think we're going to see much of it. Not you and me, anyway.'

'What are you saying? This is terrible. You can't mean it, Sis.'

'Dad took advantage of us. We were only young when the cottages were sold. You and Carol had just got married, and I had Ronnie to look after. We had no choice except to trust him,'

'Don't forget the cow money. Dad got a nice bit for selling the cows and the milk quota.'

'We should have gone to a financial adviser. Made sure it was invested properly.'

'Things were different then. It seemed the right thing to do, letting him look after the money.'

Alice was becoming agitated. 'Somehow we've got to get hold of that suitcase. We need to count the money and then find out how much is left.'

'That's exactly what Carol said. Dad wouldn't let us, though, would he?'

'We must force him. Stiffen up, Stevie. A few cross words with Dad won't hurt us. Doesn't Ma have a key? It's her bedroom as much as his, for God's sake. We need to get in there and take a look for ourselves.'

'How?'

'I suggest you start thinking of a way.' She paused and made a wry face. 'What are you looking at me like that for?'

'Just remembering something Ma said to me this morning.'

'Something good or something bad? Let me guess.'

He sat down on a chair before replying. 'She said our days as a happy family were over. She reckoned things here would never be the same again.'

Alice agreed. 'Ma was right. This changes everything. People always come to blows over money. We won't be any different. And if Dad really has started seeing Betty Hounsome again we've got even more cause to be worried. Jesus, what a mess.'

Steve gave her a brotherly pat on the shoulder before returning to his own quarters but Alice stayed sitting where she was, her arms folded and her face furrowed in concentration. Having earned her own living for many years, as well as bringing up a child as a single mother, she had more of an outside view on the world than the other members of her family who knew little of life as it was lived away from Nutwhistle Farm.

Although she closely resembled her father she had never felt much affection for him, mainly because as an independent woman she resented his easy assumption of old-fashioned patriarchal superiority. He had always held the purse strings, and drawn them tight most of the time, something she had resented even if she had never said anything. Her private opinion was that she considered her father to be a lazy sod who had done very little real work for the last twenty years of his life.

She began planning how to part him from his suitcase full of money. She was doing it not for herself, she was doing it for her son Ronnie.

5

Ronnie Knight was an invalid, or he was according to his mother who had cosseted him from birth. As a teenage single mother she was determined that her son should want for nothing and have the best of anything that was going. What young Ronnie liked was food, lots of it, and his mother piled his plate high. Ronnie also liked his armchair, his TV and his bed.

The things Ronnie did not like came to a much shorter list. First school and then work. He was only an occasional pupil, and in any case dyslexic and unmotivated, so his mother saw no point in inconveniencing him unnecessarily. Although investigated for diabetes because of concern over his obesity he was never actually diagnosed as such. His mother advised him not to take the risk of starting work because of his bad back. She thought that incapacity benefit would suit him nicely, and it did, provided by a generous government, and Ronnie was suitably grateful.

He was pleasant and polite to everyone else in the house, including Steve and Carol, his uncle and aunt. They were prematurely aged and worn down with years of constant over-work but never seemed to mind when they came in from the rain and cold, or the dusty heat of summer, and found him first at table. They would always enquire solicitously after his sore feet or whatever else was preventing him from doing any work and ask if there was anything they could do for him.

Now aged twenty-four Ronnie Knight led a congenial life and saw no reason why it should not continue indefinitely. His mother still doted on him, he was never bored or depressed, and made himself agreeable to everyone. He accepted without demur his mother's financial support and allowed her to fuss over him and do things for him just as she had done since childhood. He knew that her love for him would never waver. If he ever felt the merest twinge of guilt at hearing her drive off to her work in the early hours of the morning long before he got up himself, he hid it well.

Alice worked a long day, on her feet most of the time, and carried disproportionate responsibility for her supervisor's wage. She was dog tired when she arrived back at the farm but her first thought on coming indoors was always for her precious Ronnie, asking tenderly if the day had gone well for him before dishing up the tasty snacks she brought home every day from the supermarket to tempt his appetite.

As soon as she could find a moment to speak to him on his own she whispered, 'We've got a problem, darling. Turn the telly down for a moment and I'll tell you about it.'

'What sort of a problem?'

'A money problem. It concerns all of us, everyone in this house. Including you.'

'I haven't got any money.'

'No, and you aren't likely to have any if what your Uncle Steve tells me is true. Your Grandad has started drawing all the farm money out of the bank and keeping it in a suitcase.'

'I haven't seen him with a suitcase. Where does he keep it?'

'I haven't seen it either. Gran says he keeps it under their bed.'

'How big?'

'Not very big from what I hear but that doesn't mean anything. You can get a lot of banknotes even into a small suitcase. Fifty-pound notes don't take up much room.' She held up a finger and thumb. 'A pile this thick could be worth thousands. Even if it was only twenty pound notes it would still come to a fortune.'

Ronnie didn't see it as a serious problem, or any need to get involved. 'Grandad can do what he likes with his own money, can't he?'

Alice offered him a cigarette and they both lit up. Still whispering she said, 'Listen carefully, sweetheart. Twenty years ago, when you were a little boy, Grandad sold off the two cottages on the other side of the road. They made a lot of money for those days and he promised to give it to the family. We had a meeting and discussed it.'

'What was there to discuss?'

'Everyone dies sooner or later and Grandad said he would leave us the money in his will. He didn't want to see the farm sold or split up and we agreed that he should leave the farm to your Uncle Steve on the condition that I was allowed to live here for the rest of my life. You too, treasure. That was the agreement. And Gran too, of course, assuming that Grandad dies first.'

'Sounds good to me. Where's the problem?'

'Grandad said that he didn't want any of the money himself, he would invest it for us so that there was a nice bit to share out when he died. He reckoned that he could double it if we didn't touch the capital and allowed the interest to pile up. I know a bit about money, petal, and that was good advice. And it's why we're so worried now.'

'It's still Grandad's money. If he wants to keep it under his bed I don't see we've got the right to stop him. Or ask him why he's doing it.'

'That's not how the rest of us see things, darling. We've all been hard up for years, you know we have, but we've never asked to dip into the money. We trusted Grandad because he said he would share it out between us when he died. He told me that I was entitled to the biggest share in order to compensate me for my brother inheriting the farm. What do you think about that?'

'You've got me worried now.'

'Good. Start thinking what we can do about it.'

'Tell me again why Grandad is cashing in all the money and putting it in a suitcase. He must have a reason.'

'Because the silly old fool has gone senile, that's the only explanation I can think of. He wants to keep it under his bed and count it every day. That's what misers do, sweetheart. And it isn't funny.'

Ronnie picked his nose, his way of showing that he had put his thinking cap on. He was unconvinced. 'I wasn't laughing. Just wondering why you think Grandad is going to die. No one told me he was ill.'

Alice tapped her forehead. 'He's lost it upstairs. Dementia, Alzheimers, whatever. There's no reasoning with people once they've started to go like that. They never get better, only worse.'

'Doesn't mean he's going to die though, does it? Alzheimers doesn't kill you as far as I know.'

'Quite right, Ronnie. It doesn't. But it means that he isn't a suitable person to be looking after a large sum of money. I might go and see our solicitor and ask him what he advises.'

'That would cost money, wouldn't it?'

'Better to spend a little than lose a lot. The farm doesn't pay for itself, there might even be debts to pay off. If it has to be sold after Grandad dies the family would be split up and the money likewise. Is that what you want to happen? Because I sure as hell don't.'

Ronnie picked his nose again. 'You must have a good idea how much money Grandad has been investing. Give me a clue.'

'A lot. Times weren't always hard, darling. Prices used to be high. There were generous subsidies. Grandad sold the cows and the milk quota about the same time as he sold the cottages. He was a good man for business in his day and he caught the market just right. A million pounds wouldn't be far out.'

'I still see the money as his. Even if he promised to leave it to us in his will that doesn't mean we're entitled to any of it while he's still alive.'

'When it was all properly invested, yes. In a suitcase under his bed, no.' Alice put a hand behind her ear. 'Listen hard, Ronnie. That nasty noise you hear is the sound of alarm bells ringing. I can hear them even if you can't.'

'When you said we all get a share does that include me?'

'Of course it does, darling. I've just told you.'

'And Zoe?'

'Yes, and Zoe. Grandad promised she would get her fair share even though she wasn't born when the cottages were sold. That's what he promised and we're going to hold him to it.'

After a slow start Ronnie began to take an interest. 'Did you say the suitcase was under his bed?'

'According to Gran it is. She should know.'

Ronnie looked even more thoughtful. 'It would be on his side of the bed, I suppose. Not Gran's side.'

'He's keeping the door locked so there's no way of telling. And he's got a loaded shotgun under the bed in case a burglar tries his luck.'

'Just a thought.'

Alice gave him a kiss on the forehead. 'Have more thoughts like that, precious. If I can get hold of it first I'll make sure you have your share here and now. I don't know how we're going to do it but somehow or other we've got to get our hands on that suitcase. Before the old fool loses the lot.'

6

Almost from birth Zoe Knight had taken control over her own life. She seemed to realise instinctively that her parents had little interest in her. They were relieved and pleased when she became self-reliant from an early age. She never bothered them and they never bothered her, an arrangement that soon became permanent. Once started at school she came and went as she pleased.

The bicycle was Zoe's passport to the outside world, bought with money saved up from helping her grandfather. She rode it to school throughout her period of education, if such it could be described, and in the evenings rode it back again for kick-boxing classes, the swimming pool and meeting boys. Her parents never enquired where she was going, for the very good reason that they were not interested, and did not pretend to be. They were always preoccupied with their work on the farm and left her to organise her own affairs.

Even so they were not unfriendly. Mother and daughter had a pony apiece, with stables and a five acre paddock. Although they never rode these moth-eaten ponies they fussed over them every day, grooming them, talking to them and feeding them titbits. Zoe bagged up the stable manure and wheel-barrowed it to the farm shop for her grandfather to sell to the local gardeners. He paid her for it, but not very much, and pocketed the proceeds in his capacity as the senior farm shop partner.

Even when Zoe became a sexually active teenager it never occurred to Steve and Carol that a word of parental guidance or advice might be a good idea. She had a boyfriend named Emerson, several years older than herself, and on Fridays and Saturdays went clubbing with him until the early hours of the morning. Having made her decision to stop going to school she divided her time between helping her grandfather in his farm shop and texting loving messages to Emerson.

It was left to her cousin Ronnie to tell her about their grandfather's suitcase full of money, and he did so the next afternoon. His mother was at work in the supermarket, his granny was asleep in her chair by the kitchen stove, his aunt and uncle were tending to their animals, either strawing up, feeding round or cleaning out behind them. His grandfather had chalked the single word Closed on his blackboard outside the farm gate and driven off in his Land Rover.

So the time was right and Ronnie heaved his bulk from the TV viewing settee and headed for the stairs. These were covered in slippery brown linoleum and impossible to climb without making loud creaking noises on every tread. He waddled along the upstairs passage until he reached the door of Zoe's bedroom.

Still panting after the exertion of climbing the stairs he knocked and called out, 'Got something to tell you Zo. Can I come in?'

'I don't want to see anyone.'

Ronnie put his ear to the door. 'Not crying are you, Zo?' There was no response but he could hear her snivelling and after waiting a few moments turned the handle and went in. Zoe was curled up on her bed, her eyes red from weeping, a handkerchief clutched to her mouth. He was concerned, and said so, lowering himself heavily on to her bed and putting a hand on her shoulder. 'What's the matter? Has something happened? You can tell me, Zo.'

It took her a while to answer but eventually she sobbed, 'It's Emerson. It's always bloody Emerson.'

'He hasn't made you pregnant, has he, Zo?'

'No,' she whispered. 'It isn't that.'

'What is it then? I don't like to see you crying. Have you split up with him? Is that the reason?'

The family were somewhat in awe of Emerson, a young black man who was not only well-spoken, unfailingly polite and always elegantly dressed but came from a prosperous

36

middle-class family and was ever so slightly posh. He had been Zoe's boyfriend for two years and visited the farm on numerous occasions. He had even shared their sedate Sunday dinner around the large mahogany dining table and was treated as an honorary member of the family. Joe and Martha admired his impeccable manners and were impressed by his knowledge of what went on in the world away from Nut-whistle Farm.

Between sobs Zoe said, 'No, we haven't split up. Not yet anyway.'

'Why are you crying then?'

'Because he's going to Brazil without me.'

Ronnie's knowledge of world geography was virtually nil but he knew enough about football to be aware that Brazil was a favoured nation. It took him a while to work out the reason for Zoe's tears but he got there in the end. 'You mean you were both planning to go? Without telling anyone?'

She nodded miserably. 'It was our dream, going to Brazil. I never thought he would leave me and go on his own.'

'For a holiday? Is that what you mean?'

'No, stupid. To live.'

Ronnie scratched his ear and looked puzzled. 'What's wrong with living here?'

Zoe stopped crying and said angrily, 'Because Brazil is the most wonderful place in the whole world. Don't you know anything?'

'Emerson told you that?'

'It's true, dumbo.' To prove it she picked up a travel brochure from her bedside chair and showed it to him. She clasped her hands and sighed with longing. 'The music, the sunshine, the wonderful clothes, the lovely warm sandy beaches.'

Ronnie was unmoved. 'Holiday brochures all tell you the same. Read one and you've read them all.'

'You didn't listen, we weren't going for a holiday, we were going there to live. Emerson wants to be a Brazilian. He says it's his destiny. I want it to be my destiny too.'

'It's a long way to come back if you don't like it.'

'We wouldn't want to come back.' She opened the brochure and pointed to a photograph. 'The men are so hand-some, all tanned and proud and beautiful! It will break my heart if Emerson goes without me.'

'Have you told anyone else about planning to leave home?'

'Mum and Dad know. They aren't bothered.'

'Perhaps it's all for the best if you're not going. We wouldn't want to lose you, Zo. Not me anyway.'

'Oh Ronnie, I can't bear it not to go. They dance the night away in Brazil. Every day is a carnival.'

'I saw a programme about Brazil on the telly once, they were all paddling up the river in canoes. Snakes in the water ten feet long.'

'That's in the rain forest, dimwit. I'm talking about Rio.'

'Travel brochures only tell you the good things. Don't be hasty, Zo.'

'Emerson has been learning to speak Spanish. We've been planning it for ages. Now he says he's going on his own.'

'Doesn't he love you any more?'

'Not enough to pay for my plane ticket. How can I pay for it myself? I haven't got any money, have I? You know I haven't.'

'Emerson's got plenty of money. You're his girl friend, why can't he pay for you to go?'

'He says he can't afford it.'

'Sounds to me as if he's looking for an excuse to dump you, Zo. You're a pretty girl, you can soon find yourself another boyfriend.'

She sat up and took a swipe at him before bursting into tears and howling with misery. 'I shall never have another boyfriend as good-looking as Emerson. I love him. I want to go with him. But I haven't got any bloody money.'

'Are you sure they speak Spanish in Brazil? He could have been learning the wrong language.'

'What does it matter to me if I'm not going?'

'Would you have learnt it too?'

'I would have tried. Anything so long as I could be with Emerson.'

'Don't keep crying, Zo. I came up here to tell you something. Want to hear it?'

'No. All I want is for Emerson to love me and take me to Brazil with him.'

'It's money I want to talk to you about. Are you sure you're not interested?'

'Money? What money?'

'Some of it could be ours. According to my Mum it could.'

'I don't understand what you're talking about.'

'I'm talking about Grandad. Mum says he's flipped.'

'I know you and Auntie Alice don't like Gramps but I do. I don't want to hear anything nasty about him.'

Ronnie tapped his head. 'Mum says he's lost it upstairs. He's drawn all the farm money out of the bank and got it stashed in a suitcase under his bed.'

Zoe was impressed. 'Fancy that. I guessed something must be going on. Clever old Gramps. I wonder what he's planning to do with the money?'

'Mum says some of that money was promised to us, Zo. He got it years ago when he sold those two cottages on the other side of the road. He promised to share it out in his will, including some to you and me.'

'He isn't dead yet. Anyway, wills are private. How does she know?'

'Think about it, Zo. A few thousand quid would go a long way in Brazil.'

'How much do you reckon our share would be?'

Ronnie offered his cigarettes before replying. When they had lit up and taken the first long drag he said, 'Enough to buy your plane ticket and get you started over there. Worth thinking about.'

He certainly had her attention. She was quick on the uptake and soon came through with the questions that needed to be asked. 'Have you seen the suitcase for yourself?'

'No.'

'Or Auntie Alice? Has she seen it?'

'No. Only Gran.'

'How do you know it's true then? About it being full of money?'

Ronnie began picking his nose, evidence of deep concentration. 'Mum reckons Grandad has got something wrong with him.'

'Something serious?'

'Could be. Which means that the money might be coming our way sooner than we thought.'

Zoe clapped her hands in excitement, and then re-considered. 'You mean poor old Gramps has got to die in order for us to get our share of the money?'

'Yes.'

'That's terrible.' She bit on her handkerchief again and broke fresh tears. 'All I want to do is go to Brazil with Emerson. That's not much to ask, is it?'

'Sounds reasonable to me, Zo.'

'Gramps never spends anything on himself. No use to him, is it? All that money.'

'There's a lot of difference between having money and not having money.'

'I wouldn't know. I've never had any.' Zoe squashed out her cigarette in the bedside ashtray and eyed her cousin suspiciously. 'What would you do with your share if you had it?

'I've got something in mind.'

'Want to tell me?"

'I could get married.'

'What and live here?'

'No. Somewhere else.'

'I didn't know you had a girl friend, Ronnie. You've kept that quiet.'

'Well, I have.'

'Your Mum doesn't know then?'

'No. She hasn't found out yet and I haven't told anyone else.'

'I won't let on, honest. Going to tell me who she is?'

'I don't have any secrets from you, Zo. We've always trusted one another, haven't we?'

'You know we have.'

He heaved his bulk off the bed and stood in the doorway, still pondering on the money in the suitcase. 'Grandad seems to think he's got something wrong with him and is going to die. That's why he's taken the money out of the bank. Mum isn't sure. Has he said anything to you?'

'No, but I guessed something was happening. Yesterday, when we were in the shop, Gran and Dad were keeping watch on us from the kitchen window. They must have been talking about Gramps. Now I know why.'

'I don't want him to die either. But if he's only going to die anyway . . .'

'We wouldn't need to feel guilty if he did.'

'Exactly. You want to go to Brazil, don't you? To be with Emerson?'

'You know I do.'

'And I want to get married to my girl friend. Sounds to me like we both need that money, Zo.'

'If you do something nasty to Gramps I shall never forgive you.'

'Just thinking out loud. I'm going back downstairs now, there's a programme I want to watch on the telly. See you later.'

'Wait,' Zoe called after him as he left. 'You haven't told me the name of your girl friend.'

'I will. I promised, didn't I?'

'You keen on her then?'

'Yeah. Course I am.'

'She keen on you?'

'Says she is.'

'You shagged her yet?'

Ronnie hesitated. 'No. But I'm on a promise.'

'Emerson is a wonderful lover. I want to be with him all the time.' She renewed her weeping. 'I couldn't bear it if he

41

went to Brazil without me. I would kill myself.'

Ronnie calmed her down. 'No need to do anything silly. Things here have changed, Zo. Having money in the house has made everyone jumpy. Jumpy and greedy. We shall end up fighting over that suitcase.'

This made her stare at him in sudden alarm. 'They couldn't diddle us out of it, could they? Not if Grandad wants us to have a share?' She was referring to the adults in the house who tended to treat them as if they were still children.

Ronnie shared her concern. 'I wouldn't put it past them to try. From now on we need to look out for ourselves. If I hear anything else I'll let you know. And if you hear anything you'll let me know. We're mates, right?'

7

Men are creatures of habit and Joe Knight liked to have the same breakfast every day of his life, cooked and served for him by his wife Martha. This consisted of a fried egg sitting on a big square of fried bread, with a side order of mashed potatoes, also fried until nicely browned. In the spring when the geese were laying he chose a goose egg for his breakfast treat, otherwise a duck egg or a couple of pullet's eggs.

They were always freshly laid because Joe looked after the poultry section of the farm, not too demanding as jobs go because the birds were expected to fend for themselves most of the time. A muddy pond took care of the ducks while the chicken scratched a living in the open farmyard. When they were hungry they congregated at the back door, keeping company with the kitchen cats who crouched round a big enamel dish of sour milk. Every so often Joe would scatter a handful of corn for the hens to peck up. When this happened the local pigeons would fly across from the nearest hedgerow and join in the search until every grain had been found and eaten. The farm rats also liked to keep an eye on proceedings and would sun themselves as they watched Joe collecting the eggs every morning.

He was a little more attentive with his flock of geese, and marginally more generous with the food. They would cluster protectively around him as he crossed the yard in search of his breakfast, and appear to answer his cheery greetings with a gentle burbling chorus of honks and hisses. When the ducks, hens and geese were laying well he collected the eggs in a basket, at other times in his straw beekeeper's hat. When he went indoors for his breakfast he would already have selected his chosen egg, handing it to Martha as he drew up a chair to the table.

'Very nice,' he said, mopping his plate as he finished his daily fry-up. 'Set me right for the rest of the day that will. What you got on this morning, Martha?'

'Zoe is going to hang some washing out for me. As it's Tuesday I'm doing Shepherd's Pie and Rice Pudding for our dinner. That suit you?'

'Sounds good. How's your arthritis today?'

'About the same.'

'Don't overdo it then.' He pushed back his chair. 'Better go and open up the shop. Looks as if it might be a fine day. That brings the gardeners out. They all want sacks of manure for their winter bedding plants at this time of year.'

Martha said, 'Don't go for a minute, Joe. We need to have a talk about the money. The money in the suitcase under our bed.'

He stood awkwardly behind his chair, not sure how to react when challenged so openly by his wife. This was not something that happened very often. Trying to sound reasonable he said, 'I explained it to you, Martha. What is there to talk about?'

'A lot, I should say. What the hell are you playing at? That's what we all want to know.'

'We?'

'Steve is worried. Alice is worried. We're all worried. You owe us a better explanation than the one you gave me.'

Instead of replying he took his tin of tobacco from his jacket pocket and rolled a cigarette in his fingers. This provided him with thinking time. When he had pinched off the end he lit it with a big brass cigarette lighter in a gush of sooty flame. He was not pleased at the turn the conversation had taken and squinted at his wife through the first billow of smoke. 'You've always left the business side of the farm to me. What makes you think you could do it better?'

'Don't go all sarcastic on me, Joe.'

'You must have blabbed to the others. How would they know about it otherwise?'

'Of course I told them. We're a family, they have a right to know. You should have told us last Sunday when we were all sitting round the dinner table together. Why the secrecy?'

'Don't glare at me like that, Martha. Trust me. I know what I'm doing.'

'I doubt that very much. Tell me again why you think you're going to die.'

He looked embarrassed and shifted uneasily from foot to foot. 'You didn't need to tell that to the others. That was between me and you, Martha. Husband and wife. I thought you had the right to know first.'

'What are you proposing to die of, Joe? You must have some idea.'

'Not being rude to me, are you, Martha? This is a very serious matter we're talking about. I'll thank you not to take it lightly.'

'We're all on edge over the money. Taking it out of the bank and stuffing it in a suitcase is a crazy way of behaving. You've made a will, let the lawyers handle it so that it all gets done properly.'

'Too late for that, my dear. I've got the money together, I've split it up how I want it split up, and that's what's going to happen. You know I don't trust lawyers.'

'And we don't trust you. Where does that get us?'

'Not a very nice thing for a wife to say to her husband.'

'Joe, you need to see a doctor. That funny turn you had just after Christmas must have done something nasty to your brains. You wouldn't be talking crap like this otherwise.'

'Actually I'm talking good sense. There's not much to be gained from investing money these days. Interest rates are rock bottom and the banks are cleaned out and run by the government. Seems to me my money is safer where I can keep an eye on it.'

'How can it be safer under our bed than it is in a bank?'

He drew breath to argue the point but his cigarette had gone out so he relit it in a whoosh of flame and oily black smoke. 'Don't quarrel with me, Martha. I want you to have good memories of me when I'm up in the churchyard.'

This made Martha weep. She sobbed in despair. 'My poor Joe. Can't you see how this looks to other people? Telling us you're going to die, telling us you don't trust lawyers, keeping money under the bed, whatever next? You really have gone soft in the head.'

'No, I haven't. What a thing to say to your husband! Whatever has come over you today, Martha?'

'You've started locking the bedroom door. Our bedroom door. Is that any way to go on in your own house?'

Joe looked up at the kitchen clock. 'Ah well, can't stand around all day yarning, there's someone I want to go and see before I open up the shop.' At the door he put on his hat and coughed apologetically. 'As a matter of fact I've been meaning to talk to you about the bedroom door myself.'

'Leaving it unlocked would be a good start. And taking the gun away from under the bed.'

'I've got a man coming to see me from that new security firm in the town. The old mortise lock isn't up to the job so I've asked him to fit a new one, and to put in a cylinder lock as well. Double protection, Martha, you can't be too careful. And also put bars over the windows. Just in case anyone tried to climb up a ladder and get in that way.'

Martha was angry but too dispirited to argue, recognising a lost situation when she saw one. Knowing the answer in advance she whispered, 'Don't I get a key then? To my own bedroom?'

'You never go upstairs during the day. You won't be in-convenienced. Try and co-operate with me, Martha. I'm not doing this for my benefit, I'm doing it for you. For our children. For our grandchildren. To secure their future.'

'Joe, it's only fair to tell you that Ronnie and Zoe don't like what you're doing any more than the rest of us.'

'This made him angry. 'It's my money and I can do what I like with it.'

'It isn't your money. It's family money. We've all helped to earn it in our different ways and we don't want you to lose it for us. We can see it happening.'

'Why do you keep on about me losing it? I'm keeping it safe, can't you understand that?'

'You need to see a doctor, Joe. A psychiatrist. You're not right in the head.'

'That isn't a very nice thing for a woman to keep saying to her husband.'

It was Martha's turn to be conciliatory. She softened her voice and leaned out to touch his hand. 'Don't do this to us, Joe. Steve and Alice are sick with worry. What are they going to do if we have a burglary and all the money is stolen?'

'No one will be able to get into that room, Martha. The money will be safe in there. And in there it's going to stay.'

'What about when you go to the bank or the post office or the building society and come out with a wad of banknotes in your pocket? You could get robbed.'

'It won't come to that. I've got another gun in the Land Rover.'

'Joe, you're an old fool to be putting us to this worry. Put the money back in the bank and leave it there to earn some interest.'

With his hand on the door he hesitated once more. He had something difficult to say but was determined not to shirk it, having got to this stage. He said, 'I can't risk it, Martha. Can't risk anyone else having keys to the room, not even you. Sorry'

She started to cry again. 'I can't believe what I'm hearing.'

'I'll help you move your things into the spare room. A light airy room, that is, and it faces west so you'll get a nice lot of sunshine. You'll be more comfortable at night on your own. Alice's bedroom is next door so she can look in to see that you're all right. It will be for the best, trust me.'

8

Martha took the first opportunity to tell this latest item of bad news to Steve when he came in for his elevenses, and he lost no time in passing it on to his wife Carol. At this hour of the morning she was busy in the building that housed their calves. She was cleaning out their pens but stopped what she was doing when he opened the door and came in. She could see that he was angry and upset.

'Has something happened?' she asked him. 'What's Joe been up to now?' She had always called her father-in-law 'Joe', not being comfortable with 'Dad'. Nor did she expect a prize for guessing who was responsible for Steve's agitation.

'You're right, it's bloody Dad again. You're never going to believe it. This morning he told Ma she's got to move into the spare room.'

'Oh, your poor mother,' Carol said at once, briefly touching his arm in a gesture of sympathy. 'You can't mean it, turned out of her own bedroom at her time of life. This goes from bad to worse.'

'She can take her dressing table and bedside chair and some other bits and pieces. I said I'd move her stuff into the spare room after breakfast tomorrow morning. Is that all right with you?'

'I expect she will need some help in sorting out her clothes as well. We'll both have to do our best to make her comfortable.'

'Thanks, love. She would appreciate that, I know she would.'

'Glad to help. I'm only sorry it should be necessary.'

Steve shook his head in angry bewilderment. 'Forty years and more they've been married. It's almost as bad as a divorce, pushing Ma off into the spare room.'

'You're right there, love. It's the principle. Even if she will be more comfortable on her own it would still come hard to her. It would to any married woman.'

'There's worse. Dad's moving her out so that he can have new locks fitted on their bedroom door. One of the security firms from the town is coming to do the work. And put bars on the windows. What do you think about that?'

'I can hardly believe what I'm hearing. When is all this going to happen?'

'I don't know exactly when but Ma thought it would be soon. Before the end of the week.'

'Is it to keep burglars out? Or to keep us out?'

'Us, most likely.'

The calves were expecting to be fed and kept up a constant clamour of bleating and bellowing to draw attention to the fact that they were hungry. For once Steve and Carol had problems of their own and took no notice. Steve continued to shake his head in disbelief. 'Bars on the window, locks on the door! Not much like a happy home, is it?'

'Joe acted fast as soon as he knew we were on to him.'

'I'm beginning to think that Ma was right. I mean about him being funny in the head. Hiding money under the bed with a loaded shotgun is a crazy way to carry on in his own house.'

Carol gave a suppressed scream. 'You don't mean he would shoot one of us, do you?'

'Not purposely, of course not, but you can see how an accident might happen. A bit of misunderstanding in the dark, shouting, panic, and then bang! Guns can go off when you least expect them. We wouldn't be the first family to lose someone like that.'

'Don't.' Carol put her hands over her ears. 'It doesn't bear thinking about.'

Steve gave her a comforting pat on the shoulder. 'I've got some more scraping up to do. Can you manage the calves?'

'Yes, you had better get on, we're running late as it is.' She pointed. 'That white heifer calf at the far end is scouring a bit.

I know we don't usually give hay to calves but I might try a wisp or two and see what effect that has.'

'See you at lunchtime then.' At the calf-shed door he hesitated, removed his cap and worried his hair with his hand. 'There must be something we can do to stop Dad doing what he's doing. Don't know what though. It's a bugger.'

Steve and Carol were not only companionably married but also worked together all day and every day. They stayed close and were seldom out of one another's sight for more than a few minutes. They were not much interested in anyone else, nor did their conversation stray far from farming matters or the next job needing their attention.

They ate lunch on their own every day, in the privacy of their married quarters, a small internal flat devised for Joe's mother while she was alive, with her own kitchen and bathroom. Their daily lunch seldom varied, today as usual it was digestive biscuits and triangles of processed cheese washed down by mugs of scalding hot tomato soup. They usually sat around for half an hour or so before returning to work but today Carol was in no mood for rest and relaxation. She lit a cigarette and began to think aloud. 'The suitcase would be on your Dad's side of the bed, wouldn't it? That would be logical.'

'I suppose so.'

'I should like to see that suitcase for myself. Just to be quite sure there is a suitcase, and to get an idea what it looks like.'

'What did you have in mind?'

'I think we should put a ladder up and take a look. Your Dad sleeps on the side nearest the window so if it's there we should be able to see it.'

'When?'

'He doesn't open his shop in the afternoons any more. The last few days he's started going off on his own in the Land Rover. We shall never have a better opportunity.'

'Now, do you mean?'

'Why not? It's a bright sunny day so we should be able to

see inside the bedroom. If we put it off and the security firm comes to fit the bars on the windows we will have lost our chance.'

'It would be awkward if anyone saw us.'

'Not much of a risk if we're quick. How about it?'

'All right. If you say so.'

'The window is high up on that side of the house. We shall need the long ladder from the implement shed.'

'Suppose Dad came back and caught us in the act?'

'We should just have to tough it out. Ask him what the hell he's playing at. Come to think of it that might be the best thing that could happen.'

'It would be embarrassing.'

'Not nearly so embarrassing as finding ourselves bankrupt.' Carol stubbed out her cigarette in a squish of smoke and cinders. 'Come on, love. Let's not argue, I want to see that suitcase for myself. If we get the ladder down now we can be ready to carry it round the moment Joe drives out of the gate.'

The ladder was stored lengthways on the crossbeams of the implement shed rafters. It was a wooden ladder, long and heavy, but they managed to lower it down and then to hide it behind the shed where it was out of sight from the house. This took some effort after which they had to be patient and kill time until Joe left the farm.

There is nothing more tedious than waiting on the movements of someone else. Trying not to make it obvious they worked within sight of the farmhouse as much as possible, always keeping in view the long open-sided cart shed where Joe Knight garaged his crumpled but much loved Land Rover Defender. This vehicle was as filthy inside as out. For most of his life he had climbed up into the driver's seat at first light every morning and then set off on a tour of the farm. It was as much a part of him as his tattered waxed jacket, his sweat-stained beekeeper hat or his mud-encrusted boots. He didn't feel properly dressed until he was behind the wheel with his elbow on the window sill, coughing and spluttering with his first cigarette of the day.

Steve and Carol kept glancing anxiously at the sky, fearing that clouds would obscure the sun, and it was by no means as bright as when they sat down to eat their lunch. When Joe did not appear after his midday meal they guessed he must have gone up to his bedroom for a snooze. Two hours passed but just when they had abandoned hope they saw him emerge from the house, leaving it by the front door rather than the kitchen door at the back.

This was because he had a choice of staircases when leaving his bedroom and entering the long upstairs passage. If he turned right he would come down the back stairs into the kitchen, if he turned left he would go down the main staircase into the hall. When he was heading for his Land Rover he mostly used the main staircase and the front door, this being the shortest route to the old cart shed.

The moment he had driven off through the farm gate Steve and Carol hurried back to the implement shed to fetch the ladder. They had not told Martha what they intended to do and hoped that she would be dozing in her chair by the stove. To make doubly sure they were unobserved they carried the heavy ladder on a circuitous route so that they could arrive from the opposite direction after going the long way round the house. Hoisting it up to the window took a lot of strength and after satisfying themselves that it was firmly anchored in the soft earth of a flowerbed Steve volunteered to go up first.

A minute later he called down hoarsely, 'It's there, Carol.'

'Let me have a look.'

'Hold on a sec.'

'What are you doing?'

Steve was leaning dangerously sideways to examine the casement windows but came to the conclusion that there was no easy way of breaking in. He climbed down the ladder and changed places with his wife, who had been standing on the lowest rung by way of counterweight.

Carol went up in turn and pressed her face to the window. Although not easy to see inside she waited until her eyes had adjusted and then saw it for herself. Visible beneath the bedspread was the handle of a suitcase. It was the kind of lightweight aluminium suitcase that passed as hand luggage on an airline journey. She called down, 'I can see it, Steve. What shall we do now?'

'We must put the ladder back. It wouldn't look good if we were caught doing this.'

'Not so fast. I want a closer look.'

'What do you reckon, Carol?'

'Easily forced open, that's what I'm thinking. If the wrong person got hold of it.'

'We must make sure that doesn't happen.'

'Do you want to have another look?'

'No. I only wanted to make sure that it existed.'

'It exists all right. I wish it didn't.'

Lowering the heavy ladder was just as difficult as raising it but they managed without incident and carried it back the way they had come. When it was returned to its usual place in the implement shed rafters they stared at one another grim-faced. Carol said, 'I never doubted that your Ma was telling the truth. It's just that you have to see for yourself, don't you?'

Steve nodded in agreement. 'Dad's not to be trusted with all that money. I fear the worst, Carol. Should we go and see the doctor and try to get him some treatment?'

'What sort of treatment?'

'Pills. For his dementia. That's what he's suffering from isn't it?'

Carol was dubious. 'I'm not sure there are any pills that work for Alzheimers. I can't see Joe letting us take him to the surgery either. And if we went on our own and explained about the money it would look as if we were trying to get hold of it for ourselves.'

'Ma thinks he ought to see a psychiatrist.'

'An appointment would take months. We can't wait that long.'

'There must be something we can do.'

'I had a little chat with Alice last night. There's a box of old keys on the shelf in the woodshed. We were wondering if one of them would open the door.'

'Doesn't Ma have a key to the bedroom?'

'The first thing I asked her. No, she doesn't, because the room was never locked before. She said there was a spare key in the kitchen drawer but we couldn't find it when we looked. Joe must have got there first.'

'It's only an old cheap lock. One of the other keys might fit. It's worth a try.'

'I doubt if Joe would go out tonight, not after going out this afternoon. Tomorrow, perhaps. It's Alice's early turn and if Joe goes out I'll go upstairs with her and see if we can open the door. It will probably be our only chance before the new locks are fitted.'

Steve was worried about what they would do next. 'If you got in would you try and open the suitcase?'

'I don't know. I would have to ask Alice. She's more used to handling money than I am. '

'I don't like it, Carol.'

'We'll manage without you then.' She turned on him in a temper, their first angry exchange since the day they were married. 'For Christ's sake, Steve, stiffen up a bit. You and me have worked our asses off for almost twenty years so that your Dad can take life easy, and he's certainly done that. If he really has gone silly in the head we can't just do nothing and let him lose the lot. This is our future we're talking about. And without the money we don't have a future.'

9

The next evening Carol sat at her small kitchen table in the annexe rooms she shared with Steve. Her sister-in-law Alice sat beside her. They were examining a cobwebbed wooden box which contained a jumbled assortment of spare keys, looking for one that might fit Joe Knight's bedroom door. The spare key collection had been rusting away gently on a shelf in the woodshed, a brick outbuilding joined on at the end of the house and used for storing logs and kindling.

Joe had obliged by driving off in his Land Rover so they knew they would never have a better opportunity. Steve was not happy about their plan for trying to enter the bedroom and distanced himself by going off on his evening rounds. This routine involved feeding those animals that needed to be fed, strawing up, checking that all the gates were shut and the water troughs working, kissing the calves goodnight and fussing over a sick cow in a loose box. He could have done it in his sleep.

Alice and Carol were fortifying themselves with strong mugs of coffee before going upstairs to try the lock. They were aware of being the two most competent people in the house, and of the necessity for joining forces if anything was to get done. The two women were on friendly terms because neither had anything the other wanted, and understood instinctively that sisterly solidarity was in their best interests. Both were busy all day long, even if in different ways, and in the nature of busy people they could always make short work of any extra demand that came their way. At Christmas, or for any family celebration where food, cooking and organising skills were required, they managed the proceedings with the brisk orderliness of all middle-aged women used to looking after men.

The difference in their size was more apparent in the confines of the small granny-annexe kitchen. Carol was tiny compared with Alice, a much heftier woman. Carol's face was lined and weather-beaten, her hands stained, her hair badly cut and her expression on this occasion more than usually harassed. Alice worked with the public as well as handling food and this required her to be clean in her person and neat in appearance. She had nicely kept hands, her greying hair was coloured a rich auburn and after many years as a supervisor she had acquired the don't-mess-me-around attitude of someone who was more accustomed to being obeyed than argued with.

Needing to get on with it before their nerve failed they crept up the back stairs with the box of keys. They were understandably apprehensive and winced at the creaking staircase, impossible to climb in silence. Alice had collected all the other keys she could find in the house, trying to remember which doors they came from so that they could be correctly replaced. They reached the landing and turned left along the upstairs passageway which had bedrooms on both sides. First came the bathroom and lavatory, then an airing and linen cupboard, and then the largest of the bedrooms where they came to a stop outside the door. It was not only the biggest but had the best view, and was now in single occupation.

'Your poor mother,' Carol said, with feeling. 'Fancy having to move out at her time of life. Not right, is it?'

'Thank you for helping to go through her clothes. I'm afraid her chest of drawers had got into a bit of a muddle.'

'We managed. Steve is going to rig up an extra heater for her tomorrow.'

'I don't think Ma really minds. It will seem strange at first but the spare room is very comfortable and she will be next door to me if she wants anything. She knows she'll get a lot more peace and quiet on her own.'

Carol tried the door handle. 'It's locked sure enough. Thought it would be.'

'I'm glad it is. Wouldn't want Dad to leave it open when he went out, or to take the suitcase with him when he went to the pub.'

'It's still not right though. We've never had to contend with things like this before.'

They both knelt in turn and looked into the keyhole but could not see through. It was a cheap single-lever mortise lock, the metal plate discoloured with age. Alice gave the box a shake. 'You used to be able to buy keys like this from any ironmonger's shop. They fitted every lock almost. One of them is bound to be right.'

Carol selected the most likely key and handed it to her sister-in-law. 'Try this one first.'

Still kneeling Alice inserted the key. They were even more nervous now, but just as determined. For a moment it seemed they were going to be lucky first time round as the key half turned in the lock. 'Almost, almost,' Alice wept in frustration. 'Is there another one this shape?'

'This one looks hopeful,' Carol whispered, passing it to her.

Again the lock almost turned, but not quite. Nor did the next one do the trick, nor the one after that, and soon they were more than halfway through the box.

'Don't get them muddled up,' Alice whispered back. 'You're not putting the ones we've tried back in the same box, are you?'

'I think we've got them mixed up already. We should have brought a second box to put them in as we tried them.'

'Time for you to have a go,' Alice said, standing up and straightening her back. She stared in distaste at her fingers which were stained brown with rust and oil. 'I don't think we're going to be lucky.'

'Don't give up yet,' Carol pleaded, still speaking in a whisper and looking round uneasily. The upstairs passage was lit by a single dim bulb, it made them look like skulking conspirators as they rummaged in the box of keys while on their hands and knees outside Joe Knight's bedroom door. She selected another, one they had not tried before, holding it up against the light. 'How about this one?'

Alice shook her head. 'It's not long enough.'

'This one?'

'It's the wrong shape.'

There were about thirty keys in all and after separating out those which were obviously not going to fit they were left with a dozen possibles. Carol sorted through these again. 'I don't think we've tried this one yet.'

'I'm sure we have.'

'I'll try it again then, just to be sure. We can't stay up here much longer.' The key went in easily and made a half turn, once again their hopes surged and once again they were disappointed. However much Carol wiggled it in the lock it would not turn. 'It's no good,' she said, sighing in despair. 'It won't open the bloody door.'

'What's the matter now?'

'I can't get it out.'

'Let me have a try.'

Alice tried it standing up, then kneeling down again. She peered sideways into the keyhole to see why the key would not come out, but was unable to wiggle it free. It would turn from side to side but hitched up somewhere when they tried to withdraw it from the keyhole. It was exasperating and annoying. Pushing back a streak of hair from her forehead she said, 'I need a cigarette.'

'A pair of pliers would be more help. Let me have another go.'

'Don't force it, Carol. If it breaks off in the lock we're done for.'

'I shall have to go and fetch Steve. He's good with tools. He'll know how to get it out.'

'Christ, what a mess,' Alice muttered in disgust. She had not thought to wear an apron and her sweating fingers had made dirty marks on her blouse. The passage was carpeted with a hardwearing cord but outside the door there was enough dust and debris after their efforts to show that something had been going on. It was turning into a messy disaster.

Carol hurried downstairs where she pulled on her fleece and went running off into the farm buildings to find Steve. Having found him in the loose-box with the sick cow she explained the situation and pleaded with him to help. He was not keen but recognised it as an emergency and followed Carol back to the house and up the back stairs where they rejoined Alice outside the parental bedroom. The wait had not done much for Alice's frayed nerves but she was relieved to see her brother and pointed to the key in the lock.

It took Steve a few minutes to wiggle the key free and remove it from the door. Having done so he cleaned it on his sleeve and picked at it with one of the tools he had brought with him to do the job. 'I think it would go now, shall I try it again?' he enquired of his wife and sister.

'No!' they replied at the same time, and with considerable feeling.

Carol made the motion of lifting a glass to her lips and pointed downstairs. 'We all need a drink. Steve's got a bottle of white wine in our sideboard. I'll fetch the dustpan and brush to clean up here, and then I'll join you when I've finished.'

'I couldn't go through all that again,' Alice admitted when they were back in the tiny kitchen and sitting round the table with a bottle and glasses. 'Breaking and entering isn't as easy as it sounds.'

'At least we tried.'

Alice was having second thoughts. 'Even if we'd got in we would have had to force open the suitcase. Are we ready for a showdown with Dad? I don't think so.'

Carol disagreed. 'If we're not we should be. We've got to face it sooner or later. The longer we put it off the more difficult it will be. I say we should tackle him as soon as possible.'

Steve had the most to lose. He said gloomily, 'We didn't need all this grief over the money. How it's going to end I dread to think.' He poured the drinks, the ladies lit cigarettes and they contemplated a situation over which they had as yet been unable to exert any control.

Carol thought they were giving up too easily. 'Joe's an old man, we ought to be able to get the better of him if we all stick together. He shouldn't be allowed to think he can do something like this on his own without consulting us first.'

Alice was thinking along the same lines. 'Dad never believed in fattening the pig until market day. He may be old and a bit senile, and we can excuse him for that, but he's been devious as well. You can't just toddle up to the counter of a bank or a building society and start drawing out large sums of money over the counter. It would need a lot of forward planning to fill a suitcase with cash. He must have been planning this months ago and doing it little at a time so as not to arouse any suspicion. And he's got away with it.'

Steve had an admission to make, 'I had a rummage around in Dad's office today. The filing cabinet was locked. For the first time ever, I should imagine.'

'That was the right place to look,' Alice said approvingly. 'A bright idea, Stevie. Dad never throws anything away and he must have needed a lot of paperwork to keep track of all that money. Bonds, share certificates, brochures, tax returns, pass books, six monthly reports. All the fund managers send those out hoping that you'll invest a bit more with them.' She handed back her glass for a refill. 'Perhaps we should have been trying to break into that filing cabinet instead of the bedroom.'

Carol beckoned the others to lean forward. 'While we're on the subject there's another little matter we need to discuss. I know Steve doesn't like talking about it but we've shirked it long enough. '

Steve looked even more unhappy. 'What is it now, Carol? Or can I guess?'

'You guessed right. I want to know where Betty Hounsome fits into all this.'

Alice was the first to react. 'Where does Betty fit in? Nowhere, I hope.'

Carol soon disillusioned her. 'Joe calls every day at Betty's bungalow now. He's probably there at this very moment, and her husband hardly cold in his grave, poor man. She was quick off the mark as usual.'

'How could she have known about the money before we did?'

'Not unless Joe told her himself. I don't see how she could have found out otherwise.'

Alice winced. 'That makes sense. At Dad's age, and considering his state of health, he won't be visiting her to make use of her services. There must be another reason why he goes to see her so often, and it could be to do with the money.'

Carol disagreed. 'I reckon Dad is making up for lost time. Give Betty her due, she didn't see any of her other clients all the time she was married to the bookmaker. Dad might not be the only one who's been feeling deprived.'

Steve worried his hair with his hand, making it stand up on end. His wife did not like to see this visible sign of agitation and smoothed it down for him. When he had recovered his composure he said, 'I've always taken the view that if Ma didn't mind about Betty there was no point in the rest of us getting in a twist over it.'

'She's the same age as me,' Alice said glumly. 'And still wears short skirts. Looks good in them, though, you have to admit that.'

'Not as short as the skirts she wore to school,' Carol reminded her.

'She was hot stuff even then. All the men she's pleasured have had their money's worth. Dad included.'

'He's been on her visiting list a long time. How long exactly do you reckon?'

'Ever since Ma's arthritis got so bad. Ten years at least.'

Steve poured the last of the wine, shaking the empty bottle into his wife's glass. The kitchen was dimly lit and with three people in a small space it had become pleasantly warm. All three were at the end of long working day and in no hurry to move. The white wine was making them pleasantly drowsy so for a few minutes they were silent, thinking about their old schoolmate Betty Hounsome. Twice divorced and recently widowed she now lived in a posh ranch-style bungalow because she had successfully traded sex for prosperity with her succession of husbands, each one better off than the last. Blonde and blue-eyed with nice legs she had also been endowed with a bright and friendly personality. As if that was not enough she possessed a natural aptitude for getting on with men. She had found life very pleasant.

Joe Knight's past association with the frisky widow was condoned by his wife Martha following the onset of her painful arthritis in middle age. In his prime Joe had been a lusty twice-a-nighter and even in his sixties had needed sex regularly to keep him in a good mood. He was not the most adroit of lovers but reckoned to make up for it by being exceptionally vigorous. Martha may have liked it once but as her arthritis worsened his hairy-chested enthusiasm became so painful that she was forced to plead for an end to her marital duties.

She was relieved and grateful when Joe found a workable solution to their problem. Knowing that he had his wife's permission he came to an accommodation with Betty Hounsome, a local girl he had known from birth, her father being one of his village drinking buddies as a young man. Betty had always had a soft spot for Joe in spite of the difference in their ages and was happy to oblige. She was fond of sex herself and could understand his feelings at being deprived when Martha became permanently indisposed. Because of her somewhat chaotic love life and various marriages she fitted in Joe's conjugal visits as often as she could, enough to keep him satisfied until the next time she was available. Which she was again now, all day and every day, since the sudden death of her bookmaker husband.

This was the new set of circumstances exercising the imagination of the three family members gathered in Carol's kitchen. Joe Knight's intermittent adultery over many years had been condoned as a discreet and common-sense way of resolving a delicate sexual dilemma. The affair had been managed with the best of neighbourly good manners and the minimum of expense, a situation that had suddenly changed. Because of the scare over the suitcase full of money this lazy and indulgent acceptance of Joe's bit on the side was suddenly surrounded with suspicion, jealousy and bitterness.

Carol took a nervous puff at her cigarette. 'Joe used to park out of sight at the back of Betty's bungalow but now he leaves his Land Rover in her drive where everyone can see it. Make of that what you will.'

Steve's instinct had always been to defend his father when any criticism of him was made by another member of the family, even his wife. 'We can't know that he's told her about the money. He's not a great one for discussing his business affairs with other people. He doesn't trust accountants, or lawyers, or bank managers. He certainly never tells any of us what he's up to. Why should he tell Betty anything?'

His wife and sister had taken a sudden violent dislike to their playground chum and indulged themselves in a bitching match. 'Would she waste her time on Dad if she wasn't getting anything out of it?' Alice enquired of her sister-in-law.

'I doubt it. She's a smart bit of goods, is Betty. She had her head screwed on tight even at school, she could get the boys to do anything for her almost. I'm not saying she didn't deliver, because she always did, but none of them ever got it for nothing. The same with all the men in her life. When she wanted a nice new television she dated the boy from the electrical shop. When she wanted her first car she took up with one of the married men in the garage.'

'Whatever he wasn't getting at home Betty would certainly have provided it.'

'Exactly. Anything she wanted she soon found a man silly enough to give it to her. How she rewarded them is not our business but I'm sure it cost her a lot less effort than saving up her pennies like the rest of us had to.'

Alice tried to think a little more positively. 'Dad has

always been a tight-arsed old so-and-so. Betty would have to work hard to part him from very much.'

'She certainly wouldn't be satisfied with a couple of tenners under her pillow, if that's what you mean.'

'We could be worrying unnecessarily. He's never paid the full price for anything in his life, and I can't see him changing now.'

'Not even for a bunk-up with Betty Hounsome?'

'I honestly don't know. Dad has always been a mean sod, if he could get laid on the cheap he wouldn't see any need to be generous.'

Carol was not so sure. 'Men can't resist showing off. If he's really got his hands on a lot of cash it would be an easy way to impress her.'

'I don't like the sound of that. It sounds horribly true, that's why.'

'I reckon we've good reason to be worried. It's too much of a coincidence, him taking the money out of the bank and getting thick with Betty at the same time.' Carol turned to her husband and held up her empty glass. 'Go and find another bottle, love. There's some sherry in the larder, on the shelf with the pickles, at the back. I was saving it to put in the Christmas cake.'

Alice said, 'Dad was always distrustful of big institutions, my guess is that he would have spread the money into a lot of fairly small accounts. Not easy for us to track it down, or for any of the branch managers to suspect anything when he started drawing it out in cash.' She stubbed her cigarette and shifted uncomfortably in her chair. 'I wonder if he was planning to do something like this right from the start? Devious old bugger.'

Steve had always taken his father's side in any family dispute and did so once again, from force of habit. When he had found the bottle of sherry and filled the glasses he said, 'Be fair, Alice. All the money is in Dad's name, the cottages belonged to him, and most of the farm money. I know he promised to give us a share but that was only in his will. We can't really say it's our money in the suitcase.'

'That isn't true, Stevie. He told us it was family money and he promised to look after it for us. To invest it wisely. He reckoned it would double in value by the time he died.'

Carol gnawed at a ragged fingernail. 'We all believed that money was safe. For all we know he could have been drawing on it for years to keep Betty Hounsome in frilly knickers and hair spray.'

This alarmed Alice even more. 'God, I hope you're not right. If so we've only got ourselves to blame.'

'Why us? We haven't done anything wrong.'

'Oh yes we have. We all wanted a quiet life and this is the result. Dad could have handed over thousands of pounds of our money and us none the wiser. I just hope it's not too late.'

Carol sighed. 'I know Betty spends a lot on clothes and cosmetics but you have to admit it pays off for her. No one would look at me twice.'

'Not fair, is it? All those men and oceans of booze and she still swishes her ass about as if she was nineteen.'

'I've never been jealous of Betty, or wished her any harm, but if Dad really has gone soft in the head and she's taken advantage of him I shall never forgive her.'

'There's no fool like an old fool. Isn't that what they say?'

'Screwing that woman doesn't come cheap. She's always got a big pay day in mind. Whose money has Dad been paying her with? Ours, without a doubt.'

Steve was more cautious. 'I know Dad doesn't wash and shave and keep himself as smart as he used to but I wouldn't describe him as senile. I've heard what you've been saying but I don't agree with it. I don't think he would have told Betty anything about his private affairs. I still think the money is safe.'

'Safe under his bed?'

'We should have a family meeting and ask him to tell us what he's got planned for the money. So we can hear it for ourselves. No need for anyone to be rude or unpleasant.'

'When did you have in mind?'

'Alice has got the weekend off. What's wrong with raising it with him after we've had our Sunday dinner? All the family will be together. We might not have another opportunity for weeks.'

Alice and Carol looked at one another and eventually shrugged acceptance. Carol said, 'I would have liked it to be sooner but if we're all sitting down and in our places he would have to listen to us.'

'It would be only fair to tell him before the meal that we're going to ask him for an explanation.'

'So long as no one leaves the table. Steve and me will have to tell Zoe what's going on.'

Alice said, 'And I'll tell Ronnie. It needs some thinking about. Suppose Betty Hounsome's name is mentioned?'

Carol waved this aside, cigarette in hand. 'They've always known about her, both of them, Zoe and Ronnie. It won't come as a surprise.'

Steve was having second thoughts. Although he had suggested the Sunday dinner confrontation he was apprehensive ahead of the event. 'It all depends on how well Dad takes it. Being questioned, I mean. It could turn nasty.'

'Doesn't it always where money is concerned?'

'I suppose so.' Steve refilled their glasses once more. He forced a smile. 'Let's hope poor old Dad doesn't suffer the same fate as Betty's last husband.'

'I'll drink to that,' Carol said, taking a glug of the sweet brown sherry. 'The old bookie took her on at her own game but he soon ended up in a wooden overcoat. I hope Joe's got more sense than to try, at his time of life.'

Betty Hounsome's third marriage had been to a retired bookmaker with plenty of money and a weak heart. It was his wish to die happy and on the job, entering into the marriage with the declared intention of shagging himself to death, as he boasted many times in the golf club bar. Betty made sure he did exactly that, leaving her nicely placed financially in his sumptuously appointed retirement bungalow, and to the intense annoyance of his other relatives who had backed the wrong horse in the inheritance stakes.

But Steve and Alice took the point of Carol's cautionary tale. Namely that in a contest of sharp wits between the rapacious widow and the whiskery old farmer there could be only one winner, and it wasn't likely to be Joe Knight.

10

Joe Knight was lying full length on a settee. The settee was in the spacious front room of the ranch-style bungalow belonging to the recently widowed Betty Hounsome. She was sitting down on the settee, cradling his head in her lap.

He said, 'I told Martha I was going to die. I don't think she believed me.'

'That's because you still haven't told her about going to the hospital. When are you going to tell her, Joe?'

'It's difficult. I didn't tell her at the time because I didn't want to worry her. Her arthritis was terrible bad last winter, she was the one who should have gone to the hospital, not me.'

'The longer you put off telling her the more difficult it's going to be.'

'It will look bad for me. As if I was lying to her.'

'No it won't.'

'Yes it will. All I had was a couple of outpatient appointments and some tests but I still should have told her. Couldn't bring myself to admit that I had something wrong with me, I suppose. Pride, Betty. It's been the undoing of better men than me.'

'Oh Joe, you should have let me come with you. If only so that there was someone else hearing what the specialist said to you. Doctors aren't always right.'

'They're always right when you don't want them to be right.'

'I know, lover. I wish I could help you.'

'No one wants to die, do they? I certainly don't.'

'I think the doctor was a bit hard on you. If he really told you what you think he told you. Are you sure you didn't misunderstand him?'

'My own fault, Betty. I asked him to tell me the truth, and he did. I can't complain about it afterwards.'

'Just how bad is your blood pressure? Is it as high as they say it is?'

'Higher. That's why the doctor reckoned I was done for. He said I wouldn't last much longer whatever they did for me.'

'Are they sure they didn't offer you any treatment?'

'I decided long ago I would never have an operation, any sort of operation. Can you blame me?'

'Oh Joe, there's nothing to be frightened of these days. It's not too late. If Martha can't go with you then I'll come with you. We'll make some appointments and get you seen to. Let me help you, Joe.'

'It's too late for that. I'm on the way out and I'd sooner spend my last days at home than in a hospital bed hitched up to a machine with needles in my arm.'

'It won't come to that if you look after yourself. Why don't you try to stop smoking? That's what the doctor told you to do, didn't he?'

'It's my own fault to end up like this. I'm overdue, well overdue. Just living on borrowed time, that's what I'm doing.'

'Don't say things like that, Joe. It upsets me.'

'I can feel myself going, Betty. I come over all cold sometimes, I can feel my pulse slowing right down. It's going to be soon, I know it.'

'I only wish there was something I could do to help you.'

Keeping hold of her hand he said in a quavering voice, 'Being able to tell someone makes a big difference. Thank you for trying to cheer me up.'

'Don't cry, Joe. There's no need to cry.' She gave his hand a comforting squeeze.

'Poor Martha. We've been married a long time. Forty-one years. She was only nineteen.'

'That is a long time.'

'She's ten years younger than me. That means she could be a widow for ages and ages. She's bound to miss me.'

'She must see you taking your medication. Doesn't she have any idea how bad you are?' When he did not respond she gave him a prod in the chest with an accusing finger. 'Tell me the truth, Joe. You have been taking your medication, haven't you?'

He winced and shrugged. 'Sorry, Betty. I've never been one for taking pills. I made a start but soon got in a muddle and gave up altogether. Too late to worry about it now.'

'Oh Joe, it's never too late.' It was the widow's turn to cry. 'I should miss you terribly if you weren't around any more. You were such a support for me when I went through unhappy times myself.'

He muttered gruffly, 'Nice of you to say so.'

'You've worked hard all your life. There's nothing wrong with taking things a bit easier now you're seventy.'

'Three score and ten. That's what it says in the Bible, how much time we're allowed. Seemed a long way off once. But it's all I'm going to get.'

'Don't say that. Cheer up, Joe. Remember all the good times we've had together.' She gave him a playful tweak through his trousers. 'We've had some lovely tussles over the years. You really gave me what for, you rascal you! Better than most men half your age.'

Still tearful he lifted his head and gave her a kiss on the cheek. 'You're saying a lot of nice things to me today.'

Fondly she unbuttoned his shirt and ran her hand through his mat of wiry chest hair, once black but now grey at the edges. 'You're a fine vigorous man, Joe, and always have been. Martha was a lucky woman to have you for a husband.'

'It's been sad, seeing her crippled up with the arthritis.'

'Promise me that you'll tell her about going to the hospital. And what the specialist said about your blood pressure. It will help to explain it to her. She'll understand. Wives always do.'

'All right then. I promise.'

'Well make sure you do.' She slid her hand down into his trousers. 'There! How does that feel?'

'Nice. Very nice.'

'Quite sure you can't manage it?'

'Don't keep tempting me, Betty.'

'I think you could still give me a good seeing to if you were minded to take the risk. Are you sure you don't feel up to it?'

He tapped his chest, pointing to his heart. 'Quite sure, and I've got more sense than to try. Cos I don't want to end up like your last husband, that's why!'

This made the jolly widow shriek with laughter. But then she became tearful again and dabbed at her eyes with a handkerchief. 'It was very sad really. A lot of his family turned up for the funeral. They asked me if he spoke any last words.'

'And did he?'

'They asked me so I felt obliged to tell them. "*I'm coming!*" Those were the last words he ever spoke. I don't think they were much comforted though. Should I have fibbed to them, Joe?'

He thought it over. 'No, I don't think so. It wasn't a bad way to go, Betty. They should have been pleased for him. The silly daft bugger.'

11

Ronnie was once more sitting on Zoe's bed and attempting to console her. She stared forlornly into her tablet waiting for the reply that never came. Ronnie said sympathetically, 'Emerson shouldn't be doing this to you, Zo. Doesn't he ever text you back?'

She bit on her handkerchief. 'He will. I'm sure he will.'

'Why doesn't he then?'

'If I knew that I wouldn't be crying, would I?'

'I don't like to see you crying, Zo. Are you sure about him going to Brazil on his own? He could just be saying it to tease you.'

To prove Ronnie wrong she slid off the bed and went to the top drawer of her dressing table. From beneath an untidy pile of underwear she produced a red booklet, her passport, holding it up as evidence of readiness to travel. 'Emerson said he wanted me to go with him. It was going to be a wonderful adventure. I wanted it to be my adventure too.'

Ronnie was impressed on seeing the passport. 'That was clever. Do your Mum and Dad know?'

'What does it matter if Emerson is going without me?'

'These things take a long time to arrange. He might have changed his mind.'

'It was his dream, wasn't it? Of course he hasn't changed his mind.'

Ronnie picked his nose and did some thinking. 'Nor have you by the sound of it. You would still go if you had the chance?'

'Of course I bloody well would. Wash your ears out. How many more times?'

'No need to get stroppy with me, Zo. I'm trying to help you.'

72

'How can you help me? I need a lot of money to buy my plane ticket. Bloody Emerson isn't going to buy it for me, is he?'

'That's what it looks like. Not very nice of him, in my opinion, if he really is still your boyfriend.'

'What am I going to do, Ronnie? I'm desperate.'

'No one has seen him lately. I suppose Emerson hasn't gone to Brazil already?'

Zoe wept new tears. 'That's what I'm afraid of.' She pointed across the passage to her grandfather's bedroom. 'Tell me again about the money. Has Gramps really got it in a suit-case under his bed? '

'Your Mum and Dad climbed up a ladder and looked through the window. They saw it for themselves.'

Zoe stopped snivelling for a moment. She was impressed. 'People will do anything for money. I'm just starting to realise that.'

'Grandad isn't very popular right now. He's going to fuck it up for everyone.'

'Poor Gramps. I'm the only one who loves him. I don't want him to die.'

'If he doesn't die then no one gets any money. And that includes you and me.'

She sniffed and pondered. 'Well, if he's just going to die anyway . . . '

'Exactly. That's how I look at it. I need the money as much as you do.'

Zoe dried her eyes and lit a cigarette without offering him one. 'You could always get a job.'

'I'm not suited for any kind of work.'

'Who says so?'

'You've never talked to me like this before. Suddenly we're all quarrelling.'

'Emerson is an entrepreneur. He doesn't sit around dreaming. He gets out there and makes money.'

'Drug dealing. Pimping.'

'Why are you in such a bad mood today? Nothing you can

say will ever change how I feel about Emerson.'

'Being in love doesn't seem to be making you very happy.'

'What's happiness got to do with it? You don't know anything about being in love.' Ronnie had been sitting on the end of her bed but on hearing these words he struggled to his feet in a temper. Zoe hastened to calm him down. 'No need to flounce off in a sulk. You promised to tell me about your girl friend. Is it anyone I know?'

'I've got a lot of serious thinking to do. We'll talk about it later.'

'Does that mean you haven't shagged her yet? It does, doesn't it?'

'I've got a lot of time to make up, Zo. A lot of arrears. You don't need to keep reminding me.'

'You should take her out in your car. The back seats are best for making love.'

'I'll take your word for it.'

'I've done it with Emerson in the back of his car, lots of times.' Zoe heaved a dejected sigh but then cheered up for a moment and gave her cousin a friendly punch on the arm. 'And in the front seats as well. You wouldn't be able to do that, Ronnie!'

'I guess not.'

Zoe heaved another wistful sigh and laid back down on her bed again to begin another round of texting. 'My life changed when I met Emerson. If he leaves me I shall never be happy again. Ever.'

12

Alice Knight worked at a supermarket in their nearby town, a bustling market town. This ensured that she had daily contact with the outside world, or the world as it existed away from Nutwhistle Farm.

Few of her colleagues at the supermarket would have guessed how different her domestic life was from theirs. The moment she was free she returned to the farm so that she could dote on her son Ronnie. She had been born at Nutwhistle and expected to die there in the fullness of time. Her father handled the farm business but she had always kept her mother's domestic accounts and paid the housekeeping bills as well as doing most of the family shopping. Although she worked long hours she was happy most of the time.

The domestic turmoil provoked by her father's irresponsible behaviour over the suitcase was not to her liking. She had made the best of her life as a single mother, protected and secure within the family home, so the prospect of unwelcome change was bad for her nerves. Fortunately for her she was completely unaware of an even more disastrous time bomb that had started its ominous countdown. Her son Ronnie may have been a late developer but he was now in love, and love changes everything, as she would soon find out.

Wisely Ronnie kept this secret from his mother but his pleasant and stress-free life at Nutwhistle Farm was also coming to an end. His mother was a generous provider but he knew this would not extend to setting him up in a home of his own with a rival for her affection. For the first time in his life he needed money, lots of it, and this concentrated his mind on how it might be obtained. Love scuppers all preceding relationships, as countless millions of people since the dawn of time have found out the hard way. With the result that

Ronnie Knight was now a troubled young man, even if he took care not to show it, and racked his brains every day to try and find a solution to his problems.

Meanwhile he carried on as normal. He had a settled routine developed over many years and it seldom varied from the few simple activities which filled his day. After a leisurely late breakfast he drove to the town in his car every morning. If the weather was cold he headed for the magazine room in the public library, or spent an hour in the frothy-coffee shop in the market square where he conversed easily with other regulars. In the summer months he favoured a seat in the churchyard, or in the beer garden of the riverside pub. His mother provided him with generous pocket money so he enjoyed browsing in the shops. He had a wide circle of acquaintance, mostly singletons like himself, wandering about at a loose end and glad to stop for a chinwag.

Ronnie was a young man devoid of malice. He never made a wisecrack nor uttered a calumny. Those he talked with found him a good listener, attentive and always in agreement. He had discovered at an early age that being pleasant and polite would ease him through every social situation, from the job-centre to the surgery and all the other places in between where the generosity of benefits was regulated by the good impression made on officials. Because of this carefully acquired skill Ronnie was never pressed for a reason why he should be excused work and remain permanently on benefits. Social workers and counter staff were only too willing to help out such a courteous and pleasant young man. He was waved through on the nod every time, and up till now had found life an agreeable experience.

At two o'clock he returned to the farm and drew up a chair to enjoy the cooked lunch his granny had saved for him. In the summer he often went back to the town and sat watching the bowls on the bowling green, or a cricket match at the college. Sometimes he went upstairs for a snooze on his bed but mostly he just ambled along the passage to the farm's spacious living room where he anchored himself on the TV viewing settee.

Nor was he alone in pursuing this interest. His fondness for watching television was shared by his mother and his grandmother. The other members of the Knight family had other interests and mostly kept themselves to themselves but Ronnie, Alice and Martha shared this common interest and bonded closely as a threesome, spending many hours of every day in company with one another. They never tired of watching their favourite programmes, sitting side by side on the viewing settee in the big family living room. The television set had brought them together, and so far it had kept them together.

Ronnie sat on the left of the settee. His weight had flattened the cushions but it was his place and no one else ever sat there. He had a small table of his own pulled up close to the settee within easy reach of his arm. On it were packets of supermarket goodies provided by his mother, and he ate more or less continuously as he viewed, one TV snack after another. The table also contained his TV viewing guides which he studied from end to end, being extremely knowledgeable about the programmes he watched.

Martha Knight joined her grandson in the late afternoon, shuffling along from the kitchen on her two aluminium invalid sticks. Alice worked shifts at the supermarket but most days was able to sit in for at least one long session in front of the box. She sat on the right, with Martha in the middle. This was so that she and Ronnie could take an arm each to help Martha to her feet when viewing was finally over at the end of the day.

They were a talkative threesome. When a new series started they could not rest until they had identified everyone who appeared, even for a few seconds, triumphantly listing all their previous shows. When the credits came on screen they would all three lean forward intently, committing new names to memory and exclaiming over old ones. In a quiz competition on TV soaps and sitcoms a question starting with the words, 'Who played ...?' would have been answered in a chorus of three. Who played whom, when and in what, was their area of expertise. It may have been only reality shows and commercial trash TV but they were well informed about it and could put names to every face. They took it seriously, engaging in continuous debate without taking their eyes from the screen.

At every commercial break Alice would get up from the settee and bring new supplies of food from the kitchen, or make endless mugs of tea and coffee. Ronnie had always been waited on by his mother and munched contentedly on the viewing settee. He conversed affectionately with his granny and they spent their evenings in perfect harmony, three generations of telly addicts. Martha may have been the oldest, and disabled with arthritis, but her eyes were sharp and her memory undimmed. She was the arbiter in any dispute over who had played what part in any sitcom or game show going back many years, and was never proved wrong.

Although very little penetrated from the outside world when they sat three abreast on the settee, this particular afternoon was different. The unpleasant bursts of sound from an electric drill followed by hammering reached them clearly from the room above. Martha Knight found it difficult to concentrate because the room in question had been her bedroom for forty years. Locks were being fitted to keep everyone out, including her, and she was understandably tearful and upset. Alice took the unprecedented step of zapping the standby button. For the first time in living memory the image faded from the screen during an afternoon. Awkwardly they turned to face one another, having something else to talk about other than the dross in front of their eyes.

Alice said, 'Don't cry, Mum,' and put an arm round her mother's shoulders.

This only made her cry more. 'Whatever can have come over him? It's crazy.'

'Don't upset yourself.'

'How can Grandad do this to me?'

'I don't know.'

'I shall never understand it. Never.'

Ronnie picked his nose and looked thoughtful. 'How much money has Grandad got in the suitcase? Does anyone know?'

Alice said, 'That isn't the point, angel. It's the principle. We've lived together in this house all our lives and always trusted one another. Putting locks on the door and bars on the window isn't very nice, is it?'

'Grandad wouldn't be doing it if there wasn't a lot of money in the suitcase. It isn't us he's worried about, it's burglars.'

'We've never been burgled so far as I know. You're wrong there, precious. It's us he doesn't trust.'

Martha dried her tears and said, 'I don't want to hear any words spoken against Grandad. He believes he's doing it for the best. We might not like it but we shouldn't make judgements. He might have a good reason for doing it that he's not telling us about. After all, we're the only ones who know about the money.'

Ronnie disagreed, pointing upwards to the ceiling with a podgy forefinger. 'Someone else knows now.'

'The man from the burglar alarm shop, do you mean?' his mother asked him.

'Too bloody right that's who I mean.'

'Grandad wouldn't tell him anything.'

'Wouldn't need to be told, would he? He could work it out for himself.'

'If you put it like that, I suppose so, yes.'

Martha said, 'Locksmiths are always checked out by the police. Or at least they used to be.'

Ronnie was polite but unconvinced. 'Local burglars always get tipped off when there's something worth pinching. I reckon there's more risk now than there was before.'

Martha began to weep again. 'I said that things here would never be the same again. I was right, wasn't I?'

No one replied and after a decent interval the television was switched on again. Alice refilled Ronnie's mug of tea and brought in a box of their favourite jammy donuts warmed in the oven. These were soothing comfort food, deliciously sweet and sticky. They munched in triplicate, trying not to listen to the workman noises overhead, stopping their ears to the sound of the chisel as the new cylinder lock was recessed into the door frame.

What they could not know was that the security technician had drawn Joe Knight's attention to the scratches on the lock plate outside his bedroom door. When he had recovered from that little surprise he was invited to put his head through the window and view the two depressions in the flowerbed below, where a ladder had been placed.

Joe was shaken, and said so. 'You can't trust anybody, can you? Not even your own family.'

'At least two attempted entries have been made, Mr Knight. One from inside, one from outside.'

'I'll keep the curtains drawn over now that you've fixed the window bars. No one will be able to see in then, so I shall be safe from prying eyes.' He gave the curtains a tug. 'Nice and thick. Just right.'

The man from the burglar alarm shop had a wide choice of crime prevention devices in a glossy brochure and permitted himself a small smile, knowing a softened-up customer when he had one at his mercy. 'Take a look at these special offers, Mr Knight. You want to make this place burglar proof? Let me show you how.'

Joe wasn't listening, he considered he had spent too much money already and waved the sales pitch aside. There was another reason why the salesman's words fell on deaf ears and this was because Joe was experiencing a moment of truth, always an uncomfortable sensation. He had supposed that once the room was secure he could go about his business as usual with the suitcase safely locked away. Now he realised that wasn't going to happen. He would have to guard it himself, for as long as it took, which meant for the rest of his life.

When the man had gone, and he was left alone for the first time, he looked at the shiny new locks on the doors and the steel bars on the window and was shocked to realise that he had turned his bedroom, his marriage bedroom, into a prison cell. A prison cell where he had locked himself in, and would have to serve out a life sentence.

13

A few days later Joe Knight shuffled into the kitchen as usual, carrying his basket of eggs. He put the basket on the table, greeted his wife with a kiss on the cheek, rinsed his hands briefly under the kitchen tap, then drew up his chair and sat down.

Martha was about to lift the big brown family teapot when something in the way her husband was behaving caused her to stop and look at him more closely. She was right to do so. A significant moment in their long marriage was about to take place. For the first time in living memory he did not hand over his chosen egg to be fried. Instead he muttered gruffly, 'Got any porridge, Martha?'

She was so astonished that it took her a few moments to collect her thoughts. Puzzled, she said, 'What's the matter? Don't you feel like a proper breakfast, Joe?'

The long kitchen table was made from roughly hewn oak planks. Countless meals over two centuries had given it a dull lustre, polished by the elbows of many generations of farming Knights and their assorted family members. From his seat on the warm side of the table nearest the big cast iron stove Joe admitted that he had no appetite and was indeed, suffering. 'Sorry, Martha. Not up to it this morning. Fancied something milky and sweet instead.'

Still looking as surprised as she felt Martha hobbled to the big walk-in larder and returned with a packet of porridge oats. It did not take her long to cook them up with rich farm milk and plenty of brown sugar. A bowl, a spoon and then a strained silence as she returned to her easy chair and watched her husband slowly eat his first invalid meal.

'I enjoyed that,' he said when he had finished, wiping his mouth with his handkerchief. 'You make a nice bowl of porridge, Martha. I should have had it more often. Would have done me good.'

She turned to face him, her voice unsteady. 'Aren't you well, Joe?'

He lowered his gaze, finding her anguished stare uncomfortable. Eventually he mumbled, 'I took your advice, Martha.'

'I don't remember giving you any advice.'

'A few months ago now, back last winter. You said I should see a doctor. So I did.'

'You didn't tell me.'

'It took me a while to work my courage up. You know how frightened I am of doctors and hospitals. Just the smell when you go in the front door puts me right off. I'm a coward, Martha. Or at least I am where needles and injections are concerned.'

'Nothing to be ashamed of, Joe. Not if you faced up to it.'

'At the surgery I asked to see one of the new doctors. Seemed easier to talk to someone I didn't know, and who didn't know anything about me, or about the family.'

'I can understand that.'

'The news isn't good, Martha.'

'You mean it's bad?'

'Couldn't be much worse.'

'How long ago did all this start?'

'Just after last Christmas, when I had the flu. Can't remember exactly when. Didn't want to worry you, Martha. Seemed better to keep it to myself.'

'Keep what to yourself, Joe?'

'The doctor made an appointment for me at the hospital. I didn't show you the letter when it came.'

'You pick up the letters from the box every day, or meet the postman. It's your right. You don't have to show them to anyone else if you don't want to.'

'I've no secrets from you, Martha. They did some tests at the hospital, nothing painful. Let me put your mind at rest straight away. I haven't got cancer. You go downhill fast if you've got cancer.'

'I didn't expect that you had. Get to the point, Joe.'

'Don't think I'm not being straight with you but the honest truth is that I'm not exactly sure which of the things I've got wrong with me I should worry about most.'

'What sort of things are we talking about?'

'The specialist at the hospital told me I was at risk from a stroke because my blood pressure was so high. My heart is wonky, too, but not something easy to cure like a bypass or putting one of those clip things in to keep the arteries open.' He paused, squinting sideways at her. 'Why do you look so surprised at what I'm telling you?'

She shifted awkwardly in her chair. 'I thought it was your mental condition causing the trouble. Isn't that what you went to see the doctor about?'

It was his turn to look surprised. 'What gave you that idea?'

'You mean you've got heart disease as well?'

'As well as what?'

Martha sighed and wept, rubbing and kneading her thigh to ease a sudden stab of pain. She stretched out one of her legs and gazed up at the ceiling, as if hoping for a miracle cure to take place at that moment. 'Bloody arthritis. I should have gone with you, Joe. I should have spoken to the doctor myself and told him what you've got wrong with you.'

'You know you can't climb up into the Land Rover. I wouldn't ask you to. I know how painful your legs are, Martha.'

'We could have gone in a taxi. I should have been there for you, Joe.'

'There's no need to cry. You know I don't like to see you cry.'

'It's a lot to take in all at once.'

'I'm telling you the truth.'

'I know you are, Joe, and I'm sorry.'

'The head man was very nice to me, considering that I've always had a low opinion of doctors. He made his meaning plain even if he wrapped it up a bit so as not to upset me too much. I'm not long for this world, Martha. That's what it comes down to.'

'Oh Joe, that's terrible. How could he be so sure?'

'Don't upset yourself. I put off going until it was too late, just like a lot of other farm chaps I knew in the past who did exactly the same. Sorry if it's come as a shock to you.'

'Are you telling me that you're really going to die?'

'They prescribed a lot of pills. I started taking them but got in a muddle and soon gave up. Different times of day, different doses, I got mixed up between the blue ones and the yellow ones. Not that it would have made any difference.' He made a chopping movement with his hand, as though killing a rabbit. 'Could happen at any time he warned me, whether I take the medication or not.'

Martha still wept. 'You shouldn't have had to go through it all on your own. I would have come with you, you know I would, however much the arthritis was hurting me.'

'I didn't know the news was going to be as bad as it turned out to be. It didn't seem fair to worry you when you're so handicapped and in pain all the time. But you're right, I should have preferred you to be there to hold my hand, and I'm only sorry you weren't. Looking back on it.'

'What else did the consultant tell you? Didn't he give you any advice?'

'He put the wind up me good and proper, I don't mind admitting that. Advice? Only what anyone else could have told me. Avoid stress. Pack up smoking. Not to drink alcohol. Eat sensibly. And keep taking the bloody pills.'

Martha tapped her head. 'Are you sure they didn't invest-igate your mental condition without telling you? I reckon you had a stroke last winter when you were laid up. Surely they could see that you weren't quite right in the upstairs depart-ment?'

'Wasn't mentioned, Martha.' He took her hand in a gesture of conciliation. 'I'm not long for this world. I'm going to die. Don't be cross with me.'

'I'm not cross with you.'

'There's no fight in me any more. I can feel myself starting to give up. I'm on the way out, and it could be soon. I kept it from you as long as I could.'

'Don't you have anything in writing from the hospital? I should like to see something written down so that I know the names of whatever it is you've got wrong with you.'

'My desk has got in a muddle lately. I knew you would ask me that so I looked for the letter but I couldn't find it. I searched and searched. But it's there somewhere, you know I never throw anything away. You're welcome to have a look yourself.'

'Can you remember who you saw at the hospital? The consultant.'

'No.'

'Can you remember the name of the doctor at the surgery?'

'No. Can't remember that either.'

'There must be some way of finding out.'

'I wouldn't mind if you did that, of course I wouldn't, in fact it might be a good idea. If you showed me a list I could pick him out.'

'That would be a start, I suppose.'

'Good. Then if you asked to speak to him on the phone he could tell you what you want to know. Such as how long I've got left. Not that doctors are very helpful when you try and pin them down to a straight answer. Hardly surprising, is it? They're scared of being sued if they get it wrong.'

Martha was beginning to lose patience. 'Never mind about the doctors, they can look after themselves. I'm not sure you're telling me the truth, Joe. If you didn't need to have an operation you can't be all that bad. How can you be at death's door if you only went as an outpatient and got prescribed some pills?'

He winced apologetically. 'Turned it down, didn't I? Funked it in other words.'

'You had a date to go in? Which department? Was it your heart? Which specialist?' Martha threw up her apron in a gesture of despair and frustration. 'Surely you must be able to remember something about it?'

Joe fiddled around with his porridge bowl before admitting that he couldn't. 'It's no good asking me. I would tell you if I knew. I forget things all the time now.'

'Isn't that what I've been telling you?'

'Never thought it would happen to me. You can't walk and I can't remember. We've turned into a pair of old crocks, Martha.'

She kept hold of his hand, releasing it only to wipe away her tears. 'My poor Joe. Whatever will become of us?'

14

Until he ran into trouble with his health Joe Knight had been the happiest member of all his family.

He was happy because the boss of any outfit has the most reason to be happy, having the cash as well as the whip hand. But Joe was careful not to make enemies of his family, or to create jealousy. He was easy-going and indulgent, over-looking everyone else's funny little ways so that his own were overlooked in turn. He behaved affectionately to his wife Martha but never told her where he was going when he left the farm, or where he had been when he came back, still less what he had been doing. She never asked and he never volunteered the information, an arrangement that had worked well throughout their marriage.

There is an old saying in the country that good farmers make poor gardeners and Joe proved the rule in reverse, being a dud at farming but a whizz at gardening. In younger and more energetic days he enlarged the vegetable plot at the side of the house, ploughing up an extra half acre and planting thick hedges all round to shelter it from the wind. For most of his married life he had provided the household with an all-the-year-round supply of fruit, vegetables and flowers.

In its heyday his farm shop attracted a steady stream of customers and generated a cash income that kept him nicely solvent without troubling the Inland Revenue. In return his customers obtained produce not easily available elsewhere, such as home-grown tomatoes with an aromatic smell and delicious viney flavour, or bunches of sweet peas with a heady scent and gorgeous colours. His customers came for duck eggs with their turquoise silky sheen, or for jars of honey, knowing that Joe would have collected it himself from the two hives in his orchard. Where else could country parents buy baby rabbits for their children, and a hutch to keep them in? Where better to go for bundles of bean sticks cut to length, or to see for themselves cucumbers and marrows tumbling from earthy beds rich with farmyard manure. Nowhere, was the answer, and the demise of Joe Knight's hay-barn farm shop caused disappointment to many.

It was where he had sat for hours at a time, basking in summer sunshine or cosied up to the hay in winter. Now that the shop had closed the barn was cluttered with cardboard boxes and plastic trays and flowerpots no longer needed. There was a forty-five gallon oil drum overflowing with rubbish, stacks of old newspapers and magazines kept to be used as wrappers, but now in need of some drastic tidying. It was Joe's refuge and not meant to be tidy, he liked it the way it was. In addition to the slightly fermented sickly-sweet smell of the hay there was an earthy smell from the sacks of potatoes, now set aside for use by Martha in the house. Mouldering apples in a basket gave off a pleasant cidery scent to mingle with the aroma of his strong tar-weed tobacco.

In the summer months he would often stay out working in his garden until it was almost completely dark. In the winter he went up to bed as soon as he had finished his evening meal. Until the age of seventy he had been no trouble to anyone, busy with his farm shop and a few simple pleasures. He had never been known to watch television but spent time in a small downstairs room he used as the farm office. He enjoyed an occasional visit to The Shorn Lamb, the local pub, and in the more recent past he had his assignations with Betty Hounsome to look forward to.

Old bedfellows make good friends and now that he had reached the crisis age of seventy with failing health Joe sought consolation from the warm-hearted widow. In need of sympathy he found himself once more in Betty's bungalow, and again baring his soul rather than his hairy chest, which he had done quickly enough in most of their previous encounters. The widow could see that he had something serious to say and gave him time to compose himself and choose his words.

When he was ready he said, 'Well, I've done it, Betty, just like you told me to. I've told Martha about going to the hospital and why I'm not long for this world.'

'How did she take it, Joe?'

'I don't think she really believed me. It was a mistake, going to the hospital on my own. Couldn't find the paperwork to prove it to her.'

'I would have come with you, you know I would. You never told me either.'

'Brought up not to make a fuss. Brought up not to complain. My old Dad reckoned it was better to suffer in silence than let your enemies know you had something wrong with you.'

'Enemies, Joe? I didn't know you had any enemies.'

'Never admit to a weakness, that was his policy. He said that people always took advantage if they knew you had a weakness.'

'You haven't been signed off at the hospital though, have you?'

'I'm not sure. I didn't keep my last appointment, nor the one before that. Most likely they've given up on me and closed the book.'

'They wouldn't do that. Listen. Why don't I take Martha in so that she could talk to someone and get it sorted out? Your medication, I mean. I'm sure it would help if you could get started on the pills again.'

'Martha can't travel in a car. Her arthritis is too bad.'

'We might be able to do it between us. Hire a van, perhaps, and put a wheelchair in the back. No?'

'It's too late for that. But thanks for the offer.'

'You're a proud man, that's the trouble. Too proud to ask for help.'

'Maybe so. Maybe so.'

'Or too stubborn, more like it.'

Joe was slumped in an armchair, the widow curled up on the carpet and leaning against his knees. He said glumly, 'Don't be cross with me, Betty. I've been around animals all my life. I know when one of them is going to die.'

'Oh cheer up, Joe. That sounds a bit morbid.'

'True though. The animals know it too. When they've got the sign of death on them, they know. You can see it in their eyes, and the way they stand and look at you. An old ewe will go off into a corner of the field when she knows she's going to die.'

Betty reached up and took his hand. 'Is that how you feel, Joe?'

'My time's almost up. Taking pills won't alter anything.'

'You're only seventy. That isn't old these days.'

'Seventy is all I'm going to get.'

'You can't know that. You can't possibly know that.'

He stroked her hair with the back of his hand. 'Don't keep on at me, Betty. I don't want to die, for Christ's sake. I'm not wishing it on myself.'

'Oh Joe, I'm sure you've come across people who are always telling you they're going to die and never do. You could be the same and go on for years and years.'

'Not with my high blood pressure. A stroke could be fatal the doctor told me.'

The widow gave him a nudge. 'Nothing ever put you off your stroke though, did it, Joe? Not once you'd got going.'

He said huffily, 'This is no laughing matter. I'll thank you to take it seriously.'

'A war could have broken out and you would still be pounding away.'

'I thought you liked it.'

'I did. None of my husbands were much cop between the sheets. Nor a lot of other men I've been with. I've looked forward to your visits, Joe. Because I'm just as keen on it as you are and I don't want you to give it up.'

'I don't want to give it up either, it's given me up. It would be like signing my own death warrant, having sex with you again. Don't keep tempting me.'

'You need cheering up, Joe.'

He squeezed her hand. 'That's the part of dying I don't

like. No more sex. No more loving. No more pillow talk. All comes to an end when you die, that side of life.'

'It's the best side. Love makes the world go round. That's a true saying, because it does.'

'You should know, Betty.'

This made the widow laugh out loud. She jumped up and sat on his lap. 'Come on, Joe. If you can't manage it at least give me a nice hot cuddle. Something to remember you by.' She unbuttoned her blouse and placed his hand inside. 'There! How does that feel?'

'Nice.'

She kissed him on the cheek. 'We've been such good friends, Joe. I don't like to see you all down in the dumps like this.'

'I've been thinking about my family. That's what's been on my mind these last few weeks. How they're going to manage without me.'

'Do they know about your little health problem?'

'I told Martha and she told them.'

'Just as well. These things are better out in the open.'

'We've never had any secrets from one another, Martha and me. Not about anything that mattered, I mean.'

'No need to be upset, lover. You've been a good provider all these years. That's what counts.'

'It does to me. I've worked hard to keep it all together.'

'You've succeeded, Joe. You've succeeded.'

'Yes, it's nice to think of the farm staying in the family. Steve's a good boy for work, he'll hold it together for the rest of his life, just like I've done.'

'They work hard, him and Carol.'

'I've been lucky with my family. Young Zoe has always helped me with the shop. A real little treasure she is.'

'I haven't seen that boyfriend of hers around lately. Is he still on the scene?'

'Emerson? I'm not sure. I don't like to ask Zoe about her personal affairs, not now she's sixteen and grown up. That Emerson is a smart young fellow. He'll make his way in the world all right.'

'They've turned out very nicely, your two grandchildren. Lovely manners, Ronnie's got. Very pleasant and polite to speak to.'

'Him and Martha have always been close. That's a big comfort to me.'

'I'm sure it must be.'

'Yes, it's nice to know there's someone who's going to look after her when I'm dead and buried. Ronnie thinks the world of his Grandma and will do anything for her, so I don't have any worries on that account.'

'Don't talk about being dead and buried, Joe. It upsets me.'

'It upsets me too, or it does when I think about it. Some people love a good funeral, but not me. I always wondered what it would be like when it was me lying in the box and someone else singing the hymns. I reckon I shall soon be finding out.'

'Are you sure you can't manage it? One more time? Yes?'

'No.'

'Are you quite sure about that? I think you could be persuaded.'

'Oh no I couldn't'

'Oh yes you could.'

'Don't start undressing, Betty. Please.'

'Can you think of a better way to go?'

'Yes, I can. Peacefully in my sleep, that's how I want to go.'

At which the comely widow screamed with laughter. 'And so you shall, Joe, so you shall. In about twenty minutes from now I should think, judging from past performance. Hurry up and get your trousers off and I'll soon put you to sleep, my lover. You'll think you died and went to heaven!'

15

Alice had the weekend off so on Sunday morning she joined Steve and Carol in Martha's big kitchen to discuss the midday Sunday dinner. Or more precisely how best to raise the tricky subject of the suitcase under Joe Knight's bed. Steve wanted to tell his father before the meal that they intended to ask him about the money, saying it was only fair to warn him in advance. It soon became clear that Steve's nerve had failed. He was now in favour of putting off any form of confrontation until his father's intentions became known. Carol and Alice would have none of this and joined forces to brace him up.

'Dad sits farthest away from the door,' Alice pointed out. 'If we all stay put in our places and keep talking he won't find it easy to leave.'

'He likes to be listened to,' Carol added, to back up her sister-in-law. 'If we get him started on one of his pet subjects we could gradually steer the conversation round to the money. The last budget didn't do him any favours. His bottle of brandy went up by twenty-p and he's still grieving over that.'

Alice agreed. 'Quite right, Carol. He blames everything on the government so let's give him a chance to gripe about being overtaxed. Not that he's ever paid much tax, the crafty sod.'

Carol was fired up and ready to take on her father-in-law. 'I still think we're entitled to ask him for an explanation about the fortifications. Window bars are what you get in prisons and police stations, not farmhouses. We can ask him what he's hiding from us, and why he's doing it. No point in being all polite and diplomatic. We want to know, we need to know, and the best way is to ask him for some straight answers. Agreed?'

Alice did even if her brother didn't. 'We shall never have a better chance. Don't look so frightened, Stevie. I'll protect you.'

It was a wet Sunday. It began wet and became wetter, with rain trickling down the windows all day. It was also cold and dark which seemed to suit the sombre mood of the household. It was the time of year when autumn had been edged out sideways and the weather had slithered downhill into the cold clutch of a bleak windswept winter. Lights were needed in the sunless kitchen where Martha was grateful for the warmth of her trusty life-giving coke-fired Aga.

Alice stayed to help her mother cook the meal while Steve and Carol went off to toil on the farm. The rapidly shortening days of winter had signalled a steep escalation in their daily workload. For the next six months their farm animals would need constant attention to survive round until the spring grass grew again in the new year. They would be at work from early morning until late at night, feeding, bedding up and cleaning out, every day the same, over and over again, feeding, bedding up and cleaning out. They loved every minute.

The oldest part of Nutwhistle Farmhouse was very old indeed, with sagging smoke-blackened rafters and a wide fireplace and chimney. These were built with chunks of roughly squared stone and small handmade bricks. The wobbly brass door handles were worn smooth with age and the door sills were hollowed by centuries of hobnailed boots. The stone-flagged hall contained a grandfather clock, an ironbound chest and a black leather horse-hair sofa with half the stuffing missing. It had been there for many years awaiting a decision on its future, and was now likely to wait for ever.

The passages leading out of the hall, one to the back of the house, the other to the sitting room and dining room, were covered with brightly coloured strips of coconut matting to absorb as much mud as possible, and of mud Nutwhistle Farm had a plentiful supply. Overhead the ceilings bulged and creaked, there were numerous short flights of stairs to link floors on different levels, and little corner landings.

Cavernous cupboards were filled to bursting with centuries of junk. There was a barrel-vaulted cellar, an attic, a well, a cider-press room, and clutter everywhere.

Joined on to the back of the house was a covered yard. This provided a dry cobbled area where the family members could kick off muddy boots, hang up wet clothes or prop a shotgun against the wall. It was where Zoe parked her bike and where the farm cats crouched round an enamel dish, waiting for a slosh of milk from the two house cows Carol milked by hand twice a day.

Nothing was ever thrown away at Nutwhistle Farm. Old domestic appliances such as a huge iron mangle with wooden rollers, and an equally obsolete handle-operated contraption for slicing up turnips nestled side by side with other discarded family possessions in the many tumbledown outbuildings. The family did not see it as junk. There had been a policy going back many years of reluctance to discard anything which might be of some use to future generations. They were proud to have so many possessions and having paid good money for them in the past were agreed in holding on to them for as long as possible, even when they had outlived their usefulness.

To an outsider Nutwhistle Farm might have seemed dilapidated, and the way of life of its occupants to be back-ward and eccentric. This was only partly true. There was a sense of belonging to the land, and of caring for the farm, even if this took the form of not wanting change. Although they did not attend church they were conscious of the many graves in the churchyard with Knight family headstones, a reminder if they needed one that continuity went with the territory. The present family of Knights might not be highly regarded by their neighbours either as farmers or model citizens but they had been around a long time, they had survived and were not done for yet, not by a long way.

There also existed an underlying structure of routine and custom. Joe and his wife Martha were sticklers for tradition, in particular their insistence on family meals with conversation and good manners. These had always been a feature of life at Nutwhistle Farm, and still were on Sundays when everyone was expected to attend the big midday meal, and to be on best behaviour. It was Joe's chance to play the patriarch, to sit at the head of the table, to make a big thing of saying grace, and to ply the carving knife.

After the unpleasantness over the suitcase, and the sudden deterioration in his health, it was in everyone's mind that the number of remaining Sunday dinners were likely to be few. Life as they had known it was fast coming to an end.

16

On the menu for dinner at Nutwhistle Farm on this particular Sunday was a large piece of rolled brisket of beef, pot roasted slowly inside a heavy cast-iron oval-shaped casserole. The family had been brought up on this type of food and never tired of it, indeed would have rebelled in protest if offered anything else. Roast potatoes plus carrots and a cabbage, all from Joe's garden, were planned for the first course, helped down by a big jug of rich gravy. This substantial offering was followed by a home made date pudding and custard, another family favourite.

The food had to be carried the short distance from the kitchen to the family dining room. This contained a sideboard in which lived the Sunday cutlery, the place mats and table napkins, the silver cruet and the water jug and glasses. Setting the table properly was all part of the ceremony and tradition. Alice and Steve had done it for many years throughout their childhood, and carried on until Ronnie and Zoe took over. The dining room had never been redecorated in living memory, for the obvious reason that they liked it as it was. They liked the dusty velvet curtains, the faded red flock wallpaper, the threadbare Axminster carpet, the grimy oil paintings, even the fading family photographs of long dead Knights in frames on the sideboard.

Martha had hoped that Joe would spruce himself up for his Sunday dinner. In the past he had insisted on a clean white shirt to put on after his Sunday morning shave but instead he had shambled into the family dining room looking even more bewhiskered and unwashed than he had been for the past several weeks. This scruffy impersonation of a dirty old tramp did not stop him looking pleased with himself, and he presided confidently at the head of the family table. He was first into his chair and so was able to greet the others cheerily one by one as they took their seats. He gripped the table on either side with two large strong hands, as jaunty as an admiral in his barge. Then made a great show of sharpening the carving knife before he sliced up the beef.

The seating arrangements never changed. Joe presided at the top of the mahogany table with Martha on his left and Alice on his right. Steve sat next to his mother with Carol beside him. On the other side of the table Ronnie sat next to his mother and Zoe sat next to him, opposite her mother. They all liked plenty of space and spread themselves the length of the table. Although none of them went near the parish church, where so many of their ancestors were interred, all seven lowered their heads while Joe solemnly intoned the Grace. Anyone entering the room would have observed a well-behaved close-knit country family passing things to another and conversing easily as the meal got under way.

'How's your sick cow?' Joe asked Steve as the plates circulated. 'I see she's still in the loose box. Won't have to call the vet, will you?'

'She's going back with the others tomorrow. Today didn't seem right, not with all this rain.'

'Very sensible, Steve. Very sensible.' Joe turned to his granddaughter as they helped themselves to vegetables and passed the gravy boat round the table. 'Seems a long time since young Emerson joined us for Sunday dinner. When can we expect to see him again, Zoe?'

Zoe had been prepared for this question and had her answer ready. 'His father was ill. He went back to help his mother look after him. They live in London, he never told me whereabouts in London.'

'I hope that doesn't mean we won't be seeing him again.'

'Oh no, Gramps. He'll be back.'

'He's a smart lad, that Emerson of yours. Oh yes, he knows the time of day all right. Got a bright future. Give him all the best from me.' Joe could see that it was still a sensitive subject and being fond of Zoe abandoned all further attempts at conversation with her and addressed himself to his dinner instead. 'Tender as a maiden's heart,' was his verdict, holding up a forkful of pot-roasted brisket. 'You've done it again, Martha. None of those poncified cooks on the telly are half as good as you.'

After this the flow of conversation gradually died away and the remainder of the meal was eaten in an uneasy silence. Joe Knight had seized the initiative and put on a confident display as the affable yeoman farmer and head of family but that was as good as it got for him. He must have realised that any hopes he may have had of avoiding a showdown were disappearing fast. He could not fail to be aware that his daughter Alice sat grim-faced and tight-lipped on his right, waiting for an opportunity to speak. She did not intend to be distracted from her purpose and pushed away her plateful of date pudding and custard almost uneaten. Steve was becoming more nervous by the minute and if Carol had not held on tightly to his sleeve he might well have mumbled an excuse about needing to see to his sick cow and hurried from the table. Joe Knight knew he was cornered and blinked uncomfortably, having no exit strategy that would extricate him from such a tricky situation.

At which point his wife Martha began to sob.

She wept because she knew that her prediction had come true, that their happy home would never be the same again, that their tolerant and undemanding way of life was winding down to an unhappy end. Family wrangling over money was a new experience but one they would have to get used to, and she understood enough of human nature to know that the quarrels had only just begun. Martha's tears changed the mood of the gathering. Although Alice remained hostile and fired up for a showdown the others were subdued, instinctively recognising that they were witnessing a family drama that would end in tragedy.

Joe patted his wife on the hand and in a shaky voice said, 'Don't cry, Martha. There's no need to cry. You know I don't like to see you cry.'

'They want to hear it from you, Joe. Tell them about your health.'

With a flash of spirit he joked, 'Health isn't quite the word I would have chosen, Martha.'

'Ill health then. Hurry up and tell them what you've got wrong with you.'

'All right then, I will.' He folded his arms on the table and looked round slowly, making eye contact with each family member in turn. It provided him with time to choose his words. 'This isn't something any man in my position wants to tell his family. The fact is I'm coming to the end of my life. I know I'm seventy and shouldn't mind but of course I do mind. So will all of you when your turn comes.'

Carol broke the silence first. 'You don't look any different, Joe.'

'I'm not an educated man so it's no use asking me to go into details. I went to the doctor, he sent me to the hospital, I had a couple of outpatient appointments and that's more or less it. I've got high blood pressure, my heart is packing up and I'm at risk from a stroke.'

Carol wanted more information. 'They must have offered you some treatment. Tell us about your medication. People with heart trouble have all sorts of different pills they've got to take. How do we sort that one out, Joe?'

'I've never been one for taking pills.'

'Does that mean you haven't taken them?'

'I started. Soon got in a muddle.' He heaved a sigh and rasped his face with his hand. 'To be truthful I've never had any faith in doctor's medicine. Does you more harm than good in my opinion. I took some pink pills but they made me feel sick, and some yellow pills that made me constipated. Like concrete, if you want to know, I couldn't put up with that. And some blue pills that made my mouth so dry I couldn't swallow. Call me a coward if you like but if I'm going to die I would sooner do it nature's way than in a hospital bed with tubes up my nose.'

Alice had waited her turn but made it clear from the start

that she was not sympathetic. 'How soon are we talking about? If you know I think you should tell us.'

'At any time. That's what the doctor told me. I'm not as well as I look, Alice. It takes me an hour to get going in the mornings and I know that one day soon I won't be getting up at all. You'll come looking for me and find me dead in my bed.'

'You shouldn't say such things, Dad. It upsets everyone.'

'The truth often does.'

'I still find it hard to believe, if you don't mind me saying so. If you're in such a bad way why didn't you speak up sooner? You haven't been ill in bed, you haven't had an operation, we haven't seen you taking any medication. Why should we believe that you're at death's door?'

'I hope you won't regret your harsh words, Alice. When you're all stood round my grave I wouldn't want any of you to have such unkind thoughts on your conscience.'

Alice waved this aside irritably. 'We want to know what you're up to with the money. Not a recital of your ailments.'

'You're the eldest, Alice, so I guess you think that gives you the right to say these things. Maybe so, maybe so, but I won't pretend that I'm not hurt by your attitude, because I am.'

'Well?' she persisted. 'We've had the bad news, now it's time for you to give us the good news. Starting with the suitcase.'

'You don't trust me. Is that it? You don't trust your own father to do the best for you?'

'Since you ask, no. Banks and building societies were invented for people like us to keep our money in. Not a suitcase under the bed.'

Once again Joe Knight stalled for time. He flinched slightly when he saw six unsmiling faces and six pairs of eyes fixed on his. He shifted uneasily in his chair, embarrassed but defiant. 'I don't know why you're all glaring at me. Not when I'm doing my best for you.'

Alice said, 'We don't like the idea of bars on windows.

You keep asking us to trust you. Seems more like it's you who doesn't trust us.'

'Burglars, Alice. We live in dangerous times. I haven't been as security conscious in the past as I should have been. Never heard of Neighbourhood Watch? I'm thinking of starting a group for round here.'

'The suitcase,' Alice insisted. 'Get to the point. Tell us about the suitcase.'

Martha dried her tears and said, 'They've got a right to know, Joe.'

He would have gone on blustering and prevaricating, and might well have succeeded if his wife had not put her hand on his arm and said, 'Please, Joe.' He crumpled slightly and gave way, speaking in a more conciliatory tone of voice. 'Well, it's like I said. After what they told me at the hospital I realised the time would soon be coming for me to pay out the money. The money I promised you all those years ago when we sold the two cottages.'

'Go on. We're listening.'

'I'm living on credit, Alice. You see things differently when you know your time is up.'

Appealing to her better nature failed because she had lost patience long ago. 'We understand all that, Dad. We want to know what made you start drawing out the money and putting it in a suitcase under your bed. It doesn't seem a very rational thing to do. To put it mildly.'

'I've just told you. When you're on borrowed time you see things more clearly. I'm the head of the family, that gives me the responsibility for handling the finances. I'm going to die, nothing will alter that, so I started to think how to divide up the money fairly.'

'You didn't need to draw it out. You've made a will so why not leave it to the lawyers and get it done properly?'

'I've seen too many farming families split apart by arguments over a will. You know me, Alice. You know I don't like paying out money to lawyers and accountants. Usurers and tax-gatherers, that's what I call them, and I hate them all.

By the time the greedy bastards have siphoned off the expenses and paid the tax and taken their cut there isn't nearly as much left as you think there's going to be. And where has it gone? Would you be able to get any of it back? Would you buggery. Doing it my way means that everyone gets settled up fair and square with no money wasted on fees. If the government doesn't know about it they can't tax you on it, that's my family motto. I've paid enough tax in my time so you're going to get what's coming to you in cash. Any complaints?'

'You still shouldn't have taken all the money out of the bank, Joe,' his wife said. 'Not without telling us. Whatever were you thinking of?'

'Well, I was thinking of you Martha, for a start.'

'How do you make that out?'

'Because I've already split up the money. I went to the stationery shop near the bus station and bought six big brown envelopes. I counted out the money and wrote your names on the front.' He fished around in his jacket pocket and as evidence produced a felt-tipped pen, a large pen coloured black. He held it up to show them. 'This is what I used to write your names with. I wrote them on good and big so there won't be any mistake whose envelope is which.' Before anyone could speak he went on, 'There's a seventh envelope, a white one so there won't be any mix-up with the others. Want to know what's in it?' Without waiting for a reply he told them. 'It's the money to pay for my funeral and a nice headstone. I've put a note inside with the wording for the stone. Any questions?'

'It's a funny way of doing things, Joe,' his wife said, shaking her head in bewilderment.

Joe patted her hand fondly. 'There's a nice fat brown envelope with your name on, Martha,' he told her, leaning to his left and planting a kiss on her cheek. 'Course there is. The woman of the house makes it what it is, and you've worked hard every day of your life to keep us all well fed and warm and happy.'

His daughter Alice was still implacably hostile. 'What about the amounts? Is the money shared out equally or are some of us treated more equally than others?'

'Everyone's been treated fairly. And before anyone asks me the answer is 'yes,' the two nippers get their share, just as I've always promised.' He beckoned them to lean forward and managed a smile. 'Ronnie. Zoe. Thanks to your old Grandad you're both going to have a nice start in life with some money behind you. What do you think of that?'

Zoe said immediately, 'Thanks, Gramps.' She blew him a kiss, at which he smiled. He waited a few moments longer until Ronnie also made a response. His first reaction was to put up a hand to pick his nose, as he always did when about to do some hard thinking but changed his mind and put his hand down again. Unfailingly polite as always he said, 'Thanks for the kind thought, Grandad. Much appreciated.'

'It means a lot to me, having a grandson. Someone to pass on the family name.'

'It means a lot to me too, Grandad.'

This pleased him. 'Nicely said, young Ronnie. One of these days you're going to do something to make us all proud of you. I know you are.'

Alice decided this had gone on long enough and returned to the fray. 'You should have let the lawyers handle it, Dad. It's not too late. You and me can go and see Mr Vokes the solicitor, explain what has happened and get back on track again. They can reinvest the money and when the time comes things will get done properly.'

'When the time comes?'

'Well, for God's sake, you've just been telling us about being at death's door. When you die, Dad, that's what I mean. Why don't you make a new will? Have it done right so that when the time comes we all get a copy of the will and know what everyone else has had. That way there isn't any suspicion or jealousy. Which is what will happen now.'

'When the time comes?'

'I don't know why you're being so sensitive all of a

sudden. Isn't this what you've just told us you're doing, parcelling out the cash to share between us when you die?'

'You'll get more if you let me do it my way.'

'It's the wrong way. I'm all in favour of paying profess-ional people to do their jobs, and so should you be if you had any sense left.'

'Hard words, Alice.'

'They need to be.'

'Then let me remind you of something. This is my money we're talking about. I can dispose of it how I like, and that's what I intend to do.'

Alice remained obdurate to the end. 'Money in a suitcase is never safe. That's how people used to go on in the old days when there weren't any banks and they buried money in the garden, or sewed it into the mattress. You can't be right in the head to take such risks.'

Joe was beginning to sense that the others were not as supportive of Alice as she thought they were. Native cunning told him that she was ploughing a lonely furrow. He smirked, sensing victory. From his advantage position at the head of the table he held out his arms as though to embrace his family. He adopted a soothing and reasonable tone of voice.

'If you do it my way you won't have to wait for months on end while the lawyers sort things out. They won't hurry, delay is money in their pockets. When I die you'll have the money straight away, the full amount with no deductions. Don't judge me now. Wait until my funeral. You'll change your tune when you start counting those banknotes, and be glad I did what I did.'

Still dabbing at her eyes Martha said, 'I hope you didn't think we were suspicious of you, Joe.'

'My feelings aren't hurt, if that's what you mean. No, quite the reverse, in fact.' He sat back and looked pleased with himself, hooking his thumbs in his waistcoat pockets. 'We're talking about a big sum of money. I know a lot of people think I'm a backward old codger but there's plenty of smart-arse college-trained farmers round here who've gone under just because times are hard again. I didn't have it easy. I'm proud of what I've done. Investing money takes skill, or it does if you want to keep the interest piling up. I've hardly spent anything on myself these last few years but I've been stashing it away for my family. That includes you, Carol. There's a nice big packet in my suitcase with your name on it.'

'Thank you, Joe.'

'It's me who should thank you for looking after Steve so well. It will soon be twenty years you've been married and I've never heard a cross word pass between you. No man could have had a better daughter-in-law so you're more than entitled to your share.'

At this point Steve spoke up, his voice anguished. 'Alice said something about a new will. You haven't cancelled your will, have you, Dad?' His voice quavered, and he clasped his hands anxiously together.

Joe turned on him with a reassuring smile. 'No, son, I haven't. Nor will I.'

'That's a relief,' Steve whispered, wiping his face with his table napkin.

'I made my will a long time ago and it still stands. I've left the farm to you, just as I always promised.'

'Thanks, Dad.'

Joe reached down the table and gave Steve's hand a friendly squeeze. 'Your Ma and me were pleased to have a son to carry on the farm. Of course we were. My father left it to me and soon I shall be leaving it to you. Does that set your mind at rest?'

'It does. Yes.'

Carol added her thanks. 'Steve's been so worried over the money. We've got our future to think about. We want to spend it together on the farm.'

'And so you shall, my dear. So you shall,' Alice said, 'What about the rest of us? That's what we're sitting here waiting to find out.'

Her father answered with a rueful smile. 'Now I know

what it feels like to be a lawyer with all the relatives glaring at one another while he reads the will. Except that I'm not dead yet and you're behaving as though I was. Be patient, all of you. You won't have long to wait.'

Alice would have said more but he held up his hand to silence her. 'You'll get your share, Alice, and a big share it is too, to compensate you for the farm going to Steve. You can't run a farm without capital so he gets a share as well. Trust me, I've got it all worked out.'

Zoe started to cry. 'Why is everyone being so nasty to Gramps? I don't like it. I don't want him to die.'

This made Alice weep, although hers were tears of frustration. She tried to stop, furious with herself for betraying a weakness, but only cried more. Sure enough this started Martha off again and next it was Joe Knight who took out his handkerchief and started blowing his nose and dabbing at his eyes. He was visibly upset.

'I'm a man doing the best for his family. What am I doing wrong? Why is everyone so angry with me?'

It was a sad end to their Sunday dinner. Although it was not the last Sunday dinner eaten in the family dining room it was the last time that all seven Knights shared a table together. In the weeks that followed first Alice was absent, then Zoe and finally Joe, who stopped coming altogether. So it was a significant moment in the long history of Nutwhistle Farm, many years of happy and peaceful co-existence ending in tears and recrimination.

17

The occupants of Nutwhistle Farm were understandably subdued after the unhappy episode of the ill-fated Sunday dinner. They realised that none of them had emerged with much credit and kept out of one another's way as far as possible. When they met they avoided contentious topics of conversation, all equally anxious to defuse the tension that had built up over the money. Joe Knight did not like being cast as the villain of the piece and was the keenest of all to put this little spot of family bother behind him.

He had earned a reputation locally for being astute. He was poorly educated, he had never travelled, but he was a man not easily fooled. Those of his neighbours who had tried to get the better of him found to their cost that he was a lot smarter than they had given him credit for. Similarly with the many sales reps and assorted officials and advisers who had visited the farm over a period of years and made the mistake of underestimating him. Joe's long practical experience, peasant cunning and a naturally suspicious mind easily saw off those who sought to do him down.

Ten days after the fraught and edgy Sunday dinner he astounded his wife at the breakfast table by announcing that he was going to tidy the hay barn. He slurped up his porridge with every sign of enjoyment and then asked for two slices of toast. It was while crunching the toast, liberally spread with butter and marmalade, that he made his pronouncement about tidying the barn.

'Whatever has come over you, Joe?' Martha asked in astonishment, unable to conceal her surprise. 'I've never known you tidy up before.'

'There's a first time for everything. As the clergyman said to the Sunday School teacher.'

She said suspiciously, 'You're very chirpy today. What's put you in a good mood all of a sudden?'

'No particular reason. Just thought it wouldn't hurt to tidy the barn now that I'm retired and won't be opening up my shop any more.'

'About time too. How you can bear to sit there with all that rubbish round your feet I shall never understand.'

'It's easy. Sometimes I sits and thinks and the rest of the time I just sits.'

'That's an old one.'

'I prefer the old ones,' he joked, giving her waist a quick squeeze. 'You're not wearing too badly, Martha. You'll out-last me by twenty years I reckon.'

'That sounds cheerful.'

'Well, you've got to make an effort, haven't you? I've got a lot to be thankful for, all said and done. Can't be down in the dumps all the time.'

'Don't overdo it with the clearing out. Try not to lift anything heavy.'

'I've asked Zoe to give me a hand. She's a strong girl and between us it shouldn't take long.'

'What are you going to do with all the rubbish?'

'We're going to burn it. See you later, Martha.'

She looked so surprised that he pushed back his chair and left the kitchen without giving her time to ask any more questions. Keen to get on with the job he made his way quickly to the rear of the farm buildings where there was a patch of waste ground on which stood the farm incinerator. This was a simple square of chain link fencing on a platform of bricks, much blackened. Steve and Carol used it as a con-venient receptacle for empty cartons and paper sacks or any-thing else that needed to be burned. When it was full they put a match to it and the wind did the rest.

Zoe was there waiting for him, and had already begun the process of fetching the rubbish from the hay barn and piling it neatly in the incinerator. 'I've put one of those small bales of straw in to get some heat up,' she informed him by way of greeting. 'Most of the stuff from the barn is dry and should burn all right.'

'I knew I could rely on you, Zoe.'

'When do you want me to fetch the papers from your office?'

'When it's drawing nicely. Let's get a nice blaze going first.'

'That won't take long, Gramps. The wind's in just the right direction.'

'Have you brought a can of persuader, like I asked you?'

'I brought one just in case but we won't need any diesel, not with this wind. Watch.' She used her cigarette lighter on a piece of screwed up newspaper and inserted the burning spill neatly between the bricks at the bottom. Almost at once the smoke started to stream out sideways, away from the farm buildings.

'That's my girl,' Joe said approvingly. 'We've got ourselves a fire.'

'What do you want me to bring next?'

'The oil drum. Can you barrow it round? There's years and years of rubbish in that old drum. Should burn a treat. I'll help you empty it out.'

When Zoe arrived back with the oil drum they lifted it up between them and shook the contents into the wire cage. By this time the flames had taken hold and a dry south-easterly wind was racking up the temperature and the fire noise.

'Shall I sweep out the barn and bring the rest of the newspapers?' Zoe asked him.

But Joe had heard the firestorm roar and knew the time had come. He handed over a small key, the key to the filing cabinet in his office. 'The top two drawers,' he instructed Zoe. 'Just like I showed you. I've put it all in plastic bags ready. You'll have to make two journeys. It's heavy old stuff, paper, heavier than you think. Off you go. And don't answer any questions if you come across anyone while you're doing it.'

When Zoe returned with a carrier bag in each hand she said, 'You weren't kidding, Gramps. They're almost pulling my arms out of their sockets.'

He took the heavy bags from her one at a time and with a grunt of effort lifted them over the side of the incinerator cage and let them fall into the flames. 'Good girl. Nip back and get the other two. Hurry now.'

Soon the blaze was at its most ferocious, with blackened scraps of paper blowing away on the wind. When Zoe returned with the second instalment of office documents the greedy crackling flames devoured bag and contents in an instant.

'What now?' Zoe asked him.

'Bring the rest of the stuff from the barn. Let's have it looking tidy for once. Seeing that I've packed it in for good.'

They retreated again to avoid the heat from the fire and at a safe distance rewarded themselves with a roll-up. Joe handed his granddaughter the makings, she opened the pouch and expertly rolled two thin cigarettes, neatly pinching off the ends. She put them in her mouth, lit them both and passed one to her grandfather.

'What you been burning then?' she asked him. 'Go on. You can tell me. Stuff you didn't want anyone else to see, I suppose. Am I right?'

'Something like that.'

'To do with the money?'

'Could be, Zoe. Could be.'

'Burning the evidence, is that what you've been doing?'

He grinned and gave her a poke in the ribs. 'Accomplices, that's what we are. I shall say it was all your doing. I shall say you put me up to it. That you're a bad influence. How would you like that?'

She pointed to the flames, which were already starting to die down. 'Too late. It's gone for ever now, whatever it was.'

Joe returned to the fire and pushed a stick through the wire mesh to break up some charred wads of paper that were forming a clump. This created a fountain of sparks but he did it again, wanting to be sure that when it cooled down nothing would remain that could be deciphered, however small.

'We'll let it burn itself out now. Thank you for helping me, Zoe. Much appreciated.'

'Anything for you, Gramps.'

He hesitated, coughed a couple of times and then said in an embarrassed tone of voice. 'You don't look very pleased with life just at the moment. That boyfriend of yours let you down again, has he?'

She nodded miserably. 'He promised to take me to Brazil with him. Now he says he can't afford to pay for my plane ticket and he's going on his own.'

He gave her shoulder a comforting pat. 'I've always liked Emerson, although why he wants to go and live abroad among foreigners I shall never understand.'

'You would understand it if you knew what a wonderful country Brazil is.'

'It's a long way off. Supposing you didn't like it and wanted to come back?'

'If I was with Emerson I wouldn't want to come back.'

'What's Emerson got against this country?'

'Nothing. It's just that he's always had this dream of going to Rio.'

'It's good to have a purpose in life. I admire that in a man.'

'I need some money, Gramps.'

'Be patient. You won't have long to wait.'

'I wish you wouldn't say things like that. Did you know Ronnie has a girl friend now? Someone he was at school with, I think.'

'News to me, Zoe. Who is she? Anyone we know?'

'He hasn't said exactly. But he would like to get married, if only he had some money.'

'Well now, this is a surprise.' He straightened himself up and looked pleased. 'Ronnie has got more sense than to want to go and live in a country where they don't speak English. He's a bright boy, young Ronnie.'

'He needs some money, Gramps. Me too.'

'You've made my day, Zoe. Don't often hear any good news. We all need a life partner and we all need a secure future. If you and Ronnie have got it planned out then I shall die a happy man. I've worked hard to get the money together and I'm pleased that it's going to be well spent.'

'But if you've got to die before we get it that won't make either of us very happy. Couldn't you not die and let us have the money first? Ronnie and me.'

'No one wants to die, Zoe. I don't want to die. You won't want to die when the time comes. It's not a question of money.'

Zoe gave up. She had spent her short lifetime trying to wheedle money out of her tight-fisted grandfather and seldom received more than enough for a packet of cigarettes. He would pretend to be on the point of putting his hand in his trouser pocket but never actually did so, distracting her with pointless conversation. As now on this occasion, and with good reason. He said, 'Listen! That's your Mum and Dad coming back from the town. Let's shift ourselves. Don't want to waste a lot of breath on explanations.'

The sound of Steve and Carol's farm truck bumping up through the puddles and pot-holes came ever closer. It was a Wednesday morning and they were returning from their weekly shopping expedition to the town. They could not afford to be away for very long but went every Wednesday as this was the best day for buying meat from the high street butcher. Carol had a list of things to buy and shops to visit, including a street market where she stocked up on cheap fruit and veg. They needed to be back at work with least delay and scurried round in the shortest possible time.

Steve and Carol had seen the smoke from a distance and were alarmed, fearful that something had caught fire in their absence. As they neared the farm buildings they realised it was coming from their makeshift incinerator, which eased their anxiety until they saw their daughter and her delinquent grandfather hastening from the scene. Carol had a quick brain and soon worked out why. 'He's been burning something he didn't want us to see.' She pointed an accusing finger. 'Look at him hurrying away. We were just too late to stop him, whatever mischief he was up to.'

'Just like Dad,' Steve admitted in annoyance, taking a swipe at the windscreen with his cap. 'He knew it was our morning for the shops and did it while we were gone. Artful old bugger.'

'Alice is at her place of work, Mum can't see from the kitchen, so he timed it very well, didn't he. Let's go and have a look.'

They climbed down from their rugged farm truck and trudged the short distance to the back of the farm buildings. They stood in front of the incinerator cage which still shimmered with heat. Everything in it had burned away but among the glowing embers they could make out silvery flakes of fine ash which were all that remained of Joe's company brochures and financial statements. A sour cindery smell was spreading over the farm.

Steve was so obviously distressed that Carol gave him a sympathetic squeeze on the arm. 'Don't be too upset. He could have just been turning out some old papers from his desk.'

White-faced, Steve shook his head. 'Whatever he was burning he shouldn't have. He's out of control, Carol. What can we do before he ruins us all?'

18

Alice learned about the fire when she returned home to the farm after a trying day at the supermarket. Steve told her what he knew, which was that their father had announced his intention to tidy up the hay barn when he had finished his breakfast.

His sister took the point. 'It made Ma suspicious? She guessed Dad was up to something?'

'He's never worried about it being untidy before. He likes working in dirt and muddle. Yes, she was suspicious, of course she was.'

'Keep going. Tell me what happened.'

'He said Zoe was going to help him burn all the rubbish from the barn.'

'She was right to be suspicious. So would I have been.'

'Ma saw the smoke and then she heard Zoe come back into the house and go into Dad's office. She can't move very quickly but she wanted to know what was going on and shot down the passage on her two sticks and caught Zoe in the act.'

'Tell me the worst.'

'Dad had been emptying the top two drawers of the filing cabinet, which is where he keeps most of the important stuff, insurance policies and so on. He'd put it in carrier bags ready for Zoe to take round to the incinerator. She said Dad had told her not to say anything, so she didn't.'

'This goes from bad to worse, Stevie.'

'What do you suppose he was burning?'

'All the documents that would have traced back where the money came from.'

'Did he need to do that?'

'If what you tell me is true he's done it, whether he needed to or not. It means that we can never check up on how much he had invested, and how much profit he made in twenty years. Either way it was a crazy thing to do. Reckless. Criminal, almost.'

'It was his money, Sis.'

'I hope it still is his money.' She pointed to the ceiling. 'Up there in his bedroom. A great big lump sum in cash with a daft old man looking after it.' She closed her eyes and bowed her head for a moment. 'What a nightmare.'

'There must be something we can do. If we went to see his doctor, together I mean, and explained what was happening. Wouldn't they be forced to act?'

'I doubt it. But we could try, as a last resort.'

'Dementia?' Steve queried. 'Alzheimers? Is that the line we would take?'

'Doesn't trust banks, doesn't trust lawyers, doesn't trust his family, suspicious of everyone and everything. There's probably a medical term for it.'

'I could get Carol to look it up on the Internet.'

Alice lit a cigarette, squinting at her brother and waving the smoke from her face. 'Dad is probably convinced that what he's doing is right. Thinks he's the one behaving rationally and that we're all conspiring against him.'

'What would we need for an excuse? So that we could get him examined by a doctor, I mean.'

'Dad would make fools of us if we tried. Sit him down in front of a psychiatrist and he would put on a perfect act. Polite. Reasonable. Concerned for the welfare of his family. We would look like a bunch of greedy relatives scheming to steal his life's savings.'

'I don't agree with that, Sis. Those sort of people are trained to recognise the signs. They wouldn't be fooled. Not when they asked him where he was keeping the money. Under his bed with a twelve-bore shotgun! Get real. No, they would suss him out all right.'

'How else could we get an appointment with his doctor?'

'Ma might be our best bet. Worried because her husband isn't taking his medication, that might get him looked at again. And it would be true.'

Alice took a long draw on her cigarette and then squished it out in a bitter swirl of eye-stinging smoke. She said, 'We're running out of time. You know that, don't you?'

Loyal to the last, Steve rallied to his father's defence. 'Dad explained it to us, what he was doing, and why he was doing it. You never know, it might work out all right in the end.'

'I don't see it that way. Suppose he doesn't die, what happens then? Does the money stay under his bed for months on end? His nerves wouldn't stand it, and nor would ours.'

'How do you rate Dad's health at the moment?'

'I don't see much wrong with him, not physically anyway.'

'And mentally?'

'Not keeping himself clean is a bad sign but living like a pig in shit isn't the same as having something seriously wrong with you. He's always been a strong man, and a healthy man too most of the time. He could live for years.'

'What would happen to the money then? He would have to put it back in the bank, wouldn't he?'

'It's already decreased in value by not earning any interest. If you adjust for inflation it will decrease even faster the longer it stays under his bed. Something needs to happen, and happen soon.'

'Perhaps it will.' Steve made helpless gestures with his hands. 'He seems convinced he's going to die. Before Christmas, so he says. If he did, that would solve it for everyone.'

Alice agreed. 'It would. Not that I wish the cantankerous old sod any harm. But you're right, it would. '

'All right then. Suppose he does die, in his room, with the door locked. What happens next?'

'You would have to do something, Stevie.'

'You mean like forcing the door open?'

'I can't see us sending for the police, can you? The door would have to be forced open, not so easy with the new locks. Try and think. What's the first thing we do when we get into the room?'

Steve worried his hair with his hand and became agitated. 'Make sure Dad was dead, I suppose.'

'Then what?'

'Christ, I don't know. Start looking for the key of the suitcase. That would be on everyone's mind, wouldn't it?'

'Then stand round his deathbed counting the money. Do you think that's what he has in mind for us?'

Steve began to sweat, and wiped his face with his sleeve. 'You mean we ought to agree in advance how to act when he dies? Such as not opening the suitcase until we're all together?'

'Dad is entitled to a bit of dignity. We ought to sit in our places at the dining table and do it properly. You would be head of the family so it would be your duty to open the suitcase and see what was inside. Envelopes full of money with our names on, hopefully.'

'You're the eldest, Sis. I think you should do it. Or Ma.'

'We can sort that responsibility out later. Think ahead, Stevie. Do we all open our envelopes and count it out in front of one another? Or take it away to our rooms and count it in secret. We would need pens, paper, a calculator. What then? Some proper financial advice would be handy. Especially for Ronnie and Zoe.'

'That had occurred to me, actually. We wouldn't want all those banknotes scattered around the house.'

'We would need individual investment advice. It couldn't be done quickly. It would take several weeks to get it properly invested again. Longer, probably. And never be worth as much as it was before Dad broke it all up into little bits. Money works best in big lots, there's no other way of getting any decent interest. Downhill all the way, if you want my honest assessment of where we go from here.'

Steve had another worry. 'And what do we do if there's an envelope in the suitcase with Betty Hounsome's name on it?'

'Dad would have thought of that. Given it to her in advance perhaps.'

'But supposing there was an envelope with her name on?'

'It would be just another snout in the trough. Give it to her, what else could we do?'

'But is it likely?'

'No. Even Dad wouldn't do a thing like that to us.'

'You're probably right, Sis. I'm getting paranoid now.'

As they parted, Alice for the TV viewing settee and Steve to make his last round of the farm, she gripped him by arm. Pulling him round to face her she said, 'I'm relying on you, Stevie. You and the others. It's starting to worry me when I'm at work, wondering what Dad is getting up to when I'm not there to stop him.'

'Carol keeps an eye on him. Once he's up and about she never lets him out of her sight.'

'That's not good enough. I don't trust him, and nor should you. If you hear him leaving by the front door it means he's up to no good. He's a slippery customer and could be off and away in his Land Rover while you're at the other end of the farm on a tractor.'

'I don't see that we would have the right to stop him, Alice.'

'You could keep the farm gate padlocked. That would slow him down.'

'Dad would just drive it across the fields. A Land Rover will go almost anywhere. That wouldn't stop him.'

'All right then, confiscate Dad's keys if you can get hold of them. Or disable the Land Rover so that it isn't driveable. Show some guts, Stevie.'

'I'll discuss it with Carol. We'll come up with something, I promise.'

'I hope you do. If Dad ever leaves the farm and takes the suitcase with him none of us will see a penny of that money. You know that, don't you?'

19

Martha Knight had been the first to realise that the happy home would never be the same again. She had wept bitterly when telling Steve about the suitcase, knowing that their long years of amicable co-existence had come to an end. Steve thought she was overstating it but as the news spread through the house he realised that she had accurately predicted the violence of the family's reaction.

They were neither poor nor affluent, content with what they had, at ease with one another and able to lead sheltered and untroubled lives. With no forewarning of disaster they had suddenly been jerked into the real world and confronted with money troubles, just like everyone else who lived in the real world. A chill sense of insecurity cast gloom over the entire household. Their years of harmonious seclusion had come to an abrupt end.

The seven family members had never been crowded, indoors or out. The farmhouse interior had enough rooms for them all to have their own individual space, while the sprawling farmyard with its many outbuildings offered all the parking and storage capacity they would ever need. Families develop their own way of living together as congenially as possible and the seven Knights had done it better than most. To ensure that their own right to a private life was respected they had all taken care not to intrude on anyone else.

Martha was a prime beneficiary of this sensible arrangement. She was queen of the pantry and kitchen and no one encroached on her domain. Cooking meals for a big family was her reason for living, it was what she had always done, as had her mother and grandmother before her, both of them also married to farmers. She had her own easy chair beside the Aga to provide rest during the day, and constant warmth from the stove to ease her arthritis pains. With plenty of time at her disposal she managed the meals without too much difficulty, determined to retain her usefulness for many years to come. She did not see it as paid labour and until the trouble over the suitcase had been happy all day long.

One particularly cold and dark November morning Joe Knight was late down for his breakfast. Martha was just starting to get worried and about to ask one of the others to go up and knock on his door when she heard him coming slowly down the back stairs.

When he arrived in the kitchen she was shaken by the change in his appearance. He was pale and drooped, his movements slow and his voice so weak that she had to lower her head to hear what he was saying.

He said, 'Don't feel too good this morning, Martha. Reckon I've had one of my funny little turns.'

'In what way don't you feel well, Joe?'

'Just a bit shaky, that's all.' He forced a smile. 'Old age and infirmity. Catches up with us all in the end.'

'You certainly don't look very well. Sit down while I make you some porridge.'

'Don't think I want any porridge this morning, thank you, Martha.'

'What would you like then?'

'A mug of tea and a piece of dry toast. Ought to try and eat something.'

'Would you like to go in the other room and sit in an armchair?'

'No. It's nice and warm here. If you don't mind me sitting quietly.' He beckoned Martha to come closer. 'Haven't been out to collect the eggs. Don't feel up to it today. Could you ask Carol to do it for me. Tell her I would be much obliged.'

'Of course I will. And I'll ask her to collect them up every day until you feel better. Won't hurt you to take it easy for a week or two.' Martha watched as he sipped his tea and nibbled his piece of toast. She could tell that he was forcing it down and had no appetite at all. She was worried and tried to help. 'Would you like me to ring the doctor, Joe? In view of what you've told us about your medical condition. Perhaps it would be the sensible thing to do.'

'You know how I feel about doctors. The answer is 'no'. It will always be 'no'. I should be grateful if you would bear that in mind, Martha. In the event that I can't make the decision for myself I want no hospital and no doctors, ever. Promise?'

'Very well. If that's what you want.'

'It is, Martha, it is. What can a doctor tell me that I don't know already?'

'So long as you're sure.'

'I am sure, and I'm holding you to your promise. I was born in this house and I want to die here. Not in some god-forsaken side ward in a hospital.'

Martha sat down beside him and gave his hand a squeeze. 'Of course you can die at home, Joe, if that's what you want.'

'That is exactly what I want. If you let me sit here quietly I shall soon be all right. Just a nasty little turn I had. Feeling better now.'

'Do you want to go back to bed?'

'Later perhaps. Not now. What's the weather like today?'

'Steve said it was quite mild when he was in earlier. The forecast is for a fine day.'

'In that case I might go for a little walk round the farm.' He hesitated. 'We used to have quite a few walking sticks in that old umbrella stand in the hall. Couldn't see one there the last time I had a look.'

'You need a stick, Joe?'

'My legs feel as if they might let me down. Do you know where the sticks are?'

'In the cupboard under the stairs. I tried them all in turn but they were too long for me. The hospital provided me with my aluminium ones. Adjustable, they are. Perhaps you ought to be thinking of having that sort yourself.'

'Thanks for the information Martha but I'll go and have a look in the cupboard. There should be one to suit me. No, no, you needn't come to help. I'll be back when I've had my walk. Hope I'll feel better by then.'

But he didn't, nor did Martha expect him to be. She soon told the others the bad news, and they were chastened to see him walking slowly with the aid of a stick. Even Alice was forced to soften her attitude when she could see for herself that her father's health had genuinely deteriorated. No one likes to see a strong man brought low and even if she had never been particularly fond of him she was saddened to see him suddenly looking old and frail.

The unspoken thought shared by them all was surprise at discovering that he had been telling them the truth about his failing health. And it followed on from this that if he had been right about his ill health he could also be right about his impending death. Whether or not he had misinterpreted the medical warnings he had been given, and was worrying himself into an early grave, was not within their capacity to decide. It was the outcome that concerned them. He seemed convinced that he would soon die and began to act with the patient resignation of a man whose remaining days on earth had dwindled down to a meagre handful.

When he heard arrangements for the family Christmas being discussed he just smiled sadly and shook his head. 'Don't pay any attention to me. I won't be here to share it with you but I want you to promise me that you'll have the eats and a good time, just like always. That is my wish, if you would all bear it in mind, please.'

After this dire pronouncement his condition improved and when the weather was not too bad he perked up a bit and went for a longer walk than usual. The village shop was only half a mile away and he managed it more than once, mainly to buy his pouch of hand-rolling tobacco and a packet of cigarette papers. Rolling up cigarettes in his fingers, lighting them, then relighting them when they went out, was a form of occupational therapy that seemed to soothe him.

Once a week he bought the local newspaper and sat at the trestle table in the recently tidied hay barn reading every word of every page. He had always interested himself in local affairs and with plenty of time at his disposal kept up to date with the news. Although his farm shop had now been disbanded he still headed to the hay barn from force of habit. It was his special place on the farm, indeed his special place in the world. Not that it had been a proper shop needing inspection and licensing, just an extension of his back door trade, mostly bedding plants and vegetables and fruit as they came in season. The rubbish had gone up in smoke but the museum piece scales with brass weights still stood forlornly at one end of the table.

One morning after he had eaten a modest breakfast but showed no signs of wanting to go for his walk Martha said, 'The weather seems nicely settled, Joe. Why don't you put something on your blackboard and open up the shop again, even if only for a day or two? It would occupy your mind and you know how much you've always enjoyed meeting people.'

'It's too late for all that, Martha.'

'No it isn't. Zoe would be pleased to help you, you know she would.'

'There's nothing worth selling any more.'

'That's never stopped you before.' Martha hobbled across the kitchen to the dresser where she opened the top left-hand drawer. This was where she kept the box of chalks Joe used for his blackboard. She took out a new whole stick to tempt him. 'You know it would cheer you up. And the fresh air will do you good.'

'It will take more than fresh air and scenery to do me good, Martha.'

'You love talking to all the people who come to your stall. Shall I call Zoe for you? Some fresh air wouldn't do her any harm either.'

'Too late. I've chalked up the blackboard for the last time. 'Closed Until Further Notice.' That's what it says and that's what it means. Take a walk down to the gate to see for yourself if you don't believe me.'

'If only I could.' Martha returned to her chair, holding on

to the arms while lowering herself painfully. 'You said it yourself, we're a couple of old crocks, Joe.'

Gruffly he muttered, 'Didn't mean to be rude to you, Martha. It was a kind thought and a good suggestion. I'm not up to it, that's all.'

'Is there anything you want for the bedroom?'

'No, but you're right about needing to get out occasionally. I think I'll go for a little drive in the Land Rover. That will cheer me up.'

Martha was immediately alarmed. 'Oh Joe, you won't take the suitcase with you, will you?'

'I wasn't planning to.'

'Suppose you had one of your nasty little turns and there was an accident? Anyone could be first on the scene. People aren't honest any more, not like they used to be. Sod's Law, Joe. With our luck the first person to stop would be a thief fresh out of prison. His lucky day.'

'I told you, it's safe where it is and that's where I'm leaving it.'

'You've got all our life savings in that suitcase, Joe. Don't risk it.'

He pushed back his chair, no longer in a good mood. 'I don't like people telling me what to do. This is a bad time to be quarrelling with me, Martha. I would prefer us to part on good terms.'

'I'm not quarrelling with you. Just asking you to be careful, that's all. What do you mean, you want us to part on good terms? How far are you intending to go in the Land Rover?'

'I meant that you could soon be burying me.' He took down his straw beekeeper's hat from the peg on the back of the kitchen door and settled it on his head. 'I wouldn't want you to stand by my grave remembering the cross words you spoke to me.'

At which Martha wept. 'My poor Joe.' She tapped her forehead. 'What a way to end up.'

20

If he had thought through the consequences before buying the suitcase Joe would have made some preparations in advance, if only to install a television set and an armchair in the marital bedroom. This was the bedroom he had once shared with his wife Martha, and where he now spent the greater part of the day alone.

Although the bathroom was close he soon grew tired of unlocking the door, locking it behind him, and then repeating the process in reverse. He began using a chamber pot, emptying it night and morning, ignoring the comments from his family, Alice in particular, who disapproved of this arrangement.

With little to occupy his mind he passed the time slumbering restlessly on his bed fully clothed. He had brought up an old radio from his office in one of the downstairs rooms and listened to it while smoking his strong hand-rolled cigarettes. He smuggled in small food items to snack between meals but with no tap or toilet facilities the room soon got in a pickle. He would not allow any of his womenfolk inside to clean up, nor to change his bed linen, and just sat out time like an old style miser barricaded in with his hoard.

When he left the room to go downstairs he double-locked the door behind him and then kept his hand in his jacket pocket to make sure that the keys never left his possession. The other members of the family were equally on edge and more jumpy than usual, even Ronnie and Zoe were affected as they could not fail to be aware of the gathering tension inside the farmhouse. Martha had stopped having the kitchen radio on during the day so that she could hear any sounds from overhead. The creak of floorboards and the clunk of the mortise lock could be heard all over the house. All those within earshot made haste to locate him and then keep him within range so that they could be sure he was not carrying the cheap airline suitcase containing the family wealth in banknotes.

Carol was the fleetest of foot and when Joe's footsteps seemed to be heading towards the front stairs she would hare around a couple of corners and scoot down the long central passage so that she could arrive in the hall before he did. So far he had been empty-handed but the family were determined not to relax their vigilance. Until recently Steve and Carol had shared a cellphone but they now carried one each so that they could remain in contact for the few occasions during the day when their work on the farm kept them apart.

In December the weather became miserably cold and Joe began to spend his mornings in the big farm kitchen to keep warm. This irritated his wife Martha who was used to having the kitchen to herself. Over a period of years she had worked out a daily routine that made the best of her lack of mobility, and Joe's demands on her attention were a distraction she did not need. His dejected appearance and slumped body at the kitchen table were not much to her liking either, still less his lengthening beard and hair.

'What are you muttering about now, Joe?' she asked, trying not to sound too exasperated. 'It's not raining, why don't you put your coat on and go for a walk round the farm?'

'I'd only get in Steve's way.'

'It would make a change from getting in my way. Why don't you go and sit in the other room where it would be a bit more comfortable for you? Switch the telly on. Put your feet up if you don't want to do any work.'

'My working days are over. Long over.'

'I wish I could say the same. Come on, Joe, shift yourself. I need to make a start on the dinner.'

'All right then. I'll go back upstairs if I'm not wanted here.'

'You can't spend all day in that smelly old room on your own. If you can't open the window any more you should stop smoking those dreadful cigarettes of yours. You're going to get chest trouble otherwise, severe bronchitis like as not. Where are you going to hide the suitcase if they take you off to hospital for an X-Ray? I doubt if they would let you keep it under the bed with a loaded shotgun like you do here.'

'Bronchitis is the least of my health troubles. There are plenty of other things I could die of first.'

'Don't keep on about dying. It's not a nice subject of conversation.'

'How do you think I feel about it? I'm the one who is going to die, not you.'

'So you keep telling us.' As a peace offering she put a mug of coffee and the biscuit tin down in front of him but he scarcely noticed and seemed deep in thought. 'What is it, now?' she enquired, leaning on one of her sticks. 'Is something else bothering you?'

'It's what you've just said, about hiding the suitcase in a different place. Funny you should mention that because I've been thinking along the same lines myself. It isn't safe where it is. I need to find somewhere better.'

Martha finally lost patience. 'Some old men go foolish, and some old men go cantankerous, but I'm buggered if you haven't gone foolish and cantankerous at the same time.'

'I'm doing the best for my family. Be a bit nicer to me, Martha. I'm not long for this world and I should like us to part company on good terms.'

She had been drying her hands after rinsing them under the tap but threw the towel aside in a temper. 'Joe, it's time for you to back down and ask Alice and Steve to help you with the money. It's not too late. Never mind your pride and hurt feelings, you need to get that money put back into the bank, not hide it somewhere else.'

He became agitated on hearing this. He pushed back his chair and headed for the back stairs. 'You're all trying to steal it from me. I know you are.'

'Who do you mean, Joe? It's wicked to say such things.'

'I need to find a better place to hide the money, it isn't safe where it is. I've got somewhere in mind. You can tell them that from me, Martha. When they break into my room to steal the money it won't be there.'

He picked up the mug of coffee and took it with him, climbing the stairs slowly. The familiar sequence of sounds followed, the creaking floorboards, the jangle of keys and the thump of the mortise lock as it opened. Then the door slamming shut and the lock being turned from the inside.

'What is it, Ma?' Steve asked in alarm when he came in for his mid-morning snack a few minutes later. 'Has something happened?'

This was because his mother was sitting down at the kitchen table dabbing at her eyes with her apron. She said, 'It's Dad. He's in a bad way, Steve.'

'You don't have to tell me. What's he done now?'

'You aren't going to like this. He's just told me the money isn't safe where it is and he's decided to put it somewhere else.'

'Christ Almighty! He's got to be stopped. We're going to lose the lot otherwise.'

'The others won't be very happy either when they hear about it.'

'Carol certainly won't. She's feeding the pigs. I think I had better go and tell her straight away.'

He hurried from the kitchen and returned with her a few minutes later, Carol wanting to hear the bad news for herself. They both sat down at the table in their shabby working clothes, two small disconsolate figures contemplating an uncertain future.

Martha repeated what she had told Steve and then sat down beside them, still tearful. 'My poor Joe,' she sobbed. 'It's terrible to see him looking like a tramp. I hate seeing him with a beard, and his hair all long and straggly. But what can I do if he won't let me look after him?'

'If it isn't Alzheimers it's something similar,' Carol said. 'We've got to get him to a doctor. Or get a doctor to come here and see him.'

Steve didn't agree. 'There isn't any cure for Alzheimers, even I know that. And we haven't got enough money to put him in a nursing home where he could be looked after properly. I wouldn't agree to that anyway. Dad has told me more than once that he wanted to die here and we should honour his wishes.'

Martha wiped away a tear. 'My poor husband. I shall always remember him when he was in his prime. He was a strong man. Could lift and carry almost anything and worked from morning till night. This is a sad way to end up.'

'Tell us again what he said about the suitcase,' Carol pressed her mother-in-law. 'Did he give you any clue where he was going to hide it from us?'

'No.'

'He must have said something.'

'He said we were all trying to steal the money from him. That's what he said. Is it true?'

Steve and Carol exchanged anxious glances, trying not to look guilty. Carol said, 'Not to steal it exactly. But we all want to make sure the suitcase doesn't go missing.'

'It's important to me, Ma,' Steve said. 'Dad hasn't spent a penny on the farm for quite a few years now. We need thousands of pounds worth of new equipment just to replace all the machinery that's worn out. The farm won't survive without some capital expenditure so that's where my share will go, and Carol's as well. Even then it might not be enough.'

'You can have my share too. I want you to keep the farm going in your turn, of course I do. That's what sons are for.'

'Nice of you to say so. It's going to be touch and go though. Carol and me don't pay ourselves anything and that's the only reason the farm survives now. If Dad loses the suitcase, or hides it where no one can find it, we're done for. He shouldn't be putting us through all this worry.'

Carol gave his arm a squeeze. 'We must get back to work, love. We've got a lot of hungry animals to feed.'

Martha held up a hand to persuade them to stay for a few

moments longer. She had something important she wanted to say. 'I know Dad means well about sharing out the money, or at least I think he does, but none of us know how much money there actually is in that suitcase of his. There could be a lot more than we think or we could be in for a big disappointment. Either way it's my firm belief that it should all have been left to you, Steve.'

'It's the only way the farm can survive.'

'Exactly. Money doesn't last long once it's split up. Alice has got a good job and Ronnie could work if he was made to. What would Ronnie do with money he hasn't earned? Or your Zoe for that matter? But they all expect to go on living here at Nutwhistle rent free and that's where the money should stay, at Nutwhistle. Spent on the farm and spent on the house so that we can all keep going as long as possible. That's how I see it. And if there was any way I could part Joe from that suitcase and hand it straight to you, Steve, that is exactly what I would do.'

21

Without making it too obvious the four older members of the Knight family continued to monitor Joe's comings and goings between them. Only when he was safely locked into his room could they relax their vigilance. When he was not in his room they wanted to see him slumped moodily at the kitchen table, or sitting in the hay barn rolling cigarettes, anywhere so that he was in their sight.

This was always going to be difficult. Alice had her job at the supermarket, Martha was anchored in the kitchen and slept in the afternoon, while Steve and Carol of necessity had to be out and about on the farm. For anyone as artful and irresponsible as Joe Knight the odds were always going to be stacked in his favour. He was able to slip the leash and disappear from view almost at will. Usually he had only gone for a short walk, not really leaning on his stick but certainly grateful for the steadiness of foot it provided. Whichever member of the family was first to notice his absence alerted the others so that a search could begin immediately. Steve had let down two of the tyres on his father's Land Rover to make it undriveable but this had proved not to be necessary as Joe seemed to have made the decision on his own and went everywhere on foot.

'Bloody Dad, worrying us like this,' Alice complained when he was missing for longer than usual. 'He's given us the slip again, the crafty old sod. Where do you suppose he's gone? And more importantly what is he doing? That's what we need to know.'

'Betty Hounsome lives on the other side of the village,' Carol answered her sister-in-law. 'Want me to whizz round there in the truck to see if that's where he is? Where else could he have gone?'

'Betty could have driven him into the town. To have a haircut, perhaps? That would be nice. To see his solicitor? To arrange his funeral? God knows where he is or what he's up to.'

They did not have too long to wait. Joe reappeared, trudging down the lane with a plastic bag of groceries, having walked to the small convenience store in the village.

'Right out of baccy,' he informed them, showing his purchases. In addition to the tobacco he had the local newspaper, two jumbo-sized bags of crisps and a packet of Jaffa Cakes. He treated them to a sour glare, sensing their hostility. 'Where did you think I'd gone?'

He was anxious to return to the fortress bedroom and without waiting for a reply was soon climbing slowly up the back stairs. It was an old house and the ceilings creaked when anyone moved around overhead. As Martha had often remarked in jest it would be a bad place to choose for adultery or bed-hopping young lovers because anyone moving from room to room in the middle of the night would be heard all over the house. Such adventures were unlikely in the present circumstance but it helped to keep tabs on the wilful owner of Nutwhistle Farm so that he did not disappear with his suitcase containing the family fortune.

They learned to identify the sequence of sounds that began after he reached the top of the stairs. More often than not he went into the bathroom and they heard the tap run and the lavatory flush. When he came out he opened the next door along the passage, this being the big airing and linen cupboard. Martha did most of the family washing, Carol hung it out to dry and in the evenings when she was at home Alice helped with the ironing. Martha was unable to carry the finished articles upstairs so either Alice or Carol would take the big laundry basket up to the airing cupboard and arrange the items on the slatted wooden shelves. Joe's underpants, shirts and clean socks were always placed in the front so that he could help himself when he wanted a change of underwear.

Because he no longer allowed anyone access to the

bedroom, not even his wife, Martha had no option except to leave his clean sheets and pillow cases on the same front shelf. She asked him to place his soiled ones in the big drawstring bag used to collect up the week's dirty washing but he never did. This was because he had never needed to perform these humble tasks for himself. First his mother and then his wife had made his bed and cleaned his room and cooked his meals and tidied up behind him since the day he was born. Freshly laundered shirts, socks and underpants had appeared like magic in his chest of drawers for the whole of his life. Hardly surprising that he was soon in a muddle when trying to fend for himself.

His family were more than ever concerned for his appearance. This became worse day by day. On the few occasions when he was glimpsed upstairs, usually when he went into the bathroom to empty his chamber pot, it was worryingly obvious that his personal hygiene had deteriorated to the point where it was a health risk to everyone else in the house. He became increasingly dirty and dishevelled, with lengthening hair and beard. Dressed in filthy clothes, drooped and shambling, it was only too easy to believe in his gloomy prognosis of an early grave.

This came closer when he had another of his funny turns, as he called them, and did not leave his room for four days. He refused either to come out or to allow anyone else inside, and carried on a few brief conversations from behind the door. 'What do you want done with your grub, Dad?' Steve shouted, his face against the door. His father called back, 'Leave it outside. I'll come for it when I'm ready.'

They took it in turns to carry up the small items of food he asked for, leaving them on a tray outside the door. Alice joked that to save him the labour of locking and unlocking the door every time it should have a flap at the bottom, as in all the best dungeon movies. She lost patience by the fourth day and when he asked if he could have a cheese sandwich and a mug of cocoa for his supper she carried it up on a tray and hammered on his door demanding to be let in. She called out,

'Room Service! Come on, Dad. Open the door.'

She continued banging on the door until she heard him call back, 'All right, all right. There's no need to kick the door down. I'm coming.' She heard him move slowly to the door and fumble with his keys. When he had unlocked the door he opened it and put out his hand for the tray. Alice was having none of this, she turned round and used her weight and considerable strength to force her way backwards into the room.

On entering she let out a cry of disgust, 'What a stink! How can you bear it, Dad? No wonder you don't feel well.' She placed the tray on the small bedside table and pointed to the chair. 'Come and sit down and drink your cocoa while it's still hot.' She was used to being obeyed and after a few moments of token resistance her father did as he was told and sat down meekly on the bedside chair.

On looking round Alice had drawn breath to scold but softened her voice and her attitude when she saw her father looking old, frail and ill. The sickly invalid smell in the barricaded airless room told a convincing tale of infirmity and approaching death. In a less aggressive tone of voice she said, 'Your bed doesn't look very comfortable. I'll get some clean sheets and remake it for you.'

'Thanks, Alice,' he mumbled, having started to eat.

'Ma made the cheese sandwich. It's got some yellow pickle in it, your favourite.'

'Thank her for me. Tell her I'm enjoying it.'

'You don't look too good, Dad.'

'I'm better than I was. I shall come downstairs in the morning so you won't need to bring my food up any more.'

'Ma says you refuse to see a doctor. Is that right?'

'I've never got on with doctors, you know that. No point, anyway. Not now.'

'If you say so. What you need is some fresh air. Are you sure there isn't any way of opening your window?'

He made a dismissive gesture with his hand. 'You've forced your way in. Don't scold now you're here.'

136

But Alice was too busy gathering up dirty crockery and food scraps to take much notice of her father who sat watching morosely as she tidied his room and stripped off his bed. She went next door to the linen cupboard to fetch clean sheets and pillow cases and busied herself for nearly an hour remaking the bed and straightening the room. When she was finished and had piled up the tray and put it outside the door she said, 'How are you sleeping? I could bring you up a hot water bottle and some aspirins. Or anything else you need.'

'I'm fine as I am. You know me, Alice. I'm not one to make a fuss.'

Having done all she could she kissed her father goodnight and headed for the door. He was still sitting on the bedside chair but struggled to his feet and followed her to the door so that he could lock it behind her. There was a brief moment of unease. He winced apologetically as he held up the keys but turned the lock the moment she was through the door. Theirs was not a tender father-daughter relationship but at least they understood one another and she accepted his muttered thanks as the nearest he would ever come to a display of affection.

Alice was satisfied with her venture upstairs, having successfully penetrated the prison-cell bedroom, something no one else had achieved. Her insistence on remaking the bed had been with the specific purpose in mind of studying the suitcase. The suitcase! The wretched suitcase which had disrupted their family life and sabotaged their future security. She had not only seen it she had touched it, assessed its weight and photographed it on her brain. She was confident that she had its configuration programmed into her memory, its dimensions, colour, shape and a few small distinguishing features. She recognised it as a cheap type of mass-produced medium-sized airline suitcase, better still she knew the shop that sold them and was sure of being able to buy one exactly the same, most likely with a key that would fit. This was the good news she intended to pass on to her son Ronnie at the earliest opportunity.

When she returned downstairs and took the tray loaded

with dirty crockery to the kitchen sink she found that her mother, brother and sister-in-law were waiting for her. The first question they asked was not, 'How is he?' but 'Did you see it?'

Alice nodded. 'Yes, the suitcase hasn't gone awol, it's still there under the bed. Safe and sound for the moment.'

Steve breathed a huge sigh of relief. 'Thank God for that.'

'I think he was only trying to frighten us by threatening to hide it somewhere else.'

Carol was less sure. 'We can't afford to relax. He knows we're watching him but he's worked out how to dodge us and get clear away. He could sneak off with the suitcase any time he wants.'

Alice disagreed. 'I don't think the poor old sod is up to it any more.' She wrinkled her nose in distaste. 'You wouldn't believe how bad the smell was in Dad's room.'

Carol winced and spread her hands in a gesture of helplessness. 'Men are never very hygienic at the best of times. I don't suppose he notices.'

Steve was still concerned for his father. 'I'm sorry he won't let me in to see him. How bad do you reckon he was, Sis?'

'He looks terrible. To find out properly we would need to give him a bath and a haircut and shave off his beard and clean him up. Hard to tell otherwise.'

'We could be taking his food up for quite a while then?'

Alice shook her head. 'No. He said he was feeling better and would be coming downstairs tomorrow. I don't think he actually is any better, just that he wants to keep us out of his room. That's what he said, and knowing Dad, he means it.'

Carol still urged caution. 'So long as it doesn't suddenly occur to him that the suitcase might be safer under Betty Hounsome's bed. Every time he comes out of his room there's a risk of something happening or going wrong. We mustn't take our eyes off him when he's on the loose.'

'I shall have to rely on you to do that,' Alice said. She had made herself a mug of strong heavily sweetened tea to calm her nerves. 'How much money do you reckon there is in that suitcase? It would be a hell of a lot to lose.'

Carol said, 'Steve and me have been trying to work it out. There's the money from the cottages, and the money from selling the cows and the milk quota. Interest rates have been low for a long time, but not all that low. Unless Joe has been spending some of the money without telling us, or without us finding out, then we reckon it must be well over a million quid.'

Alice nodded grimly. 'I've been doing the same sums myself. There's got to be a lot more than a million. Nerve racking isn't it? To think of losing it, I mean.'

Steve leaned his head on the table and groaned in despair. 'These are hard times in farming. Prices are right down, we're losing money on the pigs and just about breaking even on the sheep. The beef trade isn't all that brilliant either. If that suitcase goes missing I shall be in Shit Street financially. I can't let it happen.'

22

The Knight family parked their assortment of vehicles side by side in a long cart shed. Several of the wooden carts still remained in their old places, most of them beyond repair.

In pole position at the end nearest to the house was Joe's crumpled dark green Land Rover. Next to it was Steve's equally battered four-by-four farm truck, in constant daily use. He and Carol also owned a modest saloon car but they used it so infrequently that it was covered in dust. Steve had once bought a second-hand small caravan just in case it might ever be possible for him and Carol to take a holiday. It suffered the same fate as their car and mouldered away next to a boat which had belonged to Joe's father. This had been bought on a similar whim and had long ago ceased to be seaworthy.

The two cars belonging to Ronnie Knight and his mother were parked side by side at the farthest end of the long cart shed. Alice had asked Ronnie to meet her by their cars late the next night so that she could show him the suitcase she had purchased earlier in the day. She opened the boot of her car so that he could take a quick look inside. It was dark and they had positioned themselves where they could not be seen from the house, but still spoke in whispers.

'Nice one, Mum,' Ronnie said approvingly. He leaned over to examine the suitcase she had bought. 'Identical, did you say?'

'I know all the shops Grandad goes to, the cheap ones mostly. As soon as I saw the suitcase in his bedroom I knew straight away where he had bought it, and I was right.'

'Brilliant. And the key?'

'It might fit, with luck. Not every suitcase would have a different lock, there would be about three patterns for a dozen suitcases. Buy enough suitcases and you would soon get one that worked.' She paused, aware that Ronnie had started to pick his nose. 'Yes, darling. What is it?'

'Might not matter about the key fitting.'

'Oh? How is that?'

'What do they do in all the spy films? Think, Mum.'

She did, and when the penny dropped gave him a kiss on the forehead. 'Of course. Just switch the suitcases. Why didn't I think of that?'

'We would need to know how heavy Grandad's is. Next time you take him up his mug of cocoa could you lift it out of the way when you make the bed? We would need to get it right.'

'I already did that sweetheart. I nudged it quite hard a few times and it felt full, and heavy.'

'That's a good start. Are you sure it's identical?'

'Absolutely positive.'

'Wouldn't this one look new? Grandad's suitcase has been around a while. How messed up did it look?'

'You're right, precious. This one is a lot more shiny. Is that a problem?'

'You'll need to rough it up a bit. You would know when it looked the same, wouldn't you?'

They were huddled in coats, their only light a dim glow from the boot compartment of the car. Still speaking in whispers Alice said, 'Leave it to me. I'll dip an old towel in some muddy water and rub it all over to take the shine off. Good thinking, sweetheart, I'll make sure it looks the same, or at least same enough for him not to notice unless he looks closely.' She paused and whispered again, 'What is it, darling? Have you thought of something else?'

'Just that to make it feel the same you ought to put the same things inside. Grandad told us about the brown envelopes, I think you should buy some more and fill them with paper.'

'Paper?'

'Yes, blank paper. Photocopy paper. Buy a few packets

and cut them up small, same size as banknotes. Put them in wads with rubber bands round them and stuff them in the brown envelopes. Attention to detail, Mum. That way the suitcase will balance right, and feel the same weight if Grandad lifts it.'

'Leave it to me, darling. Mummy will do all that for you.'

Ronnie could foresee a bigger problem. 'That's the easy part. How do we make the switch? That's the difficult part.'

She gave him another kiss. 'You're so clever, angel. I'm sure you'll think of a way.'

'Grandad doesn't wash and shave any more. If you could persuade him to go to the bathroom that might give us long enough. My room is just on the other side of the passage. I could have our suitcase ready by the door. It would only take a couple of seconds to change them over.'

'It's not that easy. Grandad always resists when you try and make him do something he doesn't want to do.'

'All right then. Fetch his razor and offer to give him a shave in his room. Work up a nice lather and shove a brushful of soap in his eyes. That would give me time to run in and out. Like I said, we only need a few seconds.'

'He's crafty, is Grandad. And suspicious. He would guess I was up to something.'

Ronnie was anxious to press on with the plan. 'That Sunday dinner time, when he told us about putting the money into envelopes with our names on, it sounded to me as if he had finished doing it. Which means he probably wouldn't need to open the suitcase up again. Not if he could see it in its usual place. It's worth a try.'

'It is, if you put it like that. It might be ages before he thought of looking inside.'

'He would be in for a big surprise if he did.'

'I'll buy the envelopes and paper tomorrow. If you think it's that urgent.'

'I do.' He took another close look at the suitcase, snapping open the locks and peering inside. They had been speaking in whispers, pausing frequently to look round in case they were overheard. He put up his hand to pull down the tailgate of her car. 'Keep it well covered up. When you've got it ready we'll think of a way of getting it up to my room. I'll keep it in the back of my wardrobe until we're able to do the switch.'

'Whatever you say, darling.'

'We might only get one opportunity. We wouldn't want to miss it by not being ready.'

Alice gave him another kiss on the forehead and put her arm round his waist. 'I'm doing it for you, treasure. I promised you I would make it up to you, and I will. The best of everything I promised you, and I can see it coming your way. Give Mummy a kiss and then we had better get ourselves back in front of the telly before anyone suspects anything.'

23

Ronnie and Zoe shared a problem and so made common cause. Zoe had to endure her teenage angst without the slightest flicker of sympathy or understanding from any of the adults in the house, including her parents. Ronnie wished to replace his doting mother with a doting wife but needed money to make the break. Keeping his romance a secret, particularly from his mother, was becoming a strain on his nerves. He and Zoe had only one another in whom to confide their problems of love and sex, or in their present circumstances, the lack of both.

Until that fateful Sunday when they sat round the family dinner table and listened to their parents and grandparents arguing about the money it had never occurred to either of them that a financial solution to their problems might be fast approaching. When they heard their grandfather talk openly about his failing health it seemed as though a miracle was about to happen. They were sorry when he told them he was not long for this world and would shortly die but could not help being excited when he declared his intention of leaving a large sum of money in cash to everyone present at the table, including them.

Zoe had clapped her hands in joy to think that she might soon be happily reunited with her boyfriend Emerson and fulfil their dream of emigrating to Brazil. And Ronnie was happy because although his mother continued to lavish affection and presents on him she could not provide what he now wanted above all else, an active sex life with his girlfriend. A timely legacy would likewise turn his dream into reality.

Having had this golden prospect dangled in front of them they were fearful that it might be snatched from their grasp before it could happen. They were aware of the escalating level of unease and suspicion in the house, and did not trust any of the adults to look after their interests. The scheming and plotting and bad feeling generated by Joe Knight's folly seemed to them to be bringing the inevitable disaster closer and more likely by the day.

'Poor old Gramps,' Zoe said tearfully. 'I'm the only one who loves him. I would never rat him out.'

'I don't see why,' Ronnie replied candidly. 'What has he ever done for you? He knew you wanted some money for your plane ticket, he could have slipped you a few hundred quid or even a couple of thousand quid with no one the wiser. That would have been a good thing to do, considering how much help you've always been to him.'

'It's not his way, is it? He's not a generous man. No farmer is.'

'If he gave it to us before he died we could thank him. Won't be able to thank him when he's dead, will we?'

'I don't like all this talk about people dying. We never did it before.'

'We didn't start it, Zo. Grandad told us himself he was going to die.'

'I need that money badly, Ronnie.'

'You aren't the only one.'

'I've haven't told you my good news. Emerson is coming back to live in the town again. One of his friends told me. He's going to share their flat.'

'You can believe it when you see him.'

'I believe it now. Emerson wouldn't tell porkies to his friend.'

No?'

Zoe aimed a punch at him. 'He said Emerson still loves me. Isn't that marvellous? I'm so happy.'

'You don't look happy.'

'I've been all packed up and ready to go to Brazil for weeks and weeks and bloody weeks. I shall do whatever Emerson wants.'

'He hasn't treated you very well, Zo.'

'You won't change my mind about Emerson. I never listen to anything bad about him. People are jealous of him because he's so clever.' She heaved a heartfelt sigh. 'I've pictured it so often in my head, what it would be like living with him in Brazil. I want it to happen. More than anything else in the world, that's what I want.'

'I hope it comes off for you, Zo, I really do. Just think, you could get on the plane and go to sleep and when you woke up you would be in Rio.'

Zoe stopped daydreaming and faced up to her present predicament. 'I'm no nearer getting the money for my plane ticket than I ever was. Gramps is my only hope. Which means that I want him to die. Isn't that an awful thing to say?'

'I'll tell you this much, Zo. If Grandad has got it wrong, and doesn't die like he thinks he's going to, then we're all in deep shit.'

'All of us? How could that be?'

'The farm can't pay its bills and owes money. Mum and me would have to find somewhere else to live. You too, Zo.'

'It won't come to that.'

'It might.'

'Where would you live if the farm was sold and we all had to leave? Tell me about your love life. Is it going anywhere?'

'No, and it won't unless I get my share of the money.'

'Not one of the girls at school is it? You can tell me. Go on.'

'I'm afraid my Mum will find out.

'You must have shagged her by now. You told me you were on a promise.'

'I still am.' Ronnie put his hands together as if in prayer and turned his eyes to the ceiling. 'Please hurry up and die, Grandad. Because Zo and me need the money.'

Zoe giggled but then repented. 'I hope no one else heard you say that. Poor old Gramps. It will serve us right if he lives another ten years.'

24

After a few sharp frosts in early December the weather settled for being cold and wet in the run up to Christmas. The days were short and Joe Knight spent most of them holed up in his insanitary bedroom, guarding the suitcase and avoiding his family. His condition was not noticeably worse, although this was difficult to assess with any degree of accuracy as he was seldom on view long enough for his loved ones to form an opinion.

He surfaced about ten o'clock every morning when he could be heard going to the bathroom. Eventually he found his way downstairs and ate a small breakfast at the kitchen table but was not inclined to talk. After this he put on his overcoat and went for a short walk. Martha watched him from the window as he trudged slowly down to the farm gate and from there into the road and out of her sight. Martha was not very happy at their neighbours seeing him dressed like a tramp, standing by the side of the road aimlessly watching the traffic pass by. Not that many of them recognised him with his beard and straggled hair and dishevelled clothes.

On other days he would mooch disconsolately around the farm for an hour or so, usually ending up in his old haunt in the hay barn. His chair and trestle table had survived Zoe's bonfire purge and he stayed there until it was time to return to the house for something to eat. After he had eaten the small lunch Martha had prepared for him he sat around for half an hour or so watching her clear up in the kitchen. When she was ready for her nap she sat down in her easy chair beside the stove and made it plain that she wanted to shut her eyes. This was usually at two o'clock in the afternoon. Joe took the hint and left her slumbering in the kitchen while he went up to his bedroom to do the same. He then stayed there for the rest of the day.

When he was safely banged up in his room the others could relax slightly but in the mornings when he was out and about on the farm they needed to be vigilant. Martha kept watch on him from the kitchen window, Steve watched from his tractor cab and Carol watched on foot as she carried out her morning duties in the calf shed and elsewhere on the farm. Even when he was sitting in his favourite place, the hay barn, they kept him under surveillance, and it wasn't easy. In the December gloom it was often hard to pick him out. The ailing Joe Knight was a ghostly figure, half concealed inside the shelter of the barn. Frequently they thought he had disappeared and then saw the flare of a match as he relit one of his finger-rolled cigarettes. These were made from the strongest black tobacco and made him cough. Sometimes they had to look twice to make sure he was there, and in spite of their vigilance he managed to elude his watchers more than once, and for a substantial period of time.

'He's given us the slip again,' Carol yelled in a panic, running to the kitchen to tell Martha. She ran out again brandishing the keys of the farm truck and was soon in hot pursuit. Sometimes she returned with him sitting on the passenger seat beside her, having intercepted him on his way to the village shop. They knew he resented being under surveillance and in spite of his various handicaps and disabilities was artful enough to disappear the moment he saw an opportunity to evade his guards.

Steve continued to agitate himself over the suitcase. His father's vague threats to find a new and better place of concealment for the money preyed on his mind. The longer he had to think about it, and do mental sums to try and work out how many thousands of pounds were needed to replace the worn out and obsolete machinery he and Carol were obliged to use, the more desperate he was to prevent the suitcase from going walkabout.

'I can't bear the worry,' he admitted to Carol when they sipped their mugs of tomato soup at lunch time. 'I want to know if the money is still in the house. It's quite a few days now since Alice saw it in his room.' He appealed to his wife. 'Couldn't you have a try?'

'What do you suggest?'

'You could offer to wash Dad's hair for him. That might get you into the room.'

'He's too far gone to be concerned about his appearance.'

'He needs a complete set of clean clothes. A bath. A haircut. All the food rubbish removed from his room. It's not unreasonable, is it? To try and persuade him to have a wash and brush up? His room must be like a pigsty by now'

''I can't see myself giving Joe a bath. Or him letting me. Sorry, love.'

This forced a smile. 'Not a pretty sight. Can't say I blame you.' He paused for thought; 'Try taking Ma upstairs with you. Dad would have to answer the door then.'

'Her arthritis is too bad. She can only manage the stairs twice a day, down in the morning and up again when she goes to bed.'

'That's when I meant. Fix Dad a nice little supper, take Ma up with you at bedtime and get her to knock on the door.'

'It's worth a try.'

'Then let's do it tonight. We're running out of time.'

Carol agreed, her face grim. 'I want to know that bloody suitcase is still there just as much as you do. Our future depends on it.' She stopped speaking, aware that her husband now had something else on his mind.

When she asked him what it was he replied, 'I've been trying to figure out how I could raise enough money to buy Mum a chair-lift for the stairs.'

'It's a nice thought, love. I was starting to wonder if the time had come for her to have a bedroom downstairs. A stair-lift would solve the problem nicely.'

'I know we need a heap of stuff for the farm but poor old Mum has suffered long enough. When Dad started talking about dying and leaving us all a wad of cash my first thought was to buy a stair-lift.'

She touched his arm. 'It would be money well spent. So we'll do it, whatever happens.'

They finished off their meal with digestive biscuits and processed cheese as usual but were soon pulling on their wellies again and returning to the fray. It had started to rain when they opened the back door. Not just ordinary rain but cold December rain blown in their face by a freshening wind beneath low clouds. They were so used to changes in the weather that they scarcely noticed and simply got on with their work. As Steve was about to climb up into his tractor cab Carol suddenly gave him a kiss. 'We'll survive all this, love. Try not to worry so much.'

'Are we on for tonight then? To make sure Dad has still got the suitcase with him?'

She pulled the hood of her anorak over her head and gave him a brief thumbs up. 'Yep. We're on. We'll do it.' Then hurried through the rain to their pig unit and began mixing up buckets of sow-and-weaner meal.

Later that evening they told Martha of their plan and asked if she would co-operate in trying to persuade Joe to let her into his room. She agreed, if not very willingly. When it was her bedtime Carol prepared Joe's supper and carried it upstairs on a tray. She put together a mug of heavily sweetened cocoa, a cheese and pickle sandwich and a packet of Jaffa Cakes, his favourite chocolate biscuits. Meanwhile her mother-in law sat down and hoisted herself slowly backwards up the stairs. When she reached the top Carol helped her to struggle painfully to her feet, something she had done many times before.

When Martha was upright again they moved along the passage to Joe's door. Carol knocked but there was no response. They put their ears to the door but could hear no sound from inside.

Martha whispered, 'He's not asleep. You could hear him snoring from the next village if he was asleep.'

Carol said, 'I'll knock again.'

When there was still no reply Martha called out, 'It's me,

Joe. Are you asleep?'

A voice called back, 'Yes. Fast asleep.' Followed by wheezy laughter.

'It's not funny, Joe.'

'Why ask a silly question then? Fancy asking a man if he's asleep.'

'Come and unlock the door. I'm just off to bed. You can say goodnight to me.'

It took a while but eventually he turned the key in the lock and opened the door. He poked his head round the door and offered his cheek to be kissed. 'Goodnight Martha. Sleep tight.'

Before he could close the door Carol said quickly, 'We've brought you something to eat. I'll put the tray down on your bedside table.'

'No need. I can take it from you.'

'We're running out of trays and plates, they must be all up here. Move aside, Joe. We're coming in.' She was wearing shoes and gave his shin a kick through the gap. It must have hurt because he moved back just far enough for her to squeeze round the door. The moment she was inside the room she pulled the door wide so that her mother-in-law could follow her in.

This was the only time Martha had been inside the marital bedroom since her eviction, and her first reaction was to put a handkerchief to her nose. 'For God's sake, Joe. How can you stand the smell? It stinks worse than a cesspit. Open a window before I suffocate.'

'You know I can't do that. Had it screwed up, didn't I. Couldn't open it even if I wanted to.'

'Oh Joe, what a state to be in! Sit down on the chair and eat the food Carol has brought you while we clean the place up.'

'Don't want it cleaned up. I didn't invite you in, you forced your way in. I'll thank you not to bellyache about it now that you're here.'

Martha began to sob. 'Whatever have you come to, Joe,

living in shit like this? It smells worse than a pig sty. Is it any wonder you aren't well?'

Carol was inclined to agree, scratching her head helplessly as she looked round the room. 'I can't do much at this time of night except to tidy up a bit and straighten the bed.' She began to load a tray with dirty mugs and plates and discarded food packaging. 'You've got your room in a real mess, Joe. I'll ask Alice to help me next time she's got a morning off. You would need to move out for a few hours while we strip the bed and hoover the floor. The room will need fumigating if we really can't open a window. You'll get food poisoning or something worse if you go on living like this. Whatever made you think it was a good idea?'

'That did,' Martha said bitterly, pointing to the suitcase which could be seen on the floor under the bed. 'Nothing has gone right in this house since the day Joe brought it home. A bad day for Nutwhistle Farm that was.'

This remark did not go down well. Joe stopped munching on his cheese and pickle sandwich and put on a show of wounded dignity. 'I asked you not to scold, Martha. It's too late, you know it is. Can't put the clock back and pretend it didn't happen. I've got to make the best of it, and so have you.'

'How much tobacco have you smoked?' Carol asked in disgust as she tipped all his fag ends on to a plate. 'It can't be good for you without any ventilation in the room.'

'Not much else to do up here.'

'Whose fault is that? You need a bath, Joe. It will have to wait until Alice and me clean the room. No getting out of it, you need plenty of soap and hot water to get rid of the smell.'

Martha agreed. 'Carol's right, Joe. A nice hot bath would do you a world of good.'

'Don't you start,' he snarled, turning on his wife. 'I won't be criticised like this, not in my own house. Show a bit of respect.'

'Joe, you need to look in a mirror. You've got food in your beard and your hair is so long you'll trip over it if you're not careful.'

'I'm a sick man, Martha. I'm entitled to my privacy.'

'Drink your cocoa and stop talking nonsense.'

Carol was even less forgiving. 'When did you last empty your chamber pot, Joe? No wonder it stinks in here.' Before he could argue the point she retrieved it from under the bed and carried it along the passage to the bathroom. Having done which, and made her point, she gave up the struggle, knowing it to be a lost cause. Martha must have come to the same conclusion because she said a brief goodnight to her husband and began hobbling from the room. Carol followed her out into the passage, pulling the door shut behind her. A few seconds later they both heard Joe turn the key in the mortise lock.

Carol was afraid that Martha would be tearful, justly so in the circumstances, but instead she was calm. 'I'm thinking of Steve,' she explained when sitting down in the safety of her new bedroom. 'You can tell him we saw the suitcase. That will put his mind at rest.'

'I'm sorry about Joe. Can't have been nice for you, seeing him like that.'

'Don't be. I understand enough about men to know that they all live their lives exactly as they please. Why Joe should choose to end up like this is a mystery to me but there's nothing we can do. I'm not going to interfere and neither should you.'

'What about cleaning his room and giving him a bath?'

'Forget it. You've got your own work to do, and plenty of it at this time of year. So have I, Alice the same. You can't help people who don't want to be helped. Leave it at that.'

'I'm afraid Joe's in a bad way.'

'I think so, too. You can see he is.'

Carol's voice trembled slightly. 'He reckoned he was going to be dead before Christmas. Less than a week.'

'I know.'

Carol kissed her mother-in-law goodnight then went slowly down the stairs carrying the stacked tray of dirty crockery retrieved from Joe's room. Her husband and sister-in-law were waiting for her in the big farm kitchen, both chastened to see the sombre expression on her face when she entered.

'You look as if you need a drink,' Alice said at once, taking the tray from her. 'Stevie, fetch the bottle of brandy from the sideboard. Carol's feeling the strain.'

Steve hurried back with the brandy and poured three drinks, pushing a glass into his wife's hand. 'Hope it didn't upset you too much,' he said anxiously. 'You're as white as a sheet.'

'It's been a long day. I'm just tired out, that's all.'

'She's knackered,' Alice said candidly. 'Dad upset her, you can see he did.'

When she had recovered slightly Carol said, 'Well at least we saw what we went for. Joe hasn't found a new hiding place, the suitcase is still under his bed.'

'That's a relief,' Steve whispered, wiping sweat from his forehead with his sleeve, something he had done many times in agitation during the last few weeks.

'How did he seem to you?' Alice enquired. 'He must have something seriously wrong with him to be going on like this.'

'I don't know. I honestly don't know.'

Steve said, 'It's a pity he didn't trust any of us enough to go with him to the hospital and hear what was actually said to him. Dad's a great one for getting the wrong end of the stick, he could have misunderstood what they were telling him. Seems to me he's just frightening himself to death. What do you think, Sis?'

'Now he knows that Mum and Carol have seen the suitcase as well as me it could make him even more jumpy. If he's planning a new hiding place he would have to move it out soon. God only knows what goes on his mind. '

Steve took the point. 'Right again, Sis. We know how suspicious he is, of all of us. If what Mum says is true Dad thinks we're all plotting together to steal it from him.'

Alice nodded agreement. Speaking forcefully she said to

Carol. 'He's not to be trusted. I can't be here all day so I'm relying on you. Watch him like a hawk, morning, noon and night. If he finds a new hiding place and then dies on us we're buggered. All of us. Well and truly buggered.'

After this glum assessment of the family fortunes Steve switched off the kitchen light and they went their various ways to bed. In the granny annexe Carol said to Steve as they undressed, 'We've shovelled enough shit on this farm to last a lifetime, you and me. The longer I have to think about it the more convinced I am that the money in that suitcase rightly belongs to you, all of it. I'm going to get it for you, Steve. And if I have to use force, I will.'

25

Alice was equally desperate to make a bid for the money in the suitcase.

She had convincingly taken the shine off the duplicate suitcase so that it no longer looked new, and filled it with brown envelopes and photocopy paper cut to size, estimating the weight to be near enough the same for her father not to notice. If he opened it, well, as Ronnie had said, he was in for a surprise. After that it would be his problem to sort out. All she needed to make it happen was a diversion that would give Ronnie time to change the suitcases over.

An evening switch was proving difficult for all sorts of reasons so she changed her shifts at the store so that she could be home earlier in the day. She calculated that two o'clock in the afternoon offered the best time slot opportunity, allowing for half an hour either way. The house was then at its quietest period of the day, with Martha snoozing in the kitchen while Carol and Steve took a tractor and trailer to feed some beef animals at the farthest field on the farm. They were usually gone for an hour.

Zoe's absentee boyfriend Emerson had proved everyone wrong by returning to the town. Although he had not yet put in an appearance at the farm the last remaining obstacle to the suitcase switch had been removed. This was because Zoe rode off on her bike every morning to meet Emerson in the town and did not return until late, if at all. Alice knew they would never have a better chance and she urged Ronnie to be ready from noon onwards every day until the optimum moment for action presented itself.

Although she had been trying to think of an alternative plan she could come up with no better idea than the distraction burglary suggested by her son Ronnie. Somehow she had to coax her father into opening the door in order for her to engage him in conversation. Ronnie would be waiting with the duplicate suitcase in his room, conveniently situated on the other side of the upstairs passage, hoping she could devise a situation that would give him the few seconds he needed to make the change. The ruse of a shave and soap in the eyes might well have worked but Joe Knight's obstinate refusal to let anyone else into his room scuppered their plan before it could be tried out in practice. He was more suspicious than ever and refused even to open his door.

Yet another afternoon came and went without success. Once more Alice knocked on his door and called out, 'I've got a ham sandwich and a can of beer for you, Dad.'

From the other side of the door he called back, 'Leave it outside.'

'I've put some mustard in the sandwich. And it's a can of Stella, your favourite.'

'I can't hear what you're saying. Go away.'

'It's me, Dad. Alice.'

'I know who it is. I heard you the first time.'

'I've got a jug of hot water and your shaving tackle from the bathroom.'

'You're not coming in.'

'I was offering to give you a shave. Open the door, Dad.'

'You're up to something. What do you want?'

'There's no need to be so aggressive. Who else is looking after you? Mum can't get up the stairs and Carol is too busy on the farm. You should be pleased that I'm offering to help you.'

'Maybe so, Alice. Maybe so.'

'Open up, Dad, the water is getting cold.'

But he would not be persuaded and Alice abandoned the attempt, exchanging frustrated grimaces with Ronnie who stood in the doorway of his room, suitcase in hand, ready to do the deed. She put her tray of goodies on the floor and went into her son's room to commiserate in person.

Polite as always Ronnie was quick with sympathy. 'Not

your fault, Mum. You tried.'

'You did your bit as well, sweetheart. Sorry it didn't come off.'

'It wasn't as easy as we thought it was going to be.'

'Can you think of a better plan?'

'Not offhand. No.'

'Bloody Grandad. He's sticking to that suitcase like shit to a blanket. We're never going to part him from it.'

Ronnie picked his nose and looked thoughtful. 'Any idea how much money Grandad's got in there? Does Uncle Steve know?'

'We've been trying to work it out. Over a million quid we reckon, well over. In cash that buys a lot of jam donuts.' She heaved a sigh. 'Think what you and me could do with that money, Ronnie. We would be set up for life.'

'I am thinking of it.'

His mother gave him a kiss and pointed to the open door of his wardrobe. 'Better hide it away again, darling. It would need quite a bit of explaining if we were caught with that suitcase. No one would believe us, would they? I'm beginning to think it wasn't such a good idea after all.'

26

It was Saturday evening at Nutwhistle Farm. Joe was safely locked away in his bedroom, Zoe had gone clubbing with Emerson and his friends and would not return until the early hours of the morning. Sitting side by side in their accustomed places on the TV viewing settee were Ronnie, his granny and his mother, in that order. They watched and they munched. It was a good evening, with programmes they all enjoyed equally, and the time passed very agreeably.

Only when the grandfather clock chimed ten did Martha wrench her attention away from the screen and point to the ceiling. 'What is it, Ma?' Alice asked.

'Grandad hasn't been to the lavatory. He usually goes once during the evening.'

Alice was unsympathetic. 'He's made it quite clear he doesn't want us interfering. Leave him to his own toilet arrangements.'

'One of us ought to go up and ask him if he's all right.'

Ronnie said, 'I heard him go about half an hour ago. I heard the lock. And then I heard him moving about, same as usual.'

'You did?'

'Yes, Gran. While we were watching Millionaire.'

She had been struggling to her feet but fell back again with a sigh of relief. 'That's all right then. Thank you, Ronnie.'

'It was during the adverts. Mum had just brought in the pizzas. I expect that's why you didn't hear him go to the lav.'

So they went to bed and forgot all about the unkempt hermit of Nutwhistle Farm until the next morning. This was Sunday morning. Alice had the day off and came down to the kitchen in her dressing gown and curlers. Steve and Carol were out on the farm, having already been at work for several

159

hours. Martha had a large pot of baked beans on the stove and a pile of toast keeping warm for anyone who wanted it. Ronnie appeared soon after his mother and ate a hearty breakfast. It was a peaceful scene, Alice read the local newspaper while drinking coffee and smoking a cigarette, Martha took her ease in the chair beside the stove and Ronnie buttered slice after slice of toast and helped himself to big scoops of beans.

Only when it was time to start thinking about preparing vegetables for the Sunday dinner did Martha point to the chair her husband sat in every morning. She said, 'I haven't heard a sound from upstairs. Alice, would you mind giving Dad's door a knock and seeing if he's all right. He's usually down by now.'

Alice folded her newspaper, stubbed out her ciggie and paid attention. 'I haven't heard him moving about either. I hope something's not wrong. I'll take him up a mug of tea and see what effect that has.'

She went up, the others waited, and then heard her come downstairs again, the mug of tea still in her hand. She shook her head. 'I banged on the door. Couldn't hear a thing.'

Martha was alarmed and struggled to her feet. 'Alice, can you help me up the stairs. Ronnie, I want you to go and find your Uncle Steve and ask him to stop whatever he's doing and come at once.'

Using her two aluminium walking aids she shuffled quickly towards the back stairs and then began the painful process of sitting down and hoisting herself slowly upwards one stair at a time. Just as she reached the top Steve came panting into the house, followed a few minutes later by his wife Carol. They raced up the stairs and between them helped Martha back on to her feet. Alice was waiting as they joined her outside Joe Knight's bedroom door.

Zoe had been woken by the commotion in the long upstairs passage and came sleepily out of her bedroom. She was wearing a red polo shirt belonging to her boyfriend Emerson, a purloined garment she had used as a nightie for over a year so that she could feel close to him, even when in bed on her own. Rubbing her eyes she said, 'Woss goin on? Is it Gramps? Has something happened to him?'

'We don't know yet,' her mother replied. 'He hasn't been down for his breakfast and we can't get him to answer the door.'

'Oh, poor Gramps. What are you going to do?'

'Dad's going to force the door open. He's gone back down to the tractor shed to fetch some tools.'

When he returned Steve asked for quiet and knelt with his ear to the door. He said, 'I think I can hear Dad breathing. I don't think he's dead.' He hammered on the door with his fist but there was no response from inside.

'My poor Joe,' Martha sobbed. 'Hurry up and open the door, Steve.'

Alice said, 'He can't be asleep, he would have woken up by now with all that banging on the door. If he's not dead he must be unconscious.'

Carol looked round at the scared faces gathered outside the door. Ronnie had joined them so there was now a quorum of family members. In a shaky voice she said, 'Those two locks the man put on look very strong. How will you get the door open, Steve?'

'The locks might be strong but the door frame isn't,' Steve replied. 'The burglar alarm man wasn't doing a proper job, he was just parting Dad from some money.' He held up a small crowbar. 'This is all you need. Watch.' He inserted the sharp end of the crowbar into the door jamb and gave a steady pull. He may have been small but he was strengthened by a lifetime of hard work and skilled in the use of tools. The rending noise was not pleasant but the wood was old and dry and put up little resistance to a steel lever expertly applied.

The moment the door was opened Alice stretched out her arms to hold the others back and shouted, 'Let Gran go first.'

They obeyed, but not for long. The moment she had hobbled painfully on her two sticks into the room the others followed in a rush. Whatever dramatic scene they expected to

161

see in front of them their expectations were met in full by the sight of Joe Knight lying on the floor beside his chest of drawers. He had blood on his head.

When his family rushed in he tried to raise himself before falling back again. His bedside chair and table were overturned, they told their own story of a stumble and fall with his head striking a solid lump of furniture. That he was very close to death was plain for all to see.

Ignoring the pain from her joints Martha sank to her knees and took her husband's hand. 'Joe, Joe,' she wept. 'My poor Joe. Can you hear me, Joe?'

Steve waited a few moments and then helped his mother to her feet. 'Stand back, Ma. We'll lift him up on to the bed. He's very cold. Suffering from hypothermia, I reckon. Hardly surprising if he's spent all night on the floor.'

He took his father's arms and shoulders, Carol and Alice took a leg each and between them they lifted him on to the bed. Alice unbuttoned his shirt and Steve wrestled him out of his jacket and removed his shoes. His breathing was shallow and laboured, his eyes fixed them with a terrified stare. Because his face was so thickly bearded it was difficult to see the degree of distortion but from his inability to speak they deduced that he had suffered the stroke he feared might happen, and with it fatal damage to his brain.

'What happened, Dad?' Steve asked him, leaning over the bed.

His father tried to sit up and his eyes swivelled from one to the other, obviously bewildered by what was happening. He made an effort to speak but produced only unintelligible sounds and lots of dribble. Clearly agitated he made another big effort to raise himself on the bed but after a few seconds abandoned the attempt and sank back again. He sighed and closed his eyes as though to sleep. There was a gasp from everyone in the room because it seemed as if they had just witnessed his death.

Steve thought so too but changed his mind when he put a hand on his father's chest and nodded to show that he was still breathing. 'Very faint,' he reported, feeling for his heartbeat. 'He's not quite dead. Won't be long, I reckon.'

'Poor Joe,' Martha wept. 'Speak to me, Joe.'

There was no response and they gradually drew back from the bed and viewed the dying man from a distance. Only then did they remember about the suitcase. Carol was the first to speak. She pointed to the empty space under the bed. 'Alice, can you see it? This is the place, isn't it?'

'That's where it was,' Alice agreed. Her voice trembled. 'Not here now, is it?'

An uneasy silence followed. Trying to sound confident Carol said, 'It must have got pushed right underneath the bed.' She knelt down, took a look and gave them the bad news. 'I can't see it.'

Alice knelt down beside her. She confirmed the bad news. 'It isn't here.'

'What do you mean, Sis, not here?' Steve said in a despairing voice. 'It must be here.'

He dropped to his knees and joined his wife and sister on the floor. The floor was thick with dust but their line of vision was clear from one side to the other. There was a chamber pot, a pair of slippers and their father's twelve-bore shotgun. But no suitcase.

Steve laid down for a better look but with the same result. When his mother let out a wail of anguish he lifted up the bedspread and blankets so that she could see for herself. 'It must be in here somewhere,' she said. 'Look on top of the wardrobe, that's where he puts things to hide them from me.'

Steve appeared dubious but carried the chair to the wardrobe and stood on it for a better look. He gave a quick shake of the head and made an agonised grimace. He handed down a bottle of brandy and a small pile of magazines. 'There's nothing else,' he told them. 'See for yourself if you don't believe me.'

'Coar, they look good,' Ronnie said, snatching the magazines from him, quickly identifying them as continental hardcore porn. He took a quick look inside and they were even better than he could have hoped. 'Brilliant! Fancy Grandad having mags like these. Not much good to him now, are they, so I'll have them.'

His mother waved this aside irritably. She was beginning to sweat and become agitated. 'Look inside the wardrobe, Stevie. I'll look in the chest of drawers.'

It took only a few frantic minutes to search the room. With so many people getting in one another's way it was a grim and chaotic ransacking of drawers and cupboards. Martha had propped Joe up on his pillows and continued to weep while he sat staring blankly from his ruined face. Ronnie sat down on the bedside chair, leafing wide-eyed through the explicit adult sex photographs.

When the search came to an end they all stared at one another in blank despair. From happiness to unhappiness only a very short period of time is required. For six of the seven Knights of Nutwhistle Farm the missing money was a catastrophe of Biblical proportions. Their faces registered equal amounts of dismay and bewilderment as they circled the bed of the seventh, the whiskery old patriarch who had broken their hearts as well as their dreams.

The only member of the family who had not spoken so far was Zoe. She did so now. She said, 'Poor old Gramps. Shall I ring for an ambulance?'

Her voice was not loud but it was heard, and the response was immediate, unanimous, and emphatic.

'No!' her father, mother, aunt, granny and cousin cried with one voice.

'No?'

'No,' her father explained to Zoe. 'He isn't quite dead yet. We need to keep him here so that we can ask him about the money when he comes round.'

'If he comes round,' Alice said apathetically, lifting a finger under her father's limp wrist. 'I reckon the poor old bugger has had it, you can see he has. He'll never talk again.'

Steve refused to believe what his eyes were telling him. Desperately he said, 'No, no, stroke victims often recover a bit before they die. It's just a case of being here when he tries to speak.'

Only Zoe seemed to have any concern for the suffering old man lying on his pillows as though already dead. She repeated her demand. 'Gramps needs to go to hospital. I think you should ring for an ambulance.'

Carol picked up Joe's keys which were on the carpet beneath the wrecked door. She stood and mused, suddenly calm. 'He locked himself in, there was no way we would have been able to do anything for him even if we knew he needed help.' She shrugged. 'Something like this was bound to happen. I knew it all along. I think we all did.'

Steve said, 'He's a tough one all right. Lying on a cold floor all night would have finished anyone else off.'

'Doesn't always pay to be strong, love. You just suffer longer.'

Alice was still thinking about the suitcase. She said to Carol, 'We know it was here on Friday night because you and Ma both saw it. Dad didn't leave the farm yesterday so he must have hidden it somewhere close. Either in the house or in one of the outside buildings. I don't see where else it could be.'

Carol agreed. 'He spent most of yesterday morning reading the local paper in the hay barn. Hardly moved until he came in for his dinner. That was about one o'clock and then he went straight upstairs to his room and stayed there. That's right, isn't it?'

Still tearful and distressed Martha nodded. 'It's a mystery to me. We should have noticed if he was carrying it under his coat but I'm sure he wasn't. He had his breakfast in the kitchen, I gave him the newspaper and he spent the rest of the morning sitting at his table in the hay barn reading it and smoking his cigarettes. I kept an eye on him from the window.'

'So where the hell is it?' Alice asked, her face grim. For once she lost patience with Ronnie and gave him a smart tap on the shoulder. 'Don't look at those things while your grandfather is lying there like that. Show a little more respect.' She turned to Zoe. 'You're not decent, put some knickers on, get yourself dressed. Go back to your rooms, both of you.'

Zoe and Ronnie did as they were told, Zoe holding her nose in a gesture of defiance, and the smell in the room was indeed truly awful and stomach churning. Alice turned to her brother. 'You too, Stevie. There's women's work to do here.' She made a wry face and indicated their father. 'He's soiled himself, we must get him stripped off and cleaned up. Can you cope on your own? Carol and me will be up here for some time.'

'Of course I can, Sis. Thank you for offering to do it.'

Making sure the two young people were not listening outside the door she said, 'If Dad survives and we put him back to bed I think one of us should sit with him.'

Steve lowered his voice. 'You mean to ask him about the money?'

'Yes. We must ask him where he's hidden the suitcase.'

Carol said, 'What's the use? He can't speak.'

'No, but I think he can hear what we're saying. We can ask him questions and tell him to nod his head.'

Carol saw the sense in this. 'It might only be for a minute or two. We've got to take it in turns right round the clock, so far as we can. Or as long as it takes.'

Still sobbing and tearful Martha said, 'I'll sit with him all the time I'm able. It's my right.'

'Of course it is, Ma,' Steve said, putting an arm round her waist. He gave her a kiss on the cheek. 'A sad day for all of us. Poor old Dad.' He took a rueful look at the door he had wrecked, picked up his tools and left the womenfolk to their work.

27

They kept up the vigil for the rest of the day, all through the night and into the next day. Steve and Carol were always dog tired at bedtime, falling asleep the moment one of them pulled the cord over their bed to switch out the light. Although they took their turns to sit at Joe Knight's bedside they were of little help because they found it difficult to stay awake and kept nodding off. When it was Martha's turn she pulled the chair close up to the bed so that she could hold the hand of her dying husband, but she too was asleep more often than she was awake.

The first few watches had the easiest time. After the ordeal of being cleaned up and put back to bed Joe was exhausted and slept for several hours. After this he had long waking periods during which he was restless and agitated, even needing to be restrained from trying to get out of bed. He soon drifted back into sleep again but every so often he would suddenly awake and try to sit up. When this happened he seemed to be trying to speak, and they all agreed when relieving one another that they believed he could hear and understand what they were saying. During these periods of apparent lucidity they repeated over and over again. 'Where have you hidden the money? The suitcase, tell us where can we find the suitcase.' Without once receiving a response.

Only Alice stayed obstinately awake on her watch and volunteered to see out the night from two o'clock in the morning until relieved by Carol at eight. Throughout this long period Alice leaned as close to her father's ear as she could get and repeated over and over again, 'The money, Dad, where have you hidden the money?'

When there was the slightest flicker of response she would redouble her efforts. 'Where have you hidden the suitcase? Is it in the hay barn? Nod your head if it's in the hay barn. Or is it in one of the other farm buildings? The tractor shed? The grain dryer? The chemical store? The old dairy? No? Is it somewhere indoors then? Squeeze my hand if it's indoors. Was that a squeeze? We shall have to search the house anyway but if you tell me now it will save us a lot of bother. In the linen cupboard? Is that where it is? Up one of the chimneys? In the wood shed? The cupboard under the stairs? In your Land Rover? Can you blink an eye if it's in your Land Rover? Do something, Dad, we need to know. We need the money, you know that, don't you? So please help. Tell us where it is.'

Every so often in response to her insistent questions about the money he became agitated, his fists clenched, his eyes bulged, he sat up and tried desperately to say something. Only strangled sounds and lots of dribble emerged, but nothing that was of the slightest help. The effort of trying to speak soon exhausted him and he relapsed back into his comatose state again.

When this happened Alice lit a cigarette and took a short rest before renewing her attack with an even greater air of desperation. 'The money, Dad. Where have you hidden the money?' When this failed she tried another line of enquiry. 'Did you buy something with the money? Something small but valuable? Diamonds, perhaps? Have you bought another property somewhere without telling us? Did you put it all back in the bank? If so, which bank? Do you have a pass book? Think, Dad. A small painting can be worth a lot of money. Ornaments can be worth thousands. Is it right here, staring us in the face? Give me some help, Dad. What sort of start is Ronnie going to have in life without his share of the money? You promised it to us, Dad. So where is it, for God's sake?'

At the promised time Carol interrupted this dismal monologue but instead of taking her place on the bedside chair she beckoned Alice to join her outside in the long upstairs passage. Alice was not sorry to abandon her vigil and kneaded her neck to show that she was stiff from sitting in one position for so long. 'What is it?' she whispered. 'Has something happened?'

Carol took her arm and led her to the landing at the top of the stairs. Although there was no one close enough to hear them it seemed natural to lower their voices. Replying in an urgent whisper Carol replied, 'No. Nothing has happened yet. But it might unless we act quickly.'

'Something serious?'

'Yes. Very serious.'

'What did you mean about quickly?'

Trying not to sound exasperated Carol said, 'Joe isn't going to last much longer. He could die at any time.'

'I know. That's why I've been trying to find out what he's done with the bloody suitcase.'

'Well stop worrying about the suitcase and start thinking what it's going to look like when the doctor comes to sign the death certificate. And what happens when he takes one look at Joe and sends for the police, and the police start asking us some awkward questions. Am I getting through to you?'

The answer to this last question was positive. Alice visibly quivered as the enormity of what Carol was telling her began to sink in. She put both hands to her head and stared at her sister-in-law in surprise and horror. 'Bloody hell,' she whispered. 'I hadn't thought of that.'

'Well start thinking of it now. Think what would go through the doctor's mind when he sees your Dad looking like a vagrant in a doss house with a big bruise on his forehead. Try to picture the faces of the police officers when they see the bedroom door hanging off its hinges. Imagine their thoughts when they see the bars on the windows. Watch them wrinkle their noses and look round at the filthy dirty room where we kept our father a prisoner. Do you fancy spending the night in a prison cell trying to convince them it was all perfectly innocent and not like that at all?'

'Jesus. No.'

'If they ever find out about the suitcase and the money

we're done for. They wouldn't need the brains of Donald Duck to put that lot together and put us all under arrest.'

'What do you want me to do, Carol?'

'We've got to get Joe cleaned up straight away. We can't risk anyone coming to the house and finding him in the state he's in now. We would be in big trouble. Accused of neglect and all sorts.'

Alice swore and blamed herself. 'I was so worked up about the money I haven't been thinking straight. Sorry, Carol. What do you want to do first?'

'We can't get him to the bathroom so we'll need a bucket to fetch the hot water to the bedroom. And plenty of it by the time we're finished. That would be a good start.'

Alice hesitated for a moment. 'Poor old Dad. I know we've got to do it but we shall probably kill him in the process.'

'It can't be helped. Better change into some old clothes, Alice. This is going to be a messy business. Rubber gloves. A long apron. Disinfectant. Oh, and bring your big pair of scissors. We shall have to cut his hair and shave his beard off.'

'I can handle that. I'll clip it down as hard as I can go and then soften it up with some shaving cream.'

And so the task of regularising the appearance of the Knight family residence at Nutwhistle Farm got under way. As Carol had accurately predicted it turned out to be a messy business. Messy and emotionally exhausting. Joe's terrified eyes watched them the whole time. He was still strong and they contained his struggles as best they could while carrying on with the grim process of cutting his hair and separating him from his beard. He kept up a constant complaint of angry but unintelligible mumbling and shouting which confused them and slowed them down.

Mercifully he did eventually quieten and they made the preparations for his bed bath. With arms bare to the shoulder and aprons wringing wet they stripped him naked and scoured him clean. 'We could have done with masks as well as rubber gloves,' Alice said ruefully as they worked on his feet, trying to soften up the ingrained dirt with soap, detergent and a stiff brush. Surrounded by buckets and bowls of soapy water, and with hair from his head and beard plastered over their clothes, they worked without rest, knowing it was a job that had to be done.

They had not expected it to be quick, nor was it, but they succeeded better than they could have hoped in restoring Joe to a more normal appearance. Although themselves exhausted and red-eyed from lack of sleep they were amazed at how different he looked when once more clean-shaven, and with his grey hair cropped and neatly parted. 'Missed my vocation,' Alice said modestly, hair dryer in hand.

'You did a good job,' Carol agreed. They could hardly recognise the finished product, now clean and sweet smelling, the rough skin on his elbows, knees and heels softened with cream. Clipping the nails on his hands and feet had been more challenging but they both had a grim vision of how Joe would look on the mortuary slab. To avoid any comeback claim of family negligence they poked all the dirt from under his nails and finished with a nail brush and soapy water. Attention to detail paid off and they began to breathe more easily as this part of their work neared completion.

They rewarded themselves in the granny annexe with coffee and biscuits, but did not slow down for long. This was because Alice knew that something else needed to be done before her father died. 'We must take the bars off the windows. Could you ask Steve to bring his tools?'

'I'll get him to do it as soon as he's finished scraping up the yard.'

'What about the door? Do you think he could replace it with one of the other doors? There must be one somewhere in the house that would fit, and wouldn't be missed. Doors are all the same size, aren't they?'

'Good thinking, Alice. I've already asked him to remove the twelve bore from under the bed. It was loaded by the way. Didn't know how we near we came to disaster, did we? Joe might easily have let us have a barrel when we were banging on the door and annoying him.'

Alice shuddered. 'It doesn't bear thinking about.'

They went back upstairs to resume their work. Steve joined them an hour later and helped to shift the heavy furniture around so that the room could be thoroughly cleaned, from the cobwebs on the ceiling to the thick dust under the bed. They worked fast, all equally dead beat with fatigue but knowing there was little to time to waste. It did not take Steve long to remove the window bars but replacing the damaged door with the one from his father's office downstairs took him over an hour. Carol went outside to cover for the farm work while Alice continued to normalise the room. As a finishing touch she fetched two brightly coloured rugs from elsewhere in the house and searched the linen chest for the prettiest bedspread. Job done.

After this Alice, Steve and Carol were forced to rest and eventually went to bed late at night, exhausted but beyond measure thankful that they had retrieved a lost situation. They looked in on Joe before turning in themselves. He had survived the long ordeal, if only just, and lay where they had left him, propped on lavender-scented pillows, near to death and scarcely breathing. They had dressed him in striped flannel pyjamas so that dead or alive he was ready to receive any visitor who came to the door.

They had agreed between them in advance that if Joe was still alive next morning Steve should ring the town surgery and ask if a doctor could come to see him. They had waited a long time to reunite Joe Knight with the medical profession and finally the moment had come. When the surgery opened for business Steve made the fateful call from his father's office. With his mother, wife and sister beside him he adjusted his voice so that he spoke in the humble, ingratiating tones of apology, supplication, pleading and deference that the surgery receptionists required before they would do anything for anybody.

It was a strategy that met with success because in the afternoon Joe Knight's registered doctor called at Nutwhistle

Farm. He asked a few questions on entering and was then taken upstairs and shown into the sick room. He entered a spacious bedroom, cosily warm, clean and bright. A bunch of invalid grapes were to hand on the bedside table, a vase of allergy friendly artificial flowers stood on the chest of drawers. Martha Knight sat on the bedside chair holding her husband's hand. It was a quiet and seemly deathbed scene, the doctor briefly pausing to note the view of pleasant countryside from the bedroom window, now free of bars.

'My poor Joe had a fall,' Martha told the doctor in a tearful voice, to explain the bruise on his forehead. 'He's not going to die, is he, doctor? Please tell me he's not going to die.'

The doctor was able to offer no such assurance. Alice and Steve came into the room for a last gathering of the dying man's immediate family. They endorsed their mother's plea for her husband to be allowed to die peacefully in his own bed. 'It's what Dad wanted,' Steve assured the doctor. Alice was quick with her groatsworth of support. 'He said it many times, Doctor.' Adding convincingly, 'Dear old Dad.'

As this arrangement suited the doctor very well he murmured his condolences in advance of the event and hastened away to the next patient in need of expert care and medical attention. But death when it arrives is never entirely welcome, and although the family now gathered at Joe Knight's bedside had no good reason for keeping him alive, they were pleased to be on hand to comfort Martha as her husband of over forty years drew his last breath.

The mood would have been sombre in any farmhouse where the main provider and head of family had just died. In this case the tension-filled weeks leading up to his death, and the loss of the suitcase full of money, made the bereavement more than usually dispiriting. There was an unspoken consensus of agreement between them that the tradition of giving thanks for a long life usefully led was not appropriate in this case. Such charitable and consoling thoughts were replaced by bitterness and resentment at his folly over the money.

Even so they were sensible country folk who flinched instinctively from any form of excess. However strongly they may have disapproved of Joe Knight's deluded and reckless behaviour in mishandling the family finances they were careful to avoid emotive words such as Crisis, Ruin, Disaster and Catastrophe when referring to the situation in which they now found themselves.

They knew it was much more serious than that.

28

Late at night, on the same day that her father died, Alice came into Ronnie's bedroom and knelt down beside the bed. She whispered, 'Are you awake, darling?'

He most certainly was awake, and did not need to ask the reason for his bedside visit. 'We've got a problem, Mum. I don't want to get caught with that suitcase in my wardrobe.'

'That's what I've come about, sweetheart. You're right, it would be terrible if one of the others saw us with it. Couldn't explain it, could we?'

'Wouldn't be easy.'

'Well?' she asked, giving him a nudge. 'Got any ideas?'

'No.'

'Is the wardrobe locked?'

'The lock doesn't work. The suitcase is right at the back, I hid it behind the longest things in there.'

'I'll take it to my room. And get rid of it as soon as I can.'

'Don't leave it too late. I heard Uncle Steve and Auntie Carol talking. They want to search the house tomorrow, including all the bedrooms.'

'Don't worry about it any more, treasure. Mummy knows what to do.'

'Will you hide it on the farm?'

'If you don't know you where it is you won't have to tell any fibs. Leave it to me. I've got somewhere in mind, a place where no one will ever find it.'

'They want to search the house first. Then the farm.'

'That will be a big job. Hundreds of places to look.'

'You had the right idea, Mum. About the suitcase, I mean. Shame we couldn't pull it off.'

'I'm gutted, absolutely gutted. What Grandad did with the money we might never know. It looks as if the silly old bugger has lost the lot. Always thought he would.' She kissed him tenderly on the forehead. 'Sleep tight, darling. A lot of the girls at work always call in sick over Christmas so there will be plenty of overtime to be had. Don't worry about the money any more. Mummy will do her best to make it up to you.'

29

There is always a lot to do when someone dies and the six remaining Knights of Nutwhistle Farm did their best in a difficult situation. They uttered a collective sigh of relief when the doctor issued a death certificate without asking any awkward questions, after which the undertaker came to take away Joe's body.

A grim event in any family history and they stood silently together in the spacious stone-flagged entrance hall as the coffin was carried down the stairs, through the front door and then slotted into the hearse waiting outside. Martha had found the last few months of her husband's life deeply distressing and although his death had come as a relief she still experienced a natural grief at the end of a long and otherwise happy marriage. She sat quietly weeping on a chair, comforted by Alice on one side and Carol on the other. Zoe and Ronnie both looked scared but still went outside to watch as the hearse was driven away.

Steve was understandably distressed when he saw his father's body leaving the farm feet first in a coffin. Joe Knight had been born at Nutwhistle and apart from a school holiday and a short honeymoon had spent his entire life there. Steve could have said the same and as he watched the funeral car swerving to avoid the potholes in the track before easing carefully through the farm gate he had to suppress a sob and brush away tears with his sleeve. 'He wasn't a bad old Dad. I shall miss him.'

Carol had wanted to begin searching for the missing suitcase even before the body was removed but was persuaded by Steve to wait until they were more organised. He had to restrain her a second time by insisting that they put their minds to arranging the funeral instead. 'There's a lot to think about. We must sit down and do it properly.'

So with Alice in tow they went back to their own part of the house and sat at the small kitchen table to discuss the funeral arrangements. Carol provided coffee and biscuits, Steve fetched a pen and a sheet of paper and Alice gave them the benefit of her advice, candidly expressed as always.

'We don't have a choice. Dad may have been a skinflint all his life, and died broke, but we've got to give the old bugger a decent funeral. The other farmers will expect it.'

'How are we going to pay for a posh funeral?' Carol enquired, having a practical turn of mind. 'We're all broke as well.'

'Undertakers always wait for their money, they don't have a choice. We'll have the funeral first and think about paying for it when we get the bill.'

Steve agreed. 'We've got to keep up appearances. And that means giving Dad the sort of funeral he was entitled to.' He picked up the pen and waited for instructions. 'What do we do first?'

Carol ticked it off on her fingers. 'We've got to go and see the solicitor and get the will started.'

Alice disagreed. 'We've got to register the death and get copies of the death certificate. Then we've got to go to the undertakers and firm up on a date for the funeral. Then we've got to choose a coffin and arrange the funeral service. They want you to do it all as a package, including ordering the headstone and the words for the inscription.'

'Won't they do that for us? Like putting a notice in the local paper and booking the church?'

'Yes, but we shall have to see the vicar and choose the hymns and write some words about Dad's life for him to read out.'

Steve was writing all this down and added a reminder of his own. 'We shall have to order the eats at The Shorn Lamb. Dad's pals will expect a good spread. He said he had put the money aside to cover his funeral expenses but that's gone as well. We shall have to pay for the food and drink ourselves,

Carol.'

'Why am I not surprised?'

'Don't forget the flowers,' Alice added. 'Ma will want to send her own. I'll do some for me and Ronnie, and you can do yours with Zoe. How does that sound?'

'Like a lot of work,' Carol groaned, putting her head in her hands. 'I need to have my hair done and buy a black skirt. Everything seems to take twice as long and cost twice as much because it's so near Christmas. And there's all the work to do on the farm, that won't go away. I don't think we can possibly cope with more. If anything else happens I shall lie on the floor and scream.'

She shouldn't have said it because next morning Zoe's boyfriend Emerson came down the back stairs into the kitchen and presented himself at the breakfast table.

30

This came as a shock since they did not know that Emerson was in the house and stared at him in complete and utter surprise. He explained that Zoe had brought him back to the farm in the early hours of the morning when everyone else in the house was asleep, and not wishing to disturb other members of the family they had spent the rest of the night in her bedroom. She was still abed and asleep but he was up bright and early at nine o'clock and had his story ready.

'Zoe is still very upset at losing her grandfather. She asked me if I would stay with her and help her through the funeral. If you have no objections, of course.'

Steve and Carol were disconcerted at Emerson's totally unexpected appearance but also overawed by his air of ease and condescension. Although he had only murmured a few words they were spoken in an impeccable English accent. Emerson was the same age as Zoe's cousin Ronnie but had been educated at a public school by his well-to-do parents. It had never ceased to puzzle Steve and Carol that their teenage daughter should have attracted a young man who was a lot more posh than they were.

In reply to his question Carol knew that she ought to speak up immediately and firmly refuse his request to stay, but could not bring herself to utter the words. Instead she mumbled, 'Nice to see you again, Emerson.'

'May I offer my own condolences? A bereavement in the family is always an affecting experience.'

'There's a lot to do when someone dies, if that's what you mean.'

'If I can help in any way please do not hesitate to ask. Zoe was very fond of her grandfather. Me too. A fine country gentleman.'

Steve and Carol blinked a bit on hearing this, as well they might. They also realised that the tall and elegantly dressed young man with the dreadlocks and the condescending manner was standing with his hand on a chair waiting for an invitation to sit down. They hesitated because the chair on which his hand rested was the chair routinely occupied by Joe Knight when he ate his breakfast in the kitchen. This had all the symbolism of inherited and devolved power, an alpha male replacement for the deceased patriarch assuming possession at the earliest opportunity.

Carol made a big effort to sound more cordial than she felt. 'It's been quite a while, Emerson. Sit down, why don't you? Tea or coffee? Something to eat?'

'Black coffee and marmalade on white toast, please. If you're sure it's no trouble.'

He sat down and brought them up to date with his news. 'I expect Zoe told you that my parents have been unwell and moved to a smaller house. They're not as young as they were and glad of my help with the move. There's always such a lot to do in a new house, more than anyone would realise who hasn't done it. But that's all behind us now and Mum and Dad are quite happy to be on their own once more.'

'I'm sure they were grateful for your help, Emerson. Good of you to bother. A lot of young people wouldn't have put themselves out to help their parents. Not these days.'

'Zoe says she has never been to a funeral before. It will be upsetting for her but she wants to go. Of course she does. It's only natural, being so close to her grandfather.'

Steve and Carol exchanged rueful glances. They were trapped in a situation of excessive work and worry, over-whelmed by the pressure of events and unable to think clearly. They distrusted Emerson instinctively and knew that everything he said was capable of almost infinite ambiguity and misinterpretation. Their natural impulse was to refuse his request to stay, and to insist that he left immediately after the funeral but they hesitated a fraction of a second too long. Emerson took their indecision for consent and Carol was left with little option except to give a sickly smile of welcome.

'You'll have to take us you find us. We're a bit upside down at the moment. For reasons you will understand.'

'You can rely on me, Mrs Knight. I won't get in your way. What a delicious cup of coffee. Yes, I would like another. Thank you. So kind.'

The loss of a dominant male followed immediately by his replacement made a dramatic impact on the whole household. Emerson's was not a presence easily ignored, and even after a mere twenty-four hours it was invested with an ominous air of permanence. The prospect of another mouth to feed on top of all their other worries was almost too much for Steve and Carol to bear.

Even so, with typical mother-hen protectiveness on behalf of her husband and daughter, Carol was determined to prosecute the search for the missing suitcase. She wanted it done with the utmost rigour and without further delay. Deprived of their share of the money she and Steve would soon be bankrupt, and the farm doomed.

She agreed to wait until Alice returned home from the supermarket so that they could go from room to room together. Martha excused herself and sat in front of the TV with Ronnie beside her for company but they both gave permission for their bedrooms to be searched. Zoe had told Emerson the sad tale of the missing money, and the brown envelope with her share inside, which explained his eagerness to take part in the search. He said, 'Shouldn't we have started outside first? Isn't that the most likely place?'

'No, we start in the house,' Carol interrupted, answering the question. 'We need to make sure it isn't indoors before we start outside. We can do that tomorrow, in the light. Right now we go through the house one room at a time. Emerson, you're the tallest, you can look on the top shelves and anywhere up high. Let's get started, we'll do the kitchen and larder first.'

They trooped along to the kitchen where they made a thorough search, starting with the two big drawers at the bottom of the dresser. Standing next to the dresser was a floor-to-ceiling cupboard with top and bottom doors. It contained crockery in the top half and saucepans and ovenware in the bottom but there was no sign of the suitcase. The searchers moved on to the two insanitary cupboards under the sink. Steve being small and agile knelt down to peer in with his lamp, but again, no joy.

The large walk-in larder was a more serious opposition. Although the suitcase would have been easily seen on one of the pantry shelves the larder floor was cluttered with old enamel bread bins, earthenware crocks, sacks of potatoes and obsolete kitchen machinery. Moving it all aside and then replacing it required effort, and in this they were considerably helped by Emerson whose health and strength were soon demonstrated. He did not creak when bending, or need to ease his back when straightening up, and soon proved to be the most active member of the search party.

'Good man,' Steve said approvingly as they went through a door into the scullery part of the kitchen where there were some heavier corpses to move aside. Every washing machine from the early days of twin tubs and spin dryers were stacked in a line, rusting and obsolete but still cherished and given space. 'There's no suitcase here,' Emerson concluded, having looked behind, inside and underneath every appliance. He was clearly disappointed and anxious to move on. He wore workmanlike jeans and a green sweatshirt with the sleeves rolled up. This made Steve extremely thoughtful. He had received no help requiring muscle and stamina either from his father or his nephew Ronnie for the best part of twenty years and it made such a welcome change that he felt himself warming to the idea that he might one day have a son-in-law who was not completely useless.

Next they tackled the cupboard under the stairs. Again Emerson was first into the fray, moving the cluttered items out one by one because he could see it was a cavernous recess that needed to be completely emptied before it could be eliminated from the search. Progress was slow, mainly because he was intrigued by the bewildering variety of domestic junk piling up behind him.

'What's this?' he enquired over and over again. 'And this? What was it used for?' The others were equally enthused, and their memories exercised, as long-forgotten treasures saw the light of day for the first time in many years.

'Oh, look Emerson!' Carol exclaimed, disentangling a wooden contraption from a metal fireguard. 'It's Zoe's first cot. Isn't that sweet?' Emerson agreed, with his arm round Zoe's waist. 'She must have been a beautiful baby to fit into that cot.' There were more oohs and aahs when Zoe's first doll's pram was also fished out of the pile and given an airing. As a search for the missing millions it had been easily diverted into a trip down memory lane.

Emerson seemed genuinely interested in the family memorabilia, although he rolled his eyes and worried his dreadlocks with his fingers from time to time, too polite to ask why so much junk had been lovingly preserved instead of put out for the bin lorry. The necessity for a heavy cast-iron mincing machine with a handle was explained to him, and the tradition in farming families of having roast beef on Sundays, cold roast beef on Mondays and minced left-over roast beef on Tuesdays made into a Shepherd's Pie, followed by a Rice Pudding for afters.

'You live and learn,' Emerson humoured them, turning the handle a few times. 'Thank goodness things have moved on since then.' When answered in a chorus that they still had Shepherd's Pie and Rice Pudding on Tuesdays he smiled politely, assuming that his leg was being pulled. He was going to find daily life at Nutwhistle Farm an interesting experience.

Long handled toasting forks were the next objects of curiosity needing an explanation, followed by an aspidistra pot and stand, heavy brass tongs and fire-irons, cans of Flit insecticide, broken deck chairs, a wartime gas mask in a box, glazed earthenware hot water containers for warming beds, a bicycle frame, a wind-up gramophone with a box of 78s, a banjo, and a commode with a chamber pot decorated in pink roses. All worthy objects for which members of the family had paid good money but there was, alas, no suitcase.

Carol let out a wail of despair. 'How are we going to get all this lot back into the cupboard again?' Then she uttered an even more desperate cry. 'There's twice as much in the attic, and ten times more in the cellar. What are we going to do, Steve?'

Emerson uttered soothing words. 'It's time for a break. Zoe will help me repack the cupboard while you make some coffee. Then I suggest we go upstairs and do the bedrooms. We'll get on quicker that way.'

Zoe clung to his arm and gazed up at his face in adoration. 'Whatever you say, Emerson, my darling.'

Alice was slightly less enraptured. She had no intention of being bossed around by her niece's young man, still less to be sent to the kitchen to brew up his refreshment. 'We're wasting time here. Leave all this rubbish, we can deal with it later. Try and think of the sort of place Grandad would have been able to get to without us seeing him. Somewhere simple like the chest in the hall. Has anyone looked in there? No? Then let's do it now.'

No such luck and after another hour ransacking all the downstairs rooms with their many cupboards and chests of drawers, all crammed with family possessions from previous generations of farming Knights, they finally trooped up the wide front stairs to the bedrooms. 'Let's start with Ronnie's room,' Alice said, leading the way. 'I hope it's clean and respectable. Zoe, Emerson, in you go. Look under the bed and on top of the wardrobe.' To help matters along she opened the wardrobe doors herself and invited everyone to examine it closely, lifting some long garments so that they could see to the back and be certain that nothing was inside.

'You can do my room next,' Zoe offered. 'I haven't got the suitcase but I want you to look. Anyway if I had the money I would share it round. We wouldn't keep it just for ourselves, would we, Emerson?'

They were spared an untruthful reply when Steve made

the same offer. 'If I found the suitcase I would own up to it straight away, I wouldn't keep it for myself. I feel the same way as Zoe. I would have done what Grandad wanted and shared it out.'

Alice sensed a mood for giving up but insisted that her room was searched next. 'I don't want this to drag on any longer than necessary. I haven't got Dad's suitcase, I don't know where it is or what's happened to it and I don't want to be under any suspicion.'

Carol responded quickly. 'Same here. Steve and me aren't holding out on you. We haven't got the bloody suitcase either but we want our place to be searched so that we're in the clear too.'

'Right, let's get on with it,' Alice said, asserting herself by opening the door of her mother's bedroom and ushering the search party inside. 'Ma wants to be included so we'll do her room next. Emerson – on your knees! You've got a lot of beds to look under.'

They continued the search for another hour, becoming increasingly dispirited in the process. They may have had some slight expectation of success when they started but somehow they all knew that the suitcase was never going to be found, not in the house anyway.

It was late at night when they went their separate ways, Steve and Carol to their married quarters, Zoe and Emerson to their love bed, and Alice to the kitchen to catch up on Ronnie's eats. Although tired out she was soon bearing a tasty snack on a tray to the TV settee. Ronnie was polite and appreciative as always but Martha Knight was tearful. 'No need to ask,' she said to Alice. 'We should have heard soon enough if you had found it.'

'It's not in the house, Ma.'

'You think it's somewhere on the farm?'

'We'll start looking as soon as it gets light in the morning.'

'Begin in the hay barn, why don't you? That's the most likely place, isn't it?'

Alice agreed that it was but the unpleasant ordeal of

searching one another's bedrooms had taken its toll on nerves and family courtesy. Although the search had been carried out so that everyone could be eliminated from further suspicion, the opposite result had gradually emerged instead.

Forty-eight hours had elapsed between breaking down the bedroom door and Joe Knight's death. There remained a lingering doubt that at some brief moment during those forty-eight hours he might have surfaced from his coma just long enough to divulge the location of the suitcase to one of the family members who had kept the vigil beside his bed. Was it possible that one of their number had been given this vital information, and if so, which one?

The thought had been present in all their minds that one of them might have already gained possession of the suitcase and was keeping quiet until things settled down again. They had been searching for a large object, one hard to conceal. On reflection they realised that the first act of a culprit would be for immediate disposal of the suitcase because even a large sum of money in banknotes would not take up much space if neatly stowed away. They had looked in the obvious places, wardrobes and chests of drawers, but passed by small items of furniture such as desks and dressing tables which were obviously too small to contain the suitcase but which might on a more thorough search have revealed the banknotes.

Which meant that the house would have to be searched again, more thoroughly this time, if all the family members were to be exonerated to the satisfaction of everyone else. Such a search was now unlikely to take place, and would have been in any case almost certainly too late. The chance of an amicable share-out was receding fast. Whatever had happened to the money, or whoever had stolen it, sufficient time had passed for the situation to be irretrievable.

Joe Knight's stash had gone for good.

31

Next morning they reassembled in the hay barn. When Zoe saw the trestle table and the old brass-weight scales, and the two wooden chairs where she had sat so often beside her grandfather, she burst into tears. It needed all Emerson's powers of persuasion to coax her to stay and help with the search. She wailed, 'I didn't want him to die. Poor old Gramps. I was the only one who loved him.'

'More to the point,' her mother said sharply, 'Is where did he hide the suitcase? If it's going to be anywhere, this is the place. I suggest we stop wasting time and start looking.'

Steve said, 'Grandad wouldn't have been able to get very high among the bales but you had better go up and have a look, Zoe.'

'I'll climb up too,' Emerson offered, and was soon following behind.

This alarmed Carol who did not bother to hide her distrust. 'You too, Steve. Up you go. Don't let those two out of your sight.'

Although referred to as the hay barn it contained mostly stacked bales of straw, used as litter for the beef cattle. Alice and Carol waited at the bottom until the other three returned safely to ground level. Only to give a negative report. The skinny black cat was up there in her nest with two of her latest kittens but the suitcase could not be found and was therefore still missing.

'Grandad wasn't very active towards the end of his life,' Steve reminded them. 'If it's in here somewhere it's got to be among all that clutter.'

He gestured round at the various items of agricultural junk which had found their way to the barn. An old seed drill, a horse-drawn hay rake, a tine harrow, a single furrow plough, two milking machine buckets and a milk churn, all rusted and thick with dust. It had been Joe Knight's forlorn hope that a customer buying a bunch of beetroots would suddenly be smitten with the urge to secure one of the museum exhibits as a garden ornament but it had never happened. Emerson pushed and pulled for the others to see behind and underneath the old farm implements but there was no sign of the missing suitcase, so with reluctance the barn was eliminated from their search list.

Steve recommended that they move on to the pig unit. 'I saw Grandad poking around in there just before he died. Got to be worth a try.'

The pig house was Emerson's first big test and the smell on entering almost sent him straight out again. 'If it's in there it can stay in there,' was his first reaction, holding his hand-kerchief to his nose. Alice, Steve and Carol were not having that and ushered him back inside for a closer hands-on tour, starting with the farrowing pen, the weaner pens, the porker pens and the food preparation area where the rations were mixed up in buckets.

'Start looking, Emerson,' Carol invited him. 'There's no need to be quite so squeamish, pig shit never hurt anyone so far as I know. Grandad grew most of his vegetables in it and none of his customers ever came to any harm, not to my knowledge anyway. How about up there, behind the water tank? There are plenty of places big enough to hide a suitcase. Don't hang around, we haven't got all day and Steve and me still have our work to do.'

Emerson made a token effort but gave up when confronted by a wheelbarrow brimming with pig manure. Steve handed him a stick and told him to poke it about, with a wink to the others. 'It could be in there somewhere, take a look.' Emerson knew when enough was enough and headed for the exit, only to be led to the silage clamp, another smell that he found equally offensive, although not so sickening as the stench from the slurry pit that was next on his tour. 'Could be down there somewhere,' Steve gave as his considered advice, urging him to kneel by the inspection cover and peer into the depths.

'Keep going, we're not done yet,' Carol said to continue Emerson's steep learning curve on the joys of penurious livestock farming in midwinter. 'This lovely machine is our muck spreader, we couldn't run the farm without it. It's about half full at the moment, fancy having a look? Use the prong to turn it over, you never know your luck.'

Emerson firmly declined the offer so Carol moved on to the two loose boxes used for sick or calving cows. When these were eliminated she pointed outside to the dog kennel, indicating with her hands that she wished it to be turned upside down. After this the hens were driven from their coops and Emerson was invited to wriggle inside and look above the perches. He emerged looking chastened but gave a thumbs down so they moved on to a paddock where a dozen or so white faced beef cattle waited patiently beside an empty ring feeder anchored in deep mud.

'No,' he said before he could be asked. 'I'm not wading through all that mud. If that's where it is it can bloody well stay there.'

It was a miserably dark morning, their noses were red with cold and their clothes wet through. At first they had scarcely noticed the slight drizzle but it had been raining steadily for some time and the search party huddled miserably inside the covered straw-yard where a younger batch of cattle fed on rolled barley were seeing out the winter. The search party was grateful for the meagre shelter it provided and watched as Steve unlocked the cake store and gestured Emerson to join him inside.

'They're well fed, our beasties. Take a good look, Emerson. It costs a lot more to feed them than it does us indoors.' He waved an arm by way of invitation. 'The choice is yours. There are plenty of places in here big enough to hide Grandad's suitcase. Start with the sacks of sugar beet pulp. When you've looked in all those you can use the shovel to turn over that big pile of brewers grains. I'm going to unlock the chemical store and have a look in there. Let's keep moving.'

Zoe was the first to protest. 'I'm cold. I'm going back indoors.' She waited for a response, aware that she was voicing the feelings of the others who were likewise, cold, miserable and fed up with a hopeless search. They longed to return to the warmth of the farmhouse kitchen where Martha would be waiting with mugs of hot milky drinks and slices of slab cake, comfort food for those much in need of comforting.

Except that Emerson still seemed eager to carry on the search, in spite of his unhappy experiences of the morning. His keenness to find the money was beginning to irritate Carol. Recent events at Nutwhistle had made her life ever more arduous and burdensome, with the prospect that things would get steadily worse rather than better. Which meant she was sufficiently disenchanted for her patience to snap. She turned on Emerson with all the menace of a striking cobra.

'You want the money so that you can go to Brazil? Is that why you're so desperate to find the suitcase?'

Zoe was scared and cried off at once. 'Oh no, Mum. Emerson's going to move in with me. That's a lot better than going to Brazil. We're not after the money. Just trying to help.'

'What do you mean, Emerson's going to move in with you? You haven't got a place of your own.'

'With us then. There's plenty of room. We won't be any trouble. I'll look after him.'

'I think you had better hear what your Dad has to say about it. You're taking too much for granted.'

'Oh Mum, you didn't want me to leave home and go abroad, did you? I know you didn't.'

'Did I have any say in the matter? You just told me you were going and now you tell me you're not going. Which is it?'

Steve said, 'We've got a right to know, Zoe.'

Zoe started to snivel and turned to Emerson for help. 'You say something.'

Emerson hastened to rescue an edgy situation. He smiled a disarming smile. 'We've had a slight change of plan. Going to Brazil didn't seem such a good idea after all.'

'You mean compared to moving in with us?'

'Oh Mum, please don't be unkind to Emerson,' Zoe pleaded.

Emerson placed a reassuring arm round her waist. 'She's not being unkind, Zoe. She's doing the right thing, looking after your interests.'

'Does that mean you can't stay?' She turned and clutched her father by the arm. 'Oh Dad, please. Emerson can stay with me, can't he?'

The last thing Steve wanted was another family crisis and a slice of teenage rebellion so he capitulated without a fight. 'Yes. It's all right by me, Emerson. You can stay with us. For the time being anyway.'

Carol was less easily talked round. 'You don't seem very upset,' she pointed out to her daughter. 'Not after all the fuss you made about wanting to go to Brazil. It was a daft idea and I shan't expect to hear of any such silliness ever again. Do I make myself clear?'

'Yes, Mum.'

'And the same goes for you, Emerson. Any more schemes like that and I'll throw you both out. Are you hearing me, young man?'

He sighed. 'We couldn't go anywhere even if we wanted to.'

'In other words you're broke too.'

'You could put it like that, I suppose.'

'I do put it like that.'

Zoe was alarmed at the way things were going and renewed her pleading for Emerson to be allowed to stay, still clutching her father's arm. 'Oh Dad, please. Emerson and me are in love. We want to be together all the time. He can move in with us, can't he?'

'I've just said he can stay, haven't I?'

Zoe immediately wrapped both arms round Emerson, her

eyes closed in rapture. 'Oh thank you, Dad, thank you. This is much better than going to Brazil. I'm going to have lovely Emerson all to myself. It's the nicest Christmas present I could ever wish for! I don't care what happens about the money now that I've got Emerson.'

32

So far so good for the first pair of Nutwhistle young lovers, which only left Ronnie to find the happiness he sought. To ensure that he was smartly dressed for the funeral his mother bought him a complete new outfit, including a dazzling white shirt, a pair of gold cuff links, a silk tie and a navy blue double-breasted Crombie overcoat. Alice was determined that when the family was on show at the church, and at the reception afterwards, her cherished Ronnie would be a credit to her many years of loving care.

On the day of the funeral there was no wind or rain to spoil the proceedings but it was gloomily overcast with a nip in the air. There is little comfort in a grave at the best of times and Joe Knight's closing ceremony was a dismal affair that matched the winter weather and the black mood of the family. They trooped into the church behind the coffin, the mournful penny-whistle continuo from the organ mingling with Zoe's sobs. Alice pushed her mother in a wheelchair, and Carol took Steve's arm, both stiffly awkward in their rarely worn best clothes.

They were doing their best to be as unobtrusive as possible but this did not apply to the two young men bringing up the rear of the family mourners. Ronnie and Emerson stole the show. Even those who secretly thought young Ronnie a lazy sod were forced to admit that his considerable bulk fitted nicely inside the expensive tailoring his mother had provided and gave him an impressive appearance. At twenty-four going on twenty-five he was in the prime of life, the picture of well-adjusted good nature. The sorrows of the day, and the troubles of the world, rested lightly on his shoulders.

He walked slowly side by side with Zoe's boyfriend Emerson, a tall slim young man of similar age and with an equally impressive appearance. He was elegantly dressed in a long red overcoat with lace cuffs. Added to his dreadlocks, jewellery and natural distinction of manner his progress up the aisle and into the front pews did not exactly go unnoticed in a church filled to capacity by plainly dressed family friends and kindly homespun neighbours.

Duty called and the farming fraternity had turned out in force to mourn the passing of one of their own. During their slow shuffle up the aisle to the front pews the Knight family had plenty of time to glance nervously around them. It seemed even colder inside the church than it was outside, and they found themselves looking at the backs of the congregation, a harvest cartload of rural yeomanry and their womenfolk huddled into overcoats, hats, scarves, gloves and boots. The mourners were a hardy lot and never shirked a good funeral but they all knew from bitter past experience that the church could have doubled up as a butchery cold store and had come prepared. A great waft of body-warmed camphor and eucalyptus drifted towards the chancel, a miasma of steaming breath and cough-drop fumes strong enough to sting the eyes.

Soon they were singing the first hymn, *All Things Bright and Beautiful*, a children's hymn that conjured up flower-strewn summer meadows, and was singularly inappropriate for the curmudgeonly old farmer in the box. The vicar had suggested it, and written the eulogy from Steve's glowing account of his father's agricultural expertise. Being a member of the Rabbit Clearance Task Force and an expert on badger gassing went down well with the predominantly rural congregation. There were nods and warm murmurs of approval for a man who obviously knew how things were done in the countryside. As the service drew to a close the well-filled pews were even beginning to generate enough warmth to moderate the tombstone chill rising from the bare stone floor.

No one likes to see a coffin lowered and a life ended but there is always a feeling of relief after a funeral. The family had done their best under difficult circumstances, the villagers and the farming community had rallied, customs had been observed and duty done. Everyone present felt they had earned the right to pile into the low-ceilinged bar of The Shorn Lamb, hands outstretched for the open fire and a warming glass of sherry. As the alcohol percolated downwards so the volume of chatter escalated until there was a pleasant hubbub of conversation. There was genuine sympathy for the family who were trying hard to be as gracious as possible to the friends and neighbours who had taken the trouble to attend.

Prominent among the mourners was the talkative Widow Hounsome, a noted chatterbox. She knew everyone present and bustled about glass in hand, giving anyone who would stand still a smacking kiss. Alice and Carol did their best to be friendly and welcoming to their old schoolmate but reserved the right to bitch about her in private. 'Did she have to wear a skirt that short to a funeral?' Carol asked her sister-in-law. 'It's not nice.'

'Be fair, Carol. I think it's the longest one she's got. Her way of showing respect.'

'I've lost count of the number of sherries she's had. Must have a hard head for drink.' And so on.

The convivial widow had been round the room once but kissed them again on the second circuit, raising her arms to include them both in an embrace. 'It was a lovely funeral, wasn't it? The vicar said some nice things about Joe, which was good. And it didn't rain, that always spoils a funeral. Pleased you had such a big turn-out, even the side aisles were full.'

'Nice of you to come, Betty,' Alice said.

'Oh, I had to, we all did. A lovely man, Joe. He deserved a good send-off.'

'Kind of you to say so.'

'He was one of our own, and he'll be missed.' She suddenly sobbed and brushed away a tear. 'I shall miss him, you know I will. I can hardly believe he's gone.'

'Thank you for your flowers. Very generous.'

'He was such a good gardener himself, I know he would have liked to see some nice flowers.' She gestured with her empty glass. 'I'll just grab a refill and then I'll have a word with Martha. It's terrible to see her in a wheelchair. Poor Martha. What a sad day for her.'

When she had gone Carol and Alice resumed their discussion. 'Well?' Alice said. 'What do you reckon, Carol? Did she act as if she had the money?'

'No. I don't think she did.'

'I don't think so either. Didn't seem embarrassed at talking to us or look guilty, did she?'

Carol sighed. 'She looks good. Even in black.'

'Particularly in black. Men think it's sexy, the silly sods.'

'In the bedroom, maybe. At a funeral? I don't think so.'

'Poor old Mum, crippled up with arthritis. Betty didn't have much competition, did she?'

There could be no argument over that and with the crowd beginning to thin out they joined the other members of the family who were saying farewell to the stragglers. They began edging unobtrusively but firmly towards the car park. At which point in the proceedings Steve found himself detached from his family and steered by the elbow to a secluded corner of the long saloon bar.

The man doing the steering was another farmer, but not any farmer, it was the farmer whose land adjoined that of Nutwhistle. His name was Foxwell, Freddie Foxwell, and although his farm was much bigger and more modern he was always careful to treat Steve as though they were landowners of equal status on the few occasions when they met socially.

'Need to expand,' he whispered to Steve as they looked out of the saloon bar window. He waved in the general direction of their respective farms. 'Need to grow a lot more maize for the pheasants. Best cover there is, maize. I grow it with a bit of millet mixed in. Works a treat.'

Steve was always nervous and ill at ease when his patrician neighbour condescended to speak to him. He replied politely, 'We grow a lot of maize ourselves. Makes good silage for the beef cattle.'

Still keeping hold of his sleeve Freddie said, 'I know this isn't the time and place to talk business but we don't meet very often these days so I thought I would let you know which way I was thinking.'

'Thank you for telling me.'

'I really do need to expand. Should you ever think of selling up.'

'Kind of you to come to Dad's funeral,' Steve mumbled.

'He was a good neighbour. My Dad liked him, you know that, and they got on well together. Now they've both been gathered in so it's between you and me to sort out the future.'

'I won't be making any decisions about the farm for a long time yet.'

'Of course not, and I wouldn't expect you to. But when things have settled down again I should appreciate it if you would bear my offer in mind.'

'I can't see myself selling the farm, Freddie.'

'Just the land, I don't want the house. I'll pay top whack for the fields and the little copse. That will leave you with the farmhouse and about five acres so that you can have your own space. Promise me you'll think about it, Steve.'

'I'll talk it over with Carol.'

'Do that,' his next door neighbour urged him, finally releasing his elbow. 'You know my number when you need to get in touch.'

He exited The Shorn Lamb in purposeful strides and zoomed off in his Range Rover, leaving a disconsolate Steve to rejoin his family. 'What was all that about?' his wife Carol asked him but Steve was too dispirited to reply. He said, 'We're done here. Let's get back to the farm. Is Ma ready to be loaded up?'

Alice Knight rejoined them, still pushing her mother in a wheelchair. She looked cold and exhausted. They had found the funeral an ordeal and were all equally desperate to return to the warmth and sanctuary of Nutwhistle farmhouse. The dismal day was nearing an end but had one further twist to unfold.

Looking all round Alice asked, 'Where's Ronnie? Why isn't he here?'

A good question and one soon to be answered, although not in any way his mother would have wanted. Because just at that moment there was a distraction, and a general turning of heads. The last remaining people in the car park were exchanging farewells but stopped talking and turned to watch as Betty Hounsome came sailing out of The Shorn Lamb's front door. The frisky widow was heading towards her sleek black low-slung Mercedes sports car, a wedding gift from her late bookmaker husband, and a prized possession.

From teenage days onward Betty had owned a succession of sports cars, and long ago mastered the art of getting in and out to maximum effect. Whether lowering herself down into the driver's seat or levering herself up again, she did so in a way that engaged the attention of any man who might be watching, and in her case there was usually more than one because she had a fan club of admirers wherever she went.

With her short skirt disappearing in the direction of her waist, and her shapely under-thighs spread wide, swivelling her legs in and out of the car was a spectacle that would have enthused a convention of gynaecologists. The burst of applause which followed, even if silently expressed, was usually rewarded with one of Betty's winning smiles, and for a really special occasion, an encore. This took the form of kneeling up, bending over and leaning across into the passenger seat to ferret around for a mislaid item. A show-stopper.

So no one was surprised at the buzz of excitement which increased in volume as she made her final farewells and approached the shiny black Mercedes. Most of the men present had seen the getting-in and getting-out exhibition many times before but were still keen to see it again, and even in front of their wives did not pretend indifference. Nor did the Widow Hounsome disappoint her audience, flashing her smile as well as her thighs before driving off with a wave.

Except that on this occasion her performance was upstaged. The attention of the soberly clad mourners was directed instead to her passenger, not someone they had expected to see driving away seated beside the sprightly widow.

Most surprised of all were the residents of Nutwhistle Farm. They had seen Ronnie and Betty Hounsome in conversation at various times during the proceedings but were absolutely gobsmacked to see them emerge from The Shorn Lamb arm in arm. To say that they were bewildered would have been the understatement of the century. There was jaw-dropping disbelief in all directions as the comely and triumphantly smiling widow kept her gloved hand tucked through the arm of Ronnie Knight's expensive new overcoat. Ronnie had an even more smug expression on his face. Omitting any farewells or explanations to his family he ensconced himself proudly in the passenger seat of the widow's Mercedes as they sped away to the deceased turf accountant's opulent ranch-style bungalow.

When they had disappeared from sight Zoe Knight was the first to speak. Keeping a tight hold of her own young man in case he disappeared as well she said, 'Wasn't Ronnie the quiet one? Imagine that! He wouldn't tell me the name of his girl friend and now I know why. Who would have believed it?'

Martha, Steve and Carol were more concerned for the effect on Ronnie's mother who had just seen her idolised son drive out of her life, and they all knew that it would be for ever and a day. If losing the money was a tragedy of Biblical immensity this was a small personal tragedy of infinite pathos, ingratitude and rejection.

They thought poor Alice Knight did well to weep, and weep she did.

33

The shock of Joe's death and Ronnie's defection had profoundly unsettled the other residents of Nutwhistle Farm. Not to mince words it had knocked them sideways.

The winter months passed in a daze and it was early spring before they had sufficiently recovered to take stock of their precarious financial situation. After paying for the funeral the coffers were empty and the farm began to look even more run-down and derelict than it was before. Martha's arthritis was just as painful but the plans for buying her a stairlift had been permanently shelved for lack of funds. Alice worked overtime at the supermarket to earn extra money, while Steve and Carol looked more thin and exhausted than ever.

There was a shining exception to all this doom and gloom because Zoe was now happily pregnant. Her delight in looking forward to the birth of her baby made life more bearable for the others, particularly for her grandmother. Martha Knight was just as excited as Zoe herself and occupied her time knitting tiny cardigans and romper suits. Emerson was looking forward to being a proud Dad and turned out the cupboard under the stairs to rescue the cot, the playpen and the doll's pram. There was every prospect of some happier times to come.

Towards the end of March the weather began to warm up and Emerson ventured out of the house and went for short walks round the farm. He still had lingering hopes of finding Joe Knight's missing suitcase and began poking around in the untidy sprawl of farm buildings. These included the old milking parlour, the old dairy and the old cowshed, all filled with farmyard junk of one sort or another, as nothing had been thrown away since the Crimean War.

One day Emerson was taking his morning constitutional

when he met Steve and Carol as they were returning to the house. It was lambing time and they had been up most of the night. When they stopped to exchange niceties and enquire after Zoe's health and wellbeing Emerson detained them with a question. 'What do you call the building that's propped up on stones like mushrooms?'

Although almost dead on his feet through lack of sleep Steve's natural politeness obliged him to give an answer. 'It's the old granary. Years ago it was where they stored the wheat crop until it could be sold. Staddle stones they're called. Designed to keep rats out.'

Carol wanted to know why he had asked. 'Come on, Emerson. You must have a reason.'

In response to her challenge he smiled and made a languid gesture with his hand in the direction of the staddle stones. 'In the ground just behind them there's a round board with a big car battery on top. I wondered what was underneath.'

'It's the well.'

'The farm has a well?'

'Not now, years ago, before we had piped water.'

'A deep well?'

Carol was still suspicious. 'Where is all this leading, Emerson?'

'Oh, nothing.'

'Nothing my ass. Don't hold out on us. You wouldn't be asking if you didn't have something in mind. What is it?'

'Just that you never thought of looking down the well when we were searching for the suitcase.'

Steve and Carol suddenly felt less tired and stared at one another in wide-eyed surprise. 'Bloody hell,' Carol whispered. 'He's right you know. Never thought of it, did we?'

Even though starving hungry, dog tired and urgently needing to visit the bathroom Steve could not suppress a flicker of hope. Trying not to sound too optimistic he said to Carol, 'It wouldn't hurt to take a look. Would it?'

She agreed that it wouldn't, so accompanied by Emerson

they were soon standing by the circular well cover. This had been crudely fashioned from an old stable door, roughly sawn to the diameter of the well, and soddened by years of rain. It was plastered with dead leaves and surrounded by mud and weeds. As Emerson had described it was anchored in place by a large and heavy vehicle battery, removed from a derelict farm tractor.

Carol put out an arm to restrain the young man who seemed as though he wished to dive down the well head first in search of the money. She uttered a warning instead. 'Don't get too close, Emerson. If you fell through I doubt if you would come up again. Not alive, anyway.'

Steve was trying to put himself in his father's place. 'Dad would have had the same problem. Easy enough to lower the suitcase down the well but how would he get it up again?'

'On a length of string?' Emerson suggested. 'Rope? I've seen lots of rope around the farm in different places.'

'Dad was a sick man. I don't think he would have been up to doing all that.'

'He wouldn't have needed to lower the suitcase to the bottom. Just a few feet so that it was out of sight.'

'That makes sense,' Carol agreed. 'Can't see how he would have done it though.' She moved closer and put out a foot to nudge the heavy lead battery.

'It's been moved recently,' Emerson said, pointing. 'See? There's a dark area where it has been standing for a long time but the battery doesn't quite fit over the mark. Whoever moved it didn't put it back in exactly the same place.'

'He's right again,' Steve said. He was starting to become emotional. 'Could this be it?' he asked his wife in a trembling voice. 'After all these months? Dad's money? It would be like a miracle.'

'There's only one way to find out.'

'I'll help you,' Emerson offered, lifting off the tractor battery, which was much heavier than he had expected. He and Steve then knelt and began prising the circular well cover up out of the mud. The wood was thick, and surprisingly heavy. When it was removed the circular brickwork of the well-head was revealed, and the deep hole in the ground. This was a tapering black cylinder with no discernible bottom. All three took an involuntary backwards step, then when their nerves had recovered leaned over and looked down.

With no sun and an overcast sky it was difficult to see to the bottom. 'Drop a stone in,' Carol suggested, then found one and dropped it in herself. There came the expected splash but it was preceded by a metallic clunk.

'Don't get too excited,' Steve cautioned. 'Dad threw a lot of rubbish and junk down the well when it was first boarded up. We've had a wet winter, the water level would be high enough to cover most of it.'

Carol knelt and leaned over as far as she dared. 'I can see the top of a paint tin.'

Emerson knelt beside her. When his eyes had adjusted to the blackness at the bottom he said, 'I can see something else just sticking up above the water. Something shiny.'

Steve joined them and agreed with Emerson. 'I can see it too.'

Carol was unconvinced. She was cold, hungry and exhausted, and beginning to lose patience. 'I want my breakfast. Cover it up again, Steve. We're wasting time here.'

'We've looked everywhere else. I don't see that we've got anything to lose now that we've got this far.'

'Even your Dad wouldn't have been daft enough to throw his suitcase down the well. Why would he want to? There's nothing tied on anywhere, he wouldn't have been able to pull it up again, so there would have been no point. You stay here if you want to but I'm going in for a hot drink and something to eat.'

Steve refused to leave. In spite of his fatigue he was fired up with curiosity and determined to continue the search. 'Emerson, would you run back to the yard and fetch my lamp, please. You know the one I mean? The big black lamp I use round the farm. It's on the seat of my truck.'

Emerson soon returned with the lamp, and this time Zoe

was following close behind. She whooped with joy and excitement. 'Have you really found where Gramps hid the suitcase? Brilliant! We all get our money and Ronnie's share too. He doesn't deserve it any more. I won't tell him if you don't.'

Once again they knelt and peered down into the well. Steve switched on his powerful lamp and the beam shone right to the bottom. The sides of the well were wet which diffused the beam but there was sufficient overhead daylight to reflect off the water at the bottom. This time there was general agreement. On top of the water they could see the empty paint tin and beside it, unmistakeably, the outline of a suitcase. They raised a cheer and stood back, hardly daring to believe that their quest was over. Carol wept and hugged her husband. 'If anyone deserved some good luck, you did, love.'

Zoe clapped her hands. 'Emerson will go down and fetch it. We can lower him on a rope, can't we?'

Carol said, 'No. I'm the lightest. I'll go down.'

His hunger and lack of sleep forgotten, Steve couldn't wait to get on with it. He said to Zoe, 'We need to find something for Mum to stand in on the way down. Any ideas?'

It was a rhetorical question because if there was one commodity that Nutwhistle Farm could provide better than anywhere else on the planet it was two hundred years of discarded agricultural junk. Even so it took an hour of anxious searching before they found what they wanted at the back of the old milking parlour. This was a small square galvanised water tank that had once been part of the dairy equipment when they had a herd of cows. Steve used his steel rule to measure the dimensions and gave the thumbs up to indicate that it would not only go down the well but allow Carol sufficient room at the side to retrieve the suitcase.

Emerson helped Steve to carry the tank to the farm workshop so that holes could be drilled and handles made on either side to take the rope. While they worked Steve explained how wells were dug and maintained.

'One of my Dad's uncles was a well digger, from a family

of well diggers. They probably dug this one, or enlarged it, or repaired it. In the olden days they dug the well before they built the house. Had to. No sense in trying to run a farm without a supply of water.'

'Thank you for explaining it to me.'

'Most of the wells round here are about three foot wide, like ours, or a bit wider if there were two chaps digging. They used props to shore it up and then built the wall from the bottom. Skilled work. I've never heard of a well caving in.'

'Is it safe for Carol to go down? It won't collapse on her, will it?'

'I put my faith in Dad's uncle. People did a good job in those days.'

It was another hour before Steve was ready for Carol to make the descent. The empty tank was secured to the front of the farm tractor by a long rope and Emerson helped him to ease it over the edge to make sure that the rope would hold. He then acted as go-between, relaying signals to Steve in the tractor cab, the tractor being at the furthest extremity of the rope. He then eased the tractor forward until Carol was able to step in, then repeated the process until she was able to hold on to the rope with her head below the level of the bricks. Emerson knelt by the side of the well as Carol slowly disappeared from view, gesturing to Steve in the tractor cab that it was going to plan. They had folded a big piece of rick-cover tarpaulin into a pad to prevent the rope chafing against the edge. When the bucket hitched up on the wall Emerson was able to free it by wiggling the rope away from the side. When she reached the water Carol held up her hand. Emerson relayed the information to Steve who immediately applied the handbrake and jumped down from the tractor cab. 'Can you see it?' he called down to his wife. 'Any joy?'

'It's dark and bloody cold,' she called back up the shaft. 'It's narrower down here, not much room to work.'

'Can you see the suitcase?'

'I can see some empty paint tins and a lot of other junk. The suitcase must be right underneath. That's a bugger.'

'Can you move anything out of the way?'

'There isn't room for me to kneel down. Can you lower me a stick? Something stiff like a drain rod?'

Slightly less optimistic now they did as she asked, tying a brass-ended drain rod to a ball of string and lowering it down. As soon as it reached Carol they could hear the sound of splashing water, the rattling of tins and plenty of swearwords as she attempted to dislodge the rubbish and work the suitcase out to the side.

Emerson was alarmed to see the rope jiggling about and hear the bucket banging against the sides of the well. He said to Steve, 'That tank is too heavy for the rope. What are you going to do if it breaks, or if she dislodges some bricks and the well caves in?'

'You're right, this isn't working, we shall have to try another way.' Having made the decision Steve called down the well. 'That's enough, Carol. We're pulling you up.'

'Not yet. Wait.'

Hearing a fresh outburst of swearing he asked, 'What's the problem now?'

'The bloody lamp needs charging. It's so faint I can hardly see a thing.'

'How near are you to the water?'

'Can you lower me a bit more? I think that might do it.' Steve went back to ease the tractor forward a few more inches. When he returned to the well-head and kneeled beside Emerson he was just in time to hear his wife's excited shrieks. She shouted in triumph, 'It's here! It's here! I can see it. I can touch it.'

Steve leaned so far over the side that he was at risk of joining her head first in the bucket. 'Is there room to reach it? Do you need a tool of any sort? A hook? Can we do anything?'

'Yes, you can pull me up. I've got it. Did you hear me? I've got the suitcase!'

Zoe clapped her hands in delight and hugged Emerson so hard that they almost toppled into the well together. Steve inched the tractor carefully backwards and away from the well, hauling his wife up to the surface in the process. As soon as her head and shoulders appeared above the well-head Emerson helped her to safety.

She stepped out of the bucket and was unsteady on her feet for a few seconds. She was shivering with cold, wet, muddy and exhausted. Then with a beaming smile she held up the suitcase like a sporting trophy and shouted, 'Taraah!'

Zoe was so excited that she ran on ahead to tell her granny. By the time her parents and Emerson arrived in triumph with the suitcase Martha had hobbled out to meet them, leaning on her two aluminium sticks. It was a very emotional moment. Steve put his arms around his mother and said in a choked voice, 'We've got it, Ma. Dad's suitcase. It's a bit wet but it wasn't all under the water so the money should still be all right.'

Martha was entitled to be similarly moved, and she was. 'My poor Joe. Whatever was he thinking about to throw the money down the well?' She screwed a finger into her forehead. 'He must have been even more farther gone than we thought.'

They crowded round the kitchen table. Steve tried the locks but had his Stanley knife ready and when they would not open simply ran the knife round the rim and removed the top in a matter of seconds. With a hiss of indrawn breath they stared down at the brown envelopes, dismayed to see that there were no names written on the outside. With the smile wiped from his face Steve tore open the first envelope to expose wads of slightly sodden blank paper.

The other envelopes were opened to reveal still more blank white paper roughly cut to the size of banknotes. The feeling of bewilderment, frustration, anger and disappointment was even more acute than on the day when they had broken down the door to Joe Knight's room and realised that the suitcase was missing. For several hours afterwards they were numbed and silent as they struggled to take in the implications of this latest kick in the teeth for a family already reeling from the shock of Joe's death, Ronnie's desertion and their dire financial situation.

'How are we going to break the news to Alice?' Steve enquired of his wife and mother. 'She's going to be absolutely devastated when she sees the trick Dad played on us.'

They did not have long to wait. When Alice Knight returned to the farm tired and weary after a long day on her feet at the supermarket she called out as usual, 'It's only me, Ma,' and entered the kitchen carrying her daily bag of shopping.

When she saw the suitcase on the table beside the wads of blank paper she uttered a scream and fell to the floor in a dead faint. She was a heavy woman and the thud rocked the house on its foundations and made the windows rattle. It was a bad ending to a bad day in the history of Nutwhistle Farm.

34

With this last despairing hope of easy riches gone for good Emerson resigned himself to finding some form of gainful employment. Work was not on the agenda, there had to be some more agreeable way to utilise his various talents. He was well educated, articulate, devious and manipulative, which led to the obvious conclusion – politics. One day he read in the local newspaper how much district councillors earned in fees and expenses. He lowered the newspaper in amazement and experienced his own personal Road to Damascus moment. To earn money by sitting at a committee table, dutifully raising his hand when given the chairman's nod, was a way of life he knew would suit him perfectly.

Emerson acted at once to take the first steps to his new life. As soon as he had finished breakfast Zoe sheared off his dreadlocks, leaving him with neatly parted short hair. Later the same day he purchased a sober dark grey suit and a glossy pair of black shoes. In the evening he knotted a true-blue tie round his neck and joined the Conservative Party. Next morning he informed Zoe that she was about to become a respectable married woman and fixed up a register office wedding.

Although carried out with the briefest of celebrations it was undeniably legal and several months ahead of the birth of their baby. Only a handful of guests received invitations. A bemused Steve and Carol were back at work within the hour, while the happy couple spent their honeymoon staying put at Nutwhistle Farm. It happened so fast that Zoe had to pinch herself to believe she was now a teenage bride, soon to be a mother, that the ring on her finger was real, and that Emerson was serious in pursuing a political career.

For any ambitious young man there will always be an

opening in politics. So it proved for Emerson, and his career trajectory was spectacular. He became a local activist and within a short space of time was selected to fight a council bye-election, a safe Conservative seat on a Conservative led district council. He was launched and on his way, onwards and upwards. From that day forward he was scarcely at home for more than a few minutes, just long enough to change his clothes before heading off to the next party function. They were overjoyed to have him, straight out of the guidelines from Central Office. Young, bright and public school educated but miraculously non-white, ethnically perfect in every way. He was soon working his way up the dinner party ladder, making all the right friends, allies, contacts and the occasional enemy at each gathering of the faithful.

His talent lay in dressing the part of the upwardly mobile politician, and he never got it wrong. He could do smart casual for the constituency barbecue, his dark suit, waistcoat and blue tie were perfect for the finance and general purposes committee, and for all formal occasions he wore his dinner jacket as naturally as though he didn't know he had it on. Even if he had received his education at one of the less famous public schools it had still given him the priceless asset of good manners and a very acceptable Home Counties accent.

Better still he had a young, tall and pretty wife, a child born in wedlock, and a good address. The sitting Member of Parliament was due to stand down at the next general election and when the list of candidates to replace him was drawn up Emerson's name led all the rest. It was a rural constituency and Nutwhistle Farm looked just the ticket on his campaign literature. Emerson's impeccable dress sense served him well and photographs of him in his tweed cap, waxed jacket and buttery cord trousers, whether worn with wellies or brown brogue shoes, proclaimed him as every inch the young squire. On the farm he tried hard not to talk down to Steve and Carol, but failed. Visitors to the farm could be forgiven for assuming he was a well-to-do young landowner giving instructions to two harassed employees.

Nutwhistle Farm sounded even better in conversation. Seated at the head of a committee table Emerson would ease back an immaculate cuff, glance at the time on his watch and murmur, 'It's late, I should be heading back to the farm. We're drilling our maize crop at the moment. Need to see how they're getting on.' His campaign photograph in cap and tweeds was taken among a group of Steve's white-faced beef cattle, with the caption, 'A Better Deal for the British Farmer.' Similar stirring slogans appeared as straplines, such as 'Hands off our countryside,' and 'Bring back Hunting.'

Emerson was the darling of the constituency.

35

Life goes on, as it always does, even for the beleaguered occupants of Nutwhistle Farm. And with life comes change. For Alice Knight, still stunned and perpetually grieving for the loss of her son Ronnie to the warm embrace of the Widow Hounsome, change came in the shape of a new bacon hand at the supermarket.

He was recently widowed, although only in his early fifties. He was a small man, meek and mild in manner but his sexual preference was for large-framed strong-minded women. Alice Knight fitted the bill exactly. She was a big handsome woman who made the best of herself with an expensive hair-do and good quality clothes. Although she carried plenty of weight it was nicely distributed. As a supervisor she stood no nonsense from staff, management or customers. The new man lost no time in wooing and pursuing her in a determined courtship.

Having accepted that Ronnie was never coming back Alice had her own future to arrange and gave the bacon hand's proposals serious consideration. Life at Nutwhistle Farm was miserable, and likely to get worse. She had never expected to be offered such an easy escape route, one that might never come her way again, and she clinched the deal before her beau had a chance to change his mind. He owned a modern detached house in a good road so she moved in immediately, resuming her sex life after a break of twenty-seven years. In due course she became a married woman, another new experience. Old maids make devoted wives so she put the past behind her and concentrated on making nice to her husband, building a successful marriage in the process.

Nothing and no one is immune from change. Having adjusted to Joe Knight's death, Ronnie's defection and the surprise departure of Alice, the remaining inhabitants of Nutwhistle Farm were braced and ready for the next mass exodus.

After living with his in-laws rent free for five years Emerson also left suddenly, taking his wife and three young children with him. Affluent friends in the party had fixed him up with a more suitable house, in an area of the constituency nearer to London. As a fast rising politician who would one day be able to distribute favours of his own, and widely tipped to become the country's first black prime minister, Emerson knew that his cronies were laying up treasure for the future and accepted their offer without demur. He scraped the Nutwhistle mud from his shoes and decamped with scarcely a backward glance. The farm had served its purpose so he told Zoe to pack up their things and order the removal lorry. Zoe had never been close to her family and willingly obeyed, leaving her childhood home with little regret. She was as infatuated as ever with her successful and increasingly unfaithful husband, and would have followed him obediently anywhere he wanted to go.

Although in some ways Steve and Carol were sad to see them leave, in practical terms their absence eased the financial burden considerably. They had been subsidising and supporting Emerson since the day he moved in, plus Zoe and their three grandchildren, and once they were gone prayed that they would never want to return. In spite of her arthritis Martha had somehow coped with the extra domestic work, cooking endless meals for Zoe and her children, as well as doing most of their laundry, so she was equally relieved to see them depart.

They settled down again, a much smaller household this time, only three Knights remaining. After Joe's death Steve and Carol had shifted rooms to be closer to Martha and now that they had the house to themselves found life less of a struggle. In the evenings all three sat together and talked in front of the fire, or in the summer sat talking with the windows open, and passed the time very pleasantly. Carol took over most of the domestic work so that for the first time in her life Martha found herself with the novelty of extended leisure time, something she had never experienced before.

With hindsight this might not have been such a good idea. Constant daily toil in looking after her family had given her life its purpose. When the work stopped she entered into a period of slow but steady decline. Exactly a year after the departure of Zoe and her family Martha died. There had been no illness and no warning. One morning she did not get up and Carol found her dead in bed. She had outlived her husband Joe by only five years, worn out by hard work and the ravages of painful degenerative arthritis.

Some months before her death Steve was surprised and slightly offended when she told him that she wished to be cremated. She repeated her request several times until he promised to respect her wishes. She had never spelled out why she did not want to be buried with her husband and when the moment came Steve was minded to ignore her request, and have her buried with his father, this being a more fitting end for a farmer's wife.

No one had visited Joe Knight's grave since the day of the funeral, and it showed. In fact it was almost as overgrown and dilapidated as his farm. This was not entirely due to family neglect. The churchyard doubled up as home for ten million rabbits, industrious little miners who tunnelled and burrowed until every headstone, Joe's among them, was either sinking down or listing badly to one side. As fast as grieving relatives placed flowers and pot plants on the graves they were devoured overnight by the ever-hungry bunnies. Not so much a cemetery, more a rabbit sanctuary, the entire warren area so honeycombed that even the church was undermined and looked slightly skew-whiff when viewed north to south.

Before making a final decision Steve visited his father's grave to see for himself how much space had been left on the headstone for his mother's details to be added underneath. He was so appalled by the poor condition of the grave, and the surrounding graves, that he withdrew his objection. In accordance with her wishes Martha Knight was cremated and her ashes scattered on the farm.

Steve and Carol carried out this last sombre duty, subdued at the realisation that they were now the sole occupants of Nutwhistle Farm.

36

During the last year of Martha Knight's life, when the evenings were spent in conversation round the fire, they devoted many hours to the subject of the suitcase and the missing money. Family emotions were too raw in the first few months after Joe's death to allow for rational discussion of the mystery. Time heals even the deepest wounds and Martha had recently removed Joe's venerable beekeeping hat from the peg behind the kitchen door and taken it to her bedroom as a gesture of reconciliation and a daily reminder of her husband.

Given sufficient time even the most intractable of problems gradually delivers up a solution, and so it was over the vexed issue of the missing money and the suitcase. With plenty of time at their disposal the first inklings of what might have happened began to trickle down into their collective subconscious. Which was that Alice's son Ronnie had been the sole beneficiary of the Nutwhistle fortune. They assumed that he had removed the money and replaced it with blank paper, a reasonable deduction and not far from the truth.

Although the conclusion was reached by elimination it held up whichever arguments were deployed against it, and the longer they thought about it the more plausible it seemed. Betty Hounsome may have had a soft spot for Ronnie but not nearly enough to want to support him. Their discussions inched towards a basic premise, namely that he would have needed a substantial dowry to prosecute his successful suit of the high maintenance widow. It was the only explanation that worked.

But how had he managed it? How much money had there been in the suitcase? Did he have the strength of character and common-sense gumption not to fritter it away? And if so had he acquired the expertise necessary to invest the money profitably? Did the Widow Hounsome know about it at the time, and if not had she found out since? Short of asking Ronnie these questions in person, and receiving truthful answers, they were doomed never to know.

Surprisingly, having worked out the identity of the culprit, they were admiring rather than bitter and resentful, and even wished him the luck which had eluded other members of the family. They had long since adjusted to the loss of the money, and accepted that it was never coming back, so there was nothing to be gained by indulging in an orgy of recrimination.

'Zoe was right when she said that Ronnie was the quiet one,' Carol conceded, referring to the remark she made after the funeral. 'Wouldn't have suspected him in a month of Sundays, would we? The idle sod.'

As for Betty Hounsome her previous three marriages had not brought marital bliss along with their financial benefits. And although pleasurable at the time none of her many affairs and liaisons had conferred lasting happiness either. Competitive sex is dual-edged, wounding both sides equally, but until she chummed up with Ronnie Knight it was the only kind of sex she knew. Much to the general astonishment, and in spite of the age discrepancy, her fourth marriage was surprisingly successful and set to last the course.

This was because Betty found Ronnie's placid temperament much to her liking. Living with a man who never looked for trouble was a new and welcome experience. His lack of aggression, in the bedroom as elsewhere, made for a relaxed and companionable marriage. They saw eye to eye on just about everything and were always out and about together, best buddies as well as happy bedmates. 'As thick as thieves, those two,' one of their neighbours summed them up, an astute observation which succinctly described the close bonds of loyalty and affection which quickly developed between them.

To a young man as conciliatory and unthreatening as Ronnie Knight the sexual imperative when it came had been a life-altering experience. Nothing in his untroubled and pampered former life had prepared him for the testosterone surge he experienced when he lay in bed at night and allowed his thoughts to linger on the delights of having sex with the frolicsome widow. He knew with utter certainty that the opportunity to free himself from his mother, and to underwrite his marriage and future happiness, would never come again. He knew it to his very soul, and knew also that only one decisive act was needed to make his dreams come true.

Everyone else in the house needed the money, and they needed it as badly as he did. But were they prepared to act forcefully enough to get it? He thought not, and eliminated them one by one. His mother's hopes of switching the suitcases was never going to work and she had no better plan. Steve was a timid man who had never been able to stand up to his father, and was unlikely to do so at this time in his life. As for his Aunt Carol she had never shown him much affection, or taken any interest in him, and he saw no point in considering her feelings at such a critical point in his own affairs. She was slightly braver than her husband in dealing with the old man but not desperate enough to seize the suitcase by force, so he ruled her out as a serious contender.

Zoe was too fond of her grandfather to carry out any act that would hurt him, which only left his granny. Ronnie was not quite so sure about her. On the settee beside him she muttered a lot under the breath, enough to convince him that she had lost patience with her wilful and smelly old husband, and blamed him for everything that was going wrong at Nutwhistle Farm. But did she feel strongly enough to bump him off ? He was coming to the conclusion that she did, and that the old guy knew it too. This was the reason why he had thrown her out of the bedroom, and kept her locked out, afraid of what she might do to him in his sleep, given the chance.

Ronnie's own hopes of making a successful bid received an unexpected boost with the return of Zoe's boyfriend Emerson. He had obeyed the law of the bad penny by turning up when least expected, and was lodging somewhere in the town. A young man always generous with the truth. Where he had been in the meantime, or what he had been up to, he would never disclose. Zoe lost no time in tracking him down and thereafter was absent from the farm for most of the day and much of the night.

Her absence from the house during the day removed the last obstacle to Ronnie's plan, and it was a simple plan, to take the money by force some time during the early hours of the afternoon. His mother had come to the same conclusion but their earlier plan to switch the suitcases had failed. This time he was acting alone and so he waited quietly in his bedroom, which was on the other side of the upstairs passage from his grandfather's room.

Silently and patiently he waited. His mother was at work in the supermarket, his granny was slumbering in her easy chair beside the kitchen stove, while Steve and Carol had taken a tractor and trailer to the farthest extremity of the farm. A dozen curly-coated white-faced Simmental beef steers were clustered in distant mud around a ring feeder, patiently waiting for them to arrive with their daily rations, and they were always gone for at least an hour.

Even so it was not until the fourth day of his midday vigil that Ronnie Knight's moment of destiny finally arrived. He heard his grandfather unlock the door of his bedroom. This was because there had been not the slightest sound from anywhere in the house for so long that Joe thought it was safe to venture out for a quick trip to the bathroom. This was a mistake, the last he would ever make. Ronnie's one brief moment of lifetime opportunity presented itself and he did not hesitate. He crossed the passage, pushed his grandfather back into the room and hit him on the head with the piece of wood he had brought with him for the purpose. It was a mahogany chair leg wrenched from some derelict furniture in one of the junk-filled barns.

He reasoned that the mark left by the blow would be similar to that caused by striking his head on the bedroom chest of drawers after a fall. He knew that he was only going to have this one chance and struck with such force that his grandfather dropped straight to the floor. Ronnie pulled him closer to the chest of drawers and laid down the bedside chair and table to make it seem as though he had stumbled over them to cause his fall. Confident that his family would never call the police he simply walked out with the suitcase, locking the door from the outside.

He drove in his car immediately to the town's industrial estate where there was a Lock and Store building. A week previously he had signed for one of the small steel box units, paid his rent and became an account holder with total discretion assured. All he had to do was log himself in, go to his box, unlock it, place his grandfather's suitcase inside and lock it again. He was back at Nutwhistle Farm and sitting in his customary seat on the left side of the TV settee in less than an hour. During the evening he lied to Martha, telling her that he had heard his grandfather use the bathroom. This ensured that no alarm was raised until the following morning.

The next day when the door was broken down he was last in and simply dropped the keys on the carpet close to the door. Simple solutions are the best solutions, and so it proved on this occasion. Ronnie's nerve almost failed him when he saw that his grandfather was still alive, if only just. It was a nasty fright but fortunately for him Joe Knight was unable to speak, or even to point an accusing finger, and the moment of danger passed.

How did Ronnie deal with his million plus, in used notes? The Widow Hounsome had learned from her three previous marriages that it is best not to ask too many questions about how and when money was acquired. Ronnie proved a surprisingly quick learner and with a new computer was soon into online banking and investment. The laws on money laundering being strict it took him many months to squirrel the cash into as many accounts as possible but it was a pleasant problem to occupy his mind and before long he was building a useful portfolio and showing a profit. He would remain comfortably solvent for the rest of his life.

He experienced no remorse either then, or after, nor did he

see any reason to share his good fortune with those who had failed to match his bold bid for the prize. He had won it fair and square to purchase a lifetime of happy wedlock with the shapely widow. Too bad for his cousin Zoe, too bad for his lavender-scented granny, and worst of all it was too bad for his doting mother.

What had she expected – gratitude?

37

After long years of hardship and struggle in an unforgiving way of life Steve and Carol had reached the sunlit plateau of a comfortable middle age. In appearance they were just as careworn as ever because they still toiled from morning till night but they did not work for wages and were as carefree as children.

This was because they were finally living out their dream. They had what they had always wanted more than anything else, a farm of their own, all to themselves to run as they pleased. They were overdue for some luck and a welcome improvement in farm prices started putting money in the bank. Their fixed overhead costs were so low that for the first time in many years they found themselves comfortably prosperous.

Livestock farming is the most demanding form of agriculture, since all days of the year are the same to the beasts of the field. Apart from the briefest of honeymoons Steve and Carol had spent every single day of their married lives at work on the farm. They were never ill because they had no time to be ill, nor did they worry about what other people thought of them and their way of life. Holidays? The idea never came within their level of consciousness. Work is the greatest of all pleasures and every single animal on the farm was a recipient of their undivided attention, and treated as an individual in its own right. Whether a bad-tempered old sow, or a fragile day old chick, they thrived because they were loved.

Hardly any visitors came to the farm, which was the way they liked it. They were sensitive to criticism about the tumbledown condition of the outbuildings and the increasing dereliction of Nutwhistle Farmhouse. They did not see it as anyone else's business and carried on with a way of life that suited them, and which they had no intention of changing.

They inhabited a few rooms in the newer part of the house and were not overly concerned whether the rest fell down or not. Builders and developers wishing to buy the farm tried to tempt them by waving cheque books in front of their eyes, hinting that even larger sums of money were theirs for the asking. Steve and Carol contemptuously ignored all such offers and carried on with their happy way of life.

A regular but unwelcome visitor over the years had been their next door farmer, Freddie Foxwell. He was infuriated by their continued refusal to sell him their land. His demands were now stripped of all pretence at civilised behaviour and neighbourly politeness.

'Holding out for more are you?' he snarled at Steve and Carol through the window of his Range Rover. 'Look at the state of your fields. The fences. The drains. The gates. My offer ought to go down rather than up. Your farm is a disgrace.'

This wounded their pride. They had never liked Freddie Foxwell so it was easy to deny him what he wanted. He seemed incapable of understanding that they preferred Nutwhistle Farm the way it was and had no intention of leaving, or had nowhere to go if they did. Steve made his refusals as courteously as possible, explaining that he had been born on the farm, liked being the owner, and saw no reason why he should give it up. Carol was less polite. She finally lost patience and told Freddie to bugger off and not to bother coming back.

An equally persistent caller was a man they referred to as Mr Moneybags. He was a developer but had a more emollient approach than their abrasive neighbour so they gave him a slightly longer hearing when he called. His pitch was more direct, he wanted to buy the farm from them so that his building company could immediately begin smothering their two hundred acres of farmland with houses. Mr Moneybags tried hard not to wrinkle his nose at the healthy farmyard smells, and stifled heartbroken sighs when his glossy shoes sank into the glutinous Nutwhistle mud. He was dressed in a sumptuous camel-hair overcoat with a hard black hat and a white silk scarf. He was as fastidiously neat and impressively affluent as they were scruffed and dirty, their clothes and skin so deeply grimed that it would seem an impossibility for either of them ever to be completely clean again.

'We don't want to sell,' Steve told him patiently. 'We like it here. We have no plans to retire. We have no intention of leaving. You're wasting your time.'

Until now Mr Moneybags had always assumed this was just a bargaining ploy to ratchet up the price. 'You've got some nerve, you two,' he told them admiringly on more than one occasion. 'Holding out for the biggest dollar like this.' Matching action to the word he raised his hat. 'I take my hat off to you. Let's do business.'

'Sorry, we must have left a gate open,' Carol apologised as a large beef animal with a white face began rubbing itself against his huge black Mercedes, causing it to rock from side to side. She clapped her hands and drove it off, adding by way of apology and explanation, 'They're not used to visitors.'

Mr Moneybags suppressed his howl of anguish and persevered with his sales pitch. 'I wasn't very pleased when I saw your neighbour Mr Foxwell here again yesterday. You're not negotiating with him, are you? Don't tell me it's none of my business, it is my business. I'll match his price and make you a much better deal.'

Steve shook his head wearily. 'I told you, we aren't leaving. We aren't selling to anyone, certainly not to Freddie. He can grow his extra maize somewhere else. We're not selling the farm. How many more times?'

Mr Moneybags was genuinely shocked. Shocked and amused. 'What do you mean, he wants to grow maize? He wants to buy it from you so that he can make a big profit by selling it on for a housing estate. Give me a break. Deal with me direct, why not?'

'Freddie would have made a profit?' Carol asked him.

'Bloody sure he would have made a profit. Guess he never offered enough to get you interested. Guys like him are all the same, too mean for their own good.'

'Why are you telling us this?' Steve asked suspiciously.

'Because Freddie would never have sold it on to me. He's mixed up with one of the big London developers. His wife, family connections, you know how these things work. That's why I've been trying so hard to deal with you myself. Only you never listen.'

Steve looked at his watch. 'I don't want to be rude but we've got work to do. Sorry about the big dent in your car.'

'What's a dent and a wing mirror between friends? Talk to me about money. Name your price. Let's do a deal.'

'We've got a sow farrowing. Some other time.'

Mr Moneybags threw up his hands in a gesture of irritation and despair. 'You don't even want to discuss my offer?' He tried to conceal his frustration and softened his voice, as though speaking to a couple of dim-witted children. 'Explain to me why you don't want to be rich? It's not natural. When you were small didn't you ever wonder what it would be like to have as much money as you wanted?'

Steve and Carol conceded the point. 'Yes. We did.'

'Well then, so what did you think you would buy with the money? You must have known about all the nice things money can buy you.'

Steve and Carol continued to look puzzled. 'We would have bought a farm, of course. Just like the one we've got now.'

'But you would have been rich, so you wouldn't have had to do the work yourself. That's the difference. You could have employed people to do the work for you. Right?'

'No. We like doing the work. That's the part we enjoy.'

Mr Moneybags gave up, aware that they remained as mutually incomprehensible to one another as ever. He was also aware that the rogue bullock that had wandered off from the herd to vandalise his car was heading back in their direction. Not this time to trash his top-of-the-range Mercedes but because it wanted to nuzzle up to Steve and Carol, blotting its big wet nose on their clothes. Steve gave its head a friendly scratch, which encouraged it to seek attention from Carol. Obligingly she put an arm round its neck and gave it a few pats on the face. This seemed to satisfy the sociable animal and it wandered off again, still eyeing up the Mercedes but this time giving it a wide berth, much to the relief of Mr Moneybags.

He said despairingly, 'There must be something you want. We're talking millions of pounds here. You'll have to sell sooner or later. You're almost joined on to the town now.'

Steve was not impressed by this line of argument. 'People like you were always coming to see my Dad when he was alive. He thought it was a cheek. So do we, don't we, Carol?'

'But look at the state of your farm! Think of all the lovely things you could buy if you sold it to my company. Wouldn't you like to live where the sun shines every day? Cyprus, that would be nice, the best end of the Mediterranean if you want my opinion. Or Queensland in Australia? They speak English there, or mostly they do. If you really want to work you could buy a vineyard or an olive grove, ever thought about that?' He passed a hand to and fro in front of their eyes. 'You're not listening to me. Do you really want to live in all this shit for the rest of your lives?'

He neither deserved nor received an answer and soon drove away in his huge Mercedes limousine, still grieving over the crumpled side panel. Steve and Carol were sorry too, sorry that they had given up so much of their time to talk to him. It meant they had to catch up on their work before going indoors for a late lunch and were even hungrier than usual. They looked forward as always to their steaming mugs of tomato soup accompanied by triangles of processed cheese squashed over digestive biscuits. When they had finished eating they lit cigarettes and put their feet up for half an hour before pulling on their wellies and going back to work.

Two happier people it would be hard to find.

End